WHERE THEY KEEP THE SKY

Cal Heath

ISBN: 9798407968061

Cover design:
A. Almeidah and C. Heath

For my family - especially my late mum, who would have loved Kate's garden.

ACKNOWLEDGMENTS

This novel would not have come into being if it were not for the encouragement and support of Ashley Winter, Alison Saunders and Clare Owen. Thanks also to the gang at Swansea Little Theatre, who believed in my writing and helped make the audio version of *Where They Keep The Sky*. I'm grateful to Gemma Mabbett for providing Welsh translations, Jane Cummings for enthusiastic and diligent editing, and to Ed Morris and Giles and Helen Rowden for sharing their knowledge of Law and Morris Minors!

We are the sum of the people around us, and I am thankful for the love and support of Teams Heath and Farr, our extended families, and our wonderful friends in their various corners of the world.

Above all, thanks to Lance, Reubyn and Vivienne, for always being excited about my writing, and for thinking I'm cooler than I am!

Day 1 - Friday

'Rail tickets, purse, bags... Right, let's get this over with.'

Jocelyn Anderson was far from impressed to be heading to Paddington Station at six forty-five on a Friday morning for a trip *out* of London. She would usually be well on her way *into* the city at this time of morning, to the Mayfair office of the law firm at which she'd worked for seventeen years. At least Jonathan had found a window in his own busy schedule to accompany her to the station. The two of them had managed to snatch a mere handful of hours in each other's company in recent weeks, and even then, it was only to bolt down a late-night takeaway before collapsing exhausted into bed.

Jonathan closed the front door of their Bayswater Georgian apartment, gave it a push to check it was locked, and followed his wife down the steps and onto the street. The sky was overcast but the June air was humid with heat left over from the previous day. It radiated from the flagged pavements and hung in the smog of vehicle fumes and under the low blanket of cloud covering the city. They walked briskly along the streets; Jocelyn looking effortlessly executive in a tailored navy suit, with a brown leather handbag over one shoulder, a matching leather briefcase, and a Burberrys summer mac over her arm. She covered the ground quickly for her five feet three inches, and Jonathan strode alongside, sweating a little in his pinstripe suit and carrying his own briefcase and his wife's suitcase.

He looked across. Jocelyn's forehead was damp around her hairline and her jaw was set in the way it did when she was utterly focused on something. 'Sweetheart, are you sure you can handle this on your own?' His tone was gentle.

'Oh yes, it's not much - just a couple of bags,' she dismissed - then murmured to herself, 'Although it's a pain to have to travel on a Friday, but I need to be on time for Kate's funeral tomorrow morning.'

'No, I mean, are you sure you can handle this… situation. If only this had all happened a couple of weeks later, I could have come with you.'

She eased her pace and smiled back at him warmly. 'Thank you darling, but you know I can manage and I'd much rather you stay here and focus on your work. A lawyer's job is never finished! You don't need this extra faff and fuss at such short notice. And anyway, according to Aunt Kate's solicitor, it was a specific request in her will that I, the sole beneficiary, must spend three weeks at her former home, The Coach House, before deciding the fate of her estate. There's really no need for you to come.'

'Well, I trust that you know what's best.'

The air was growing warmer as the sun above the clouds moved higher, and the feeble breeze that rustled in the trees above them did little to cool the street. A stray strand of hair escaped from Jocelyn's hairgrip, blew across her eyes and plastered itself to her moist brow. She stifled a sigh and brushed it back into place. She threw Jonathan another smile to reassure him, then shifted her handbag strap to a more comfortable spot on her shoulder and marched on, Italian heels clicking in time with Jonathan's footsteps on the concrete slabs.

A three-week trip to rural Wales had not been on the cards. Jocelyn's summons to The Coach House by Kate's solicitor had come as a surprise - she hadn't spoken to Kate for over ten years - and its pressing nature had left her little time to lodge an objection: she must go there for the funeral and stay for three weeks afterwards.

She'd finally flicked off her office light at ten the previous evening, after thoroughly briefing her secretary, Trudy, and gathering as many client folders in her briefcase as she could sensibly carry. There was no time to take a holiday from work; work was going with her to Wales.

They reached a pedestrian crossing and waited for the traffic lights to bring the flow of spluttering vehicles to a pause. Jonathan raised his voice over the engines. 'An odd request by Kate though, isn't it? To go and just… *live* there. I mean, how long was it since you were last there?' The lights changed and the traffic jolted to a stop, and they crossed the road.

'Oh, well, it must be twenty - no, twenty-five years since I was actually at the house. I used to spend my summer holidays there, until I was about fifteen - you know, the age when we'd rather be in the city, near to schoolfriends and prospective boyfriends, than out in the wilds of rural Wales.'

Jonathan smiled to himself at the thought of his astute wife as a spirited teenager, chasing something other than high grades and stellar career prospects. It was hard to imagine.

'Still, Aunt Kate and I were by no means strangers,' she continued. 'My mother, Kate and I religiously exchanged Christmas and birthday greetings. Letters too, when life events were worthy of putting pen to paper - and I saw her in London from time to time, at family parties and so on, although those petered out when my mother and father divorced…' her voice trailed off.

Across the street, taxis hooted at each other and sped away. In a side alley somewhere, the rhythmic beeping of a reversing delivery lorry echoed, and then air brakes went on and voices shouted over the clatter of rear doors being opened. In the distance, cathedral bells chimed seven. Jocelyn didn't notice any of it. She'd lived in the city her entire life; she moved with its pulsing rhythm.

Jonathan adjusted his grip on the suitcase, thankful that his wife was travelling light. 'It's just part of modern-day life, I suppose; our careers sweep us up and carry us along. Then you turn around, and a decade or more has passed.'

Jonathan had moved to London from Herefordshire at eighteen years old, to study law. That was twenty-four years ago and now, at forty-two, he also moved with the city's beat - except with a faint voice in his head that whispered of greener spaces and cleaner air. He certainly never mentioned his little voice to Jocelyn. She was happy, so he was happy. Their pleasant two-bedroom home in Bayswater - with its high ceilings, velvet furnishings and art pieces from some of London's finest galleries - reflected their professional success and, with neither of them having a desire to add children to the mix, they looked forward to a prosperous future together.

That their diaries had not, in the last two years, allowed them time to be together for any meaningful amount of time except eating and sleeping was, they hoped, just a blip in their carefully mapped-out life plan.

Their footsteps echoed as they made their way down the steps into the Underground. A blast of hot air swept through the corridors past them, as a train approached from one of the dark tunnels under the capital city. Jocelyn walked in silence now, mentally rehearsing her travel schedule. Jonathan followed closely behind, being careful not to lose her in the crowd of business suits. They reached the platform and hopped quickly through the open doors of the waiting train. The doors slid shut with a hiss and they grabbed onto the bars for balance, as it sped off.

The journey to Paddington, although crowded, was short and uneventful. In the station's vast hall, Jocelyn searched for the departure boards, moving slowly against the city-bound flow of commuters. She steered Jonathan and herself to a space in the crowd and set her briefcase down between her feet. Jonathan placed the suitcase down beside her, then stood up and stretched his back.

Jocelyn squinted up at the row of boards. 'Here we go: Cardiff Central - platform eight.' She checked her wristwatch. 'Departs in fourteen minutes.' She let out a long breath. They were safely at the station with time to spare. She took the opportunity to pin the escaped strands of hair from her faux-pearl-clipped updo back into place, remove her silk scarf and put it away in her bag, and unbutton her suit jacket and shake it loose. The adjustments were just enough to cool her a little, while still maintaining her appearance.

Jonathan watched her, and when she had finished, he gently wrapped his hand around her wrist, playing with the small gold buttons on her cuff. Their relationship had a quiet strength, forged over two decades that had begun with a shared Bachelor course at university in London. Her strength of character had always inspired him, but he sometimes wished she would let down the barriers a little when it came to emotional matters.

'Ready?' he said.

Jocelyn nodded and they gathered up the bags again and weaved past the rows of turnstiles that led onto each platform and the rows of passengers waiting in front of each, until they reached platform eight. There, they found another gap in the crowd, by the side of the turnstile leading onto the platform. The huge train was already waiting at the platform, rumbling patiently while porters milled around its open doors. Without a travel ticket, Jonathan could proceed no further and so they settled beside the turnstiles to snatch a final few minutes' conversation before Jocelyn was called through.

She reached into her handbag and drew out the ticket, studying it thoughtfully for a minute. 'It will be strange to be back at the old place - especially with Kate gone.' She took a subtle breath to compose herself; she disliked being flustered - it was unprofessional.

'Yes, I can imagine it will. Kate was a remarkable woman; ninety-seven years old!'

'She really was remarkable. Mother and Kate both had such fulfilling lives, what with mother's musical career and Kate's acting. It's no wonder they struggled to be in the same country - let alone the same town - at the same time. You know, they were both utterly driven to follow their calling. That takes commitment - and sacrifice, as you and I well know.'

Jonathan looked down at his wife studying her ticket, surprised to hear her refer to their own life decisions as sacrifices. She had always seemed so certain of the choices she made.

'And of course, Kate was in fact my *great* aunt,' she said, 'My mother was Kate's niece - so there wasn't quite the obligation for us all to stay in close contact. Although we always made the extra effort because Kate had chosen to stay single and free.' Jocelyn looked up and smiled thoughtfully. 'Oh, how we adored her and her flamboyant ways! Full of adventure, and ever the storyteller.'

'I never got the impression that she expected you to stay in touch just because she lived alone,' said Jonathan, 'From what you told me about her, she sounded perfectly happy - in fact, I'd assumed she'd sought a solitary life. Otherwise, why did she head off to the Welsh hills to retire? Cl... Ll...' He wrestled with the pronunciation of the Welsh town.

'Llanfairyn. Pronounced Llan-via-rin!' Jocelyn finished. 'Well, I would imagine that Kate's career was socially demanding, so perhaps retiring to rural Wales gave her the peace and quiet she craved. I love to pronounce the name - how it rolls off my tongue like a deep velvet Madeira... Llanfairyn!'

'Well, it must be in your genes; it doesn't roll off mine!' he laughed. 'It's a dramatic lifestyle change from the international acting scene, though. Two train journeys and a twenty-odd-mile taxi ride up into a part of the Welsh mountains *I* can't even pronounce!'

Jocelyn paled visibly at his comment, and Jonathan instantly regretted making it.

'Well, she returned to her birthplace, a rather large stone house with a rambling garden at the front, at the edge of a very charming town. Well, a town-*ish*.'

Jonathan laughed at his wife's tendency to invent words when a suitable one didn't exist. He reached for the collars of her jacket, tugged them together playfully and kissed her nose. 'What's a town*ish*?'

She pulled away. 'It's bigger than a village and not quite a town - as we Londoners would think of one. One colourful, tree-lined main street, and a handful of side lanes filled with snoozy slate-tiled stone cottages - so small you could touch the roofs if you reached up on tiptoe!'

'It sounds romantic.'

'Romantic? I suppose. It's certainly sleepy. Perfect for a child; not so sure I would cope with life there as an adult.'

'What, no high-end shops?' Jonathan teased, 'Michelin-star restaurants? Theatres?'

'Goodness, no! Although… I'm not like that, am I?' She pulled a face at him. 'Well, maybe I am, a little.'

'You're wonderful and I wouldn't change you,' he soothed, 'But you are a city girl through-and-through!' He gestured to Jocelyn's high-heeled sandals, 'I hope you've packed some clothing suitable for the Welsh mountain climate!'

'Suitable clothing? I don't own any! Anyway, I'm only going to be there for three weeks, to live in the old house and then to give instructions to the solicitor to empty the house and put it on the market.'

She reached up and brushed a speck of lint from his sleeve. 'Thank goodness I have a wonderful solicitor husband to help me sort out that side of things! But no, I'm certainly not planning on braving the elements, nor rubbing shoulders with the locals - not that I have anything against the Welsh weather or the locals,' she added hastily, 'But there just isn't time and I need to get back to work as soon as possible.'

'Yes, well hopefully it will all be straightforward - whatever you decide to do with the estate. Kate's solicitor seemed very efficient when he contacted me.'

'I would imagine it will be straightforward. I mean, the house won't be worth much; it's so remote up there. We'll just have to accept the first sensible offer to tie all this up, and then life can return to normal.'

An overhead tannoy crackled into life and a cheerful East End accent announced, 'The train to Cardiff Central is departing from Platform Eight in five minutes!'

'Right, there we go,' Jocelyn picked up her briefcase. 'I'd better go through. You will take care while I'm away, won't you? Remember that there is work scheduled on the Circle and District Line on Monday - and Sandra comes to clean on Fridays, so you need to leave her money out.'

Jonathan laughed. 'How will I survive for three weeks, without you organising my life?' He gestured to a nearby porter, who came to where they were standing, reached over the barrier and took Jocelyn's suitcase from him.

'I'm not joking, Jonathan.'

'Neither am I. Fifteen years of marriage, and you have me well and truly organised like one of your work projects.' He then turned to the porter, 'This case is for the Cardiff train please.'

The porter nodded and left with the suitcase.

'One of my more challenging projects!' Her eyes flashed cheekily. 'Now I am joking, darling. So, I'll call you later when I've arrived - although goodness knows where I'll find a working telephone in that... backwater! Oh dear, I feel bad that I just described it like that, but it's what I'm thinking...'

'I'm sorry all of this is happening right now and that I can't help more.'

'It's fine, really. There is never a convenient time for death, is there?' She fed her ticket into the slot on the turnstile and pushed her way through it, then moved to the side so that she could still speak to her husband over the barrier.

Kate was gone. In the busy-ness of wrapping up work and planning this last-minute trip, it had not had a chance to sink in. Jocelyn sighed. 'You're always so wonderfully supportive, Jonathan. My rock.' She reached over the railing to embrace him, and he kissed the top of her hair. 'But don't worry; I really can manage this journey alone. All six hours of it.'

At two minutes to eight, a second porter sprang into action to call above the throb of the engine, 'The o-eight-hundred train to Cardiff Central! Boarding now!'

'Oh, now I really *must* dash! I love you. I'll see you in three weeks, when all this is done and dusted.' Jocelyn went to turn away.

'All right, sweetheart. Just… try to stay mindful that it might take longer than three weeks to arrange to have the house emptied and put on the market.'

She stopped in her tracks and turned back to him. 'Oh dear, do you think it'll be packed to the creaking rafters with junk?' Her voice started to crack. 'Oh goodness Jonathan, what am I about to face? A ramshackle old house with an overgrown jungle of a garden, six hours away in a remote in a town that *you* can't pronounce!'

'I thought Kate had some paid help with the house and garden,' he kept his voice calm.

'Well, yes…'

'The couple who have arranged to meet you with the keys - Alan and Doreen Hughes. I'm sure they would have let you know if the house wasn't fit to stay in. It may be cluttered and a bit overgrown, but I'm sure it's still habitable. Otherwise, they would have advised you to stay somewhere else.'

He gestured to the train, 'Just get yourself there safely and we'll deal with things as we need to.'

Jocelyn nodded, 'You're right, the voice of sense and reason as always. Never mind you; what am *I* going to do without *you* for three weeks? You do realise that we've chatted more this morning than we have in months. It's been…' She was cut off by a shrill whistle and the slamming of train doors. 'Right, here I go then. Call you later!

She hurried away to the nearest open door, calling behind her and waving, 'Miss you already! Goodbye!'

'Goodbye, sweetheart.'

A red-faced porter helped Jocelyn board the train, and slammed the heavy door closed after her. Then he stepped back and raised his hand to his uniformed colleagues, already holding up their hands in an All-Clear further down the platform.

A whistle blew again and the engine at the front end heaved into action, setting the train into motion with a groan. The porters along the platform stood back as the machine ground slowly past them, carriages clunking as they engaged with each other.

The train pulled away slowly at first, making a steady 'chunk-chunk' as it rolled over the track joints, down the track littered with tin cans and cigarette ends. Then the engine notched up a gear, squealing with the effort, and it picked up speed as it rolled out of the cavernous station and into the bright daylight beyond.

Jonathan stood at the barrier and watched the train, until it was a speck in the distance.

***

In the rear carriage, Jocelyn made a note of the location of her suitcase - on the lower shelf of the storage rack by the door - and then walked unsteadily in her heels down the aisle, in search of a seat. She didn't have to walk far; the train was surprisingly quiet, and she chose a forward-facing seat with a table by a window and settled into it.

She exhaled; a long, carefully controlled breath through pursed lips, and tried to let her shoulders drop. Fortunately, no one was facing her and so she was able to concentrate privately on her breathing for a few minutes until she felt settled. Then she removed her jacket, folded it carefully, and laid both it and her mac on the empty seat beside her. She pushed her briefcase between her feet, under the table. From the side pocket of her handbag, she took out a compact mirror and checked her face and hair. Satisfied, she snapped it shut, returned it to the pocket and then stowed the bag safely beneath the jacket-and-mac pile beside her.

The train swayed on through the outskirts of the city. The concrete offices and tower blocks eventually gave way to warehouses and sprawling storage yards, with branded delivery vans parked in neat rows, polythene-covered toilet bowls stacked on shipping pallets, and loads of sand and gravel being craned onto the open backs of haulage lorries. The industrial landscapes were followed by suburban ones, with rows of identical red-brick houses with square gardens housing swings and paddling pools, and flyovers lined with enormous billboard advertisements for sports cars and men's wristwatches.

Finally, they had clunked and rocked their way to the city's edge, and with another gear shift of its engine, the train increased speed again. A knot of trepidation twisted in Jocelyn's stomach as the fields and trees whistled past. She shrugged it off and reached down to pick up her briefcase from the floor. Luckily, no one had taken the seat opposite and she had the whole table to work on. She opened the briefcase and leafed through the folders.

The morning passed and they sped westward, crossing the neat counties of southern England. Jocelyn buried her head in legal paperwork to distract her from the thoughts turning over and over in her mind: she was leaving the city, and everything familiar to her, behind.

***

Jocelyn had expected the first leg of the train journey, which would take her to Cardiff, the capital city of Wales, to be unpleasant. The public transport of London with which she was familiar was almost always crowded and she accepted it - got on with life, expecting the worst and generally not being disappointed. Today though, instead of growing increasingly crowded, the carriage became quieter as the miles rolled away. The landscape across the country to the Welsh border was flat and pleasant and Jocelyn was relieved to feel herself becoming calmer. During the journey, she had managed to make enough work-related notes on her Basildon Bond writing pad to feel that the morning had been spent as productively as possible.

As they approached Cardiff Central, Jocelyn took the mirror and a coral-coloured lipstick from her handbag, quickly checked her appearance, and touched up her lips. She gathered up the paperwork hastily from the table and tucked it back into the briefcase, absent-mindedly sweeping up the mirror and lipstick as she did so. She clicked the case firmly shut and as the train drew alongside the platform, pulled on her jacket, gathered up her bags from the table and the seat, and stood up.

Cardiff Central was a bustling station, with a neon-lit underground tunnel and steps leading up to platforms filled with flustered passengers - but it was not on the scale of Paddington. A porter had lifted Jocelyn's suitcase down from the train for her, but she had had to wrestle it along the platform, down the steps and along the dim tunnel herself, which had made her hot - and reminded her that she was alone. There was a half an hour wait between trains, and she located her connecting train easily enough. It was departing from a smaller platform at the far end of the station and was already standing waiting.

This train, the one to carry her further westwards into the depths of Wales, was the smallest she could ever recall seeing; it was only two carriages long. The driver and a smiling conductor stood one on each side of the open doorway of the front carriage. They were deep in a loud, enthusiastic conversation - two song-like Welsh accents - across the platform with the man in a booth selling hotdogs, crisps and fizzy orange pop, only pausing when they greeted boarding passengers. Jocelyn bought a coffee and a packet of crisps from the man in the booth. She boarded the train, found a seat and made herself comfortable.

Only a handful of people got on behind her, so that each passenger had two seats to themselves. They all spread themselves throughout the carriage, in that polite British manner that ensured everyone had plenty of personal space. This was so unusual to Jocelyn that rather than bury herself in work notes immediately, she sat back instead and observed the scene unfolding around her - the other travellers wrestling baggage into the storage nets above their heads, the posters of seaside towns on the carriage walls, the porter closing the doors and speaking to a passenger who was making an enquiry about their ticket.

Eventually, when they departed from Cardiff Central and began their journey into the Welsh countryside, she leaned her head against the window and watched the city suburbs fall away - much more abruptly than those of London had done. The train meandered slowly westwards, and the landscape became open and rugged - a vivid contrast to the green patchwork of England. The view northwards, through the windows on the right side, was of irregular hills capped with purple heather, and short trees that had grown permanently slanted because of the prevailing wind from the sea. Southwards, through the left side window against which Jocelyn was leaning and gazing out, the ground flattened out as it stretched towards the coast.

They crossed estuaries filled with white gulls and cormorants and tall marsh grasses, and where seagulls circled and squabbled with each other in the huge open sky. The midday sun shone warm on Jocelyn's face and the train rocked her towards a slumber. Well, it was probably a good idea to rest a while, she reasoned.

This journey was the longer of the two train rides. The train chugged on, and the track wound deeper into the hills until the roads and houses fell far behind and only hills and single-track lanes filled the landscape. During the afternoon, she was roused twice; once by the refreshment trolley being wheeled noisily through the carriage, and once by the actions of the train conductor - who was carrying out an activity so unexpected, the first time Jocelyn saw him doing it she sat up and gasped in amazement: Every time the little train had to cross one of the winding roads, the driver first pulled it to a complete halt. His door would then swing open, and the cheery conductor would clamber down the rungs to the ground. He would sprint forwards and heave the big white safety barriers closed across the road, to stop the cars and make way for the train. The driver would then take the train slowly over the road, where he pulled to a stop again. Once the train was clear of the road, the conductor reopened the gates for the waiting cars, then dashed forwards, jumped back up into the train… and off they would chug again. The barriers were not automated - nor, in fact, manned in any way. Mouth ajar, Jocelyn shook her head in disbelief at the primitive rail transport system. London was feeling very far away!

She slept for the rest of the journey, clutching her handbag and briefcase close to her, and dreaming that she had fallen asleep at her office desk and that it was Trudy, not a fellow passenger, who was discussing the Farmers' Market in Brecon next Saturday.

***

Just after noon, the conductor's voice crackled a cheerful announcement over the tannoy. Jocelyn sat bolt upright; this was her destination. She kicked herself because in her laziness, she had left no time to touch up her lipstick. She stood up to slip on her jacket, looking around the carriage while doing so. All the other passengers had disappeared.

As the wheels slowed, and then screeched with a jolt to a halt, she gathered her bags and mac and headed to the luggage rack next to the door. The conductor opened the door and sunlight streamed in. He turned to Jocelyn and gestured to her suitcase, 'This one?'

'Yes, that's mine,' she nodded. The interaction was both comical and pointless because there weren't any other suitcases on the rack, nor any other passengers to disembark. The man probably used any excuse to engage with his passengers.

He took hold of the case and lifted it off the rack and down onto the platform, then turned and held out a hand to support her. 'Off somewhere nice, is it?' It was clear he wasn't going to let her go without a conversation of some sort.

'Is it what?' she said.

'Sorry?' He looked at her, smiling but unsure what to make of her response. He repeated, 'I mean, are you off to somewhere nice?'

'To Llanfairyn. I'm just hoping that my taxi is here to meet me.'

'Ah, beau-ti-ful,' - he split the word into three distinct syllables.

She took his hand and stepped down onto the platform - which was a quite a drop to make in high heels with any sort of elegance - and then planted her feet on solid ground as a cool breeze fanned her. She turned her face to it for a moment, stretched her back, then picked up her baggage and stepped away from the train.

'You have a lov-ely day, now,' the happy conductor sang, and without waiting for a reply he pulled the door closed and the train rolled away on its journey.

Jocelyn looked around. The tiny rural station stood elevated above a vast open saltmarsh. The view was uninterrupted - from the tall blue hills in the north, across the broad estuary with its network of glistening rivers winding through the mudflats, down to the ocean that lay blue and shimmering in the distance. She let her eyes sweep from the hills, down to the ocean, and then up above her head. 'So, *this* is where they keep the sky!'

The sky here was pale blue and cloudless, and the air cool and salt scented. With closed eyes, Jocelyn lifted her face up to the sun and inhaled deeply.

When she opened them again to look up and down the platform, she found it empty. In each direction, the train tracks stretched away into the distance. She was alone with her bags; only the chattering of some small birds in the undergrowth and the faint bleat of a distant sheep interrupted the quiet. Jocelyn smiled and spoke aloud to herself, 'Was I the only passenger? That's a novelty!' She slid a small suede diary from her inside pocket. 'Now, who am I looking for: Mr. Maxwell Griffiths.'

A deep, warm voice interrupted her. 'Hello! Jocelyn, is it?' The platform was enclosed by a waist-high white picket fence and from a gate behind her, a strong looking man with grey hair and a deep suntan, was beckoning.

'Mr. Griffiths?'

'That's right! Max it is.' Max was wearing a shirt with a paisley waistcoat over the top, and a red cravat around his neck. His rolled-up sleeves revealed muscular forearms, and he was wearing a wide smile as he approached.

He reached for Jocelyn's suitcase. 'Come this way Miss. Let me take your bags.'

Jocelyn nodded and picked up her briefcase.

'How was the journey?' he asked.

'It was fine, absolutely fine.'

'I'm glad to hear it!'

'No delays, no diversions, no *people*! I even had a seat for the entire journey,' she mused.

'You're not used to all of that, then?' Max's eyes twinkled, as he turned to lead the way out.

'Certainly not! I'm used to crowds and delays and Standing Room Only.' She picked up her briefcase and followed him through the gate.

'Well, you're in Wales now. You can breathe. None of your city worries here - although I can't guarantee there won't be a traffic jam of the sheep variety, but at least you won't have to stand up for that!' He laughed at his own joke.

Jocelyn inhaled and looked around her.

'Yes, you can smell the sea air coming across the saltmarsh today,' he said, 'it's a Southerly wind. Although you won't from Llanfairyn - it's about twenty miles up into the hills.'

Jocelyn paused but didn't allow her face to change. 'Ah yes, another twenty miles.'

'Don't worry, it won't take us long! The car's over here.' Max strode through the gate, and down a gravel path lined with long grass and red poppies.

Jocelyn looked around one last time. 'The sea air coming over the saltmarsh,' she repeated with a smile, before following Max down the path.

***

The small gravel car park was empty apart from an old-fashioned, but very tidy and sparkling sage-coloured car, parked beside a hawthorn in the corner.

'Where are all the people?' Jocelyn gestured around them. Birds chattered away; that was all. 'I was the only person in the carriage for the final two hours. And there's no one at the station.'

'Oh, there might have been a few passengers on the midday train. This is the three o'clock. Only three trains a day out here, Miss. We don't need any more than that!' Max headed towards the shiny old vehicle.

Jocelyn raised an eyebrow. This couldn't be the taxi, could it?

It was. Max opened the passenger door, which Jocelyn noticed had been left unlocked, and tilted the front seat forwards. He carefully manoeuvred her suitcase through the door - to protect his vehicle, it appeared, rather than her case, because he rubbed the doorframe afterwards with a handkerchief from his top pocket - and laid the suitcase on the back seat. Then he pulled the passenger seat back into position, moved to the back of the car to open a rear hatch for Jocelyn to deposit her briefcase, then closed it again with a clunk. He gestured for Jocelyn to climb in the passenger side, and she followed his instruction.

As she lowered herself in, she wondered how he ran a taxi service with this old, and very compact, vehicle. His typical passenger must travel far lighter than she did - and have lower expectations for travelling in comfort, too. She settled herself into the seat - which had grown warm from the rays of the sun - and pulled the door closed. The vehicle smelled of citrus and polished leather. Looking around at the gleaming interior, she realised that this was Max's pride and joy. She immediately felt a pang of guilt.

The driver's door opened, and Max lowered himself into his own seat with a happy sigh.

'It's a lovely car,' she said, to redeem herself. 'Thank you for coming to meet me.'

'It's a pleasure!' He turned the ignition key, pulled a mystery knob on the dashboard whose function Jocelyn could not imagine - and with a rattle they were off, reversing out of the dusty car park, and heading left onto a leafy road. They drove inland, away from the coast towards the hills. Max's window was fully open, and Jocelyn wound hers down an inch too, because the car had no air-conditioning, and she was growing hot once more in her suit.

The draught through the vehicle blew the strands of hair out of her grips again and plastered them firmly across her face, and she made a futile attempt to smooth them back into place. She fished in her handbag. Where was the compact mirror? She realised it was in the briefcase… in the boot. Oh dear; arriving at The Coach House unkempt really would not do. What on earth would the Hughes' think? 'It's very kind of you, and of Mr. and Mrs. Hughes to organise my transport!' She called over the noise of the breeze whipping past the window. She grabbed a hairgrip and re-inserted it tightly above her temple, hardly able to believe that she was attempting to fix her hair without a mirror. What a sight she must look!

'Is it too windy for you?' Max called back, grinning.

Was it better to arrive hot and dishevelled, or *windswept* and dishevelled? She smiled over at Max and fibbed kindly, 'It's fine with the windows down.'

'Very good!' he looked forwards again and carried on driving.

Clutching her handbag on her lap, Jocelyn decided that, since there was little she could do now to make herself more comfortable, she may as well surrender to the situation. For the rest of the journey towards the hills, she sat back and focused on the birdsong outside of the windows and the rumble of the tyres on the warm tarmac.

The car bumbled along between narrow hedgerows for several miles. Through gateways on each side, she glimpsed sheep and cattle grazing on sloping fields in the afternoon sun. They passed a few stone cottages on the edge of the road, and a sprawling farmhouse whose barns and outbuildings spanned both sides of the road.

'I usually bring Sophie - my collie - with me for the ride,' Max said, breaking the silence. 'I didn't today in case you were allergic.'

'I wouldn't have minded.' Jocelyn said, in another effort to be kind. She wasn't keen on dogs and her thoughts turned briefly to her Italian wool suit. Jonathan's Christmas present to her, from Selfridges; perhaps it hadn't been the best choice today. Oh well. The dog wasn't here, and the seats looked clean.

After a few miles, the gentle incline of the road grew steeper, and the gentle curves became sharp U- bends as the road turned back on itself to ascend the hillside. Some of the drops were alarmingly steep, but they didn't seem to trouble Max in the slightest. Rather than look down to the side, Jocelyn concentrated on the grey tarmac ahead and the white painted letters along the centre of the road: 'ARAF'.

'Slow!' Max laughed, pointing at the floor sign. 'As if there's a danger of us going any faster on these roads!'

The higher they climbed, the sparser the hedgerows became, until there was only the occasional clump of hawthorn, or fencing with weathered wooden posts and wire with little tufts of sheep's wool caught on it. Eventually, the car rumbled over a cattle grid, and immediately and they were on open yellow common land. The road was no longer confined by boundaries, and no longer wound back and forth, but stretched out long and flat in front of them like a ribbon across the land.

The car chugged onwards until, finally, they reached the highest point of the moor and the landscape on the other side spread out in front of them. Jocelyn gasped in awe at the panorama before her eyes. The whole horizon, for as far as the eye could see, was a layer of rugged hills - rising deep blue and dramatic in the foreground, backed in the distance by outlines of soft grey that blended with the sky. A cluster of yawning valleys converged at the foot of the hills immediately below them - sweeping arcs of yellow and green, a vast jigsaw puzzle of pastureland, stone walls and pinprick sheep.

Max, who seemed to have been waiting for the moment, grinned to himself in satisfaction at Jocelyn's reaction. He pulled the car to a gentle halt, in the middle of the empty road.

'Oh my!' she finally breathed out slowly. She sensed Max smiling at her, but she was unable to pull her eyes away from the splendour that lay beyond the car windscreen. 'The sky! It's so…wide… and blue! And the fields are… big! The sky meets the fields!'

Max chuckled, 'You'd think you'd landed straight from Mars!'

She continued to stare in amazement. 'I've grown too accustomed to brick and glass,' she breathed, scanning the horizon slowly. 'The sky is a long way up, on Regent Street. Hidden above the buildings - beautiful buildings though they are. She strained forwards to look through the windscreen, whispering to herself, 'Here… it reaches right down to the ground.'

'Well, there's plenty more of this where you're heading,' said Max with a laugh. 'I hope you like heights and space as much as you appear to; you'll be practically *in* the sky in Llanfairyn!'

Max waited until Jocelyn sat back and looked at him with an approving smile, then he put the car into gear with a crunch, and they set off again. He was in no rush as they meandered across the moor. He trundled along in his own happy world, while Jocelyn drank in the passing scenery. For a while, neither spoke. Sometimes, the road edge was bordered by deep open ditches - black soil that had baked dry and cracked in the sun and whose water had evaporated long ago, and sometimes by low stone walls covered in yellow lichen, where sheep lay resting in the shade.

On the flat parts of the moor, peaty plateaus rose above the rushes, and all around them, small birds darted between the waving brown grasses, flirting with each other. Max rested an elbow on the open window frame, and laid one hand lightly on the wheel, the breeze brushing his face.

'I love it up here,' he said, 'I've lived here my whole life - well, apart from a brief dalliance with Cardiff when I was eighteen. Didn't last long.' He carried on smiling and looking around him.

'I've only ever lived in London,' said Jocelyn.

The car seemed to be moving at a walking pace now. Jocelyn briefly wondered whether she was paying Max for the taxi ride by the mile, or by the hour. Then she checked herself; it didn't matter, there was nothing to rush for really, and growing impatient wasn't going to speed things up. 'Allow yourself to enjoy the moment,' she told herself - repeating words Jonathan had begun to gently use on her, whenever he sensed she was growing frustrated.

On across the common Max drove, the sky around them empty but for a large circling hawk of some kind. Further on still, the land on the left side of the road dropped away steeply, into a valley that cradled a huge dark lake with a sweeping stone dam at one end. The still waters reflected a fringe of pine trees along the lake's edge.

'The town's reservoir,' Max explained.

Finally, they had crossed the vast moor, and the road began to drop down into the valley on the other side. A few miles along, the road split into two and a fat, gnarled tree sat in the middle of the fork. Its heavy branches formed a canopy across both routes. In front of it stood a crooked wooden signpost with Welsh-sounding names on it, and Max indicated and took the left branch. They descended further, past a coppice of pine trees, and over the bridge of a river.

Jocelyn looked out of the side window as they crossed the bridge. The river had dried up and was now a bed of pebbles and dust - a deep groove carved down the side of the hill from the top of the moor. A few sheep dozed among the stones. Everything seems to be snoozing around here, she thought.

A little while ahead, their narrow road intercepted a larger main road, forming a T-junction. The approach to the junction was a long, sloping decline. 'Just hold on for this part, Missy!' Max indicated left, then strained up in his seat and put all his weight on the brakes, locking his legs in front of him as he did so. Instead of slowing, the car carried on forwards, and Max swung out wide around the corner onto the main road - without giving way, or apparently slowing at all.

Jocelyn heard him suck in his breath. It all happened too quickly for her to react in any way other than to grab her handbag, which had slid between the seats, squeeze her feet closed on the briefcase - which was threatening to fly over into Max's footwell - and afterwards, to push herself up from Max's left armpit back into her seat.

Max exhaled slowly and resumed his grin, as they trundled safely off down the main road. 'Pesky drum brakes; these cars! They always get me just there, at that junction!'

They crossed another cattle grid and finally left the common behind, heading down into pasturelands once more. The fields were now enclosed again by wire fences and hedgerows. Max slapped a hand contentedly on his thigh. 'That's my favourite run, from Llanfairyn down to the coast and back. I'm always happy for an excuse to drive over the moor to the sea!'

Jocelyn stole a glimpse at her watch. The twenty-two-mile drive from the railway station had taken the best part of an hour. She suspected it would have been a lot quicker if the weather had been less glorious.

They rounded a bend and the hedges parted, and she finally glimpsed the old town nestled by the wide river. The big old stone bridge, with its double arch across the water. The rows of slate rooftops between the trees. The church spire, rising tall in the town centre. Jocelyn felt a rise in her stomach. She hadn't been here for so long, and yet it was still the same, still snoozing in the sun like everything else. Waiting for her.

Her emotions were confused. Excitement at being here again, and at the prospect of seeing the old house. Then apprehension; she was so far from home, and Kate wasn't here to greet her. She was discreet with her reactions, inhaling deeply and silently and then letting out her breath slowly, and always with a fixed smile.

The vehicle ambled over the river, whose tumbling water looked cool and strangely inviting, then past what looked like a recreation ground and then a gateway, where a pony chewed on a blade of grass and shook its head sleepily to dislodge flies. The town was rising around them now, and they approached a row of tiny painted cottages with stone-walled gardens. Kate's house was just past the cottages, right on the outskirts of town, she remembered.

Almost there.

It had been so long since she'd been here last. Now, with Kate gone and the Coach House empty, she was merely a stranger - wasn't she? In a strange town, a long way from the comforting throb of London. As the car rumbled to a halt, she took a breath, lifted her chin and straightened her shoulders.

***

The Coach House was exactly as she had remembered it. It was a tall stone building, standing elevated on the corner of a T-junction where the road from the common met the main street that led into town. It was painted white, and perfectly symmetrical with a chimney on each end, four sash windows and a door in the centre. An open wood-and-slate porch over the door was covered with a tangle of vines with dainty yellow and pink flowers.

'So, here we are!' Max pulled on the handbrake.

Jocelyn straightened her hair and jacket and stepped out of the car. The afternoon air was still, and a chorus of children's voices floated from across the street. She stopped and tilted her head to listen, recognising neither the song, nor the language in which they were singing. 'What beautiful singing!'

'It's the choir, in the school over the way there.' Max nodded to a low building surrounded by sycamore trees and a tall hawthorn hedge, further on up the road.

'And they are singing in Welsh?'

'Of course!' He moved around to the passenger side of the car and began the task of wrestling the suitcase back out again - wiping his brow for a minute, then continuing to wiggle it through the opening carefully, so as not to damage the car.

Jocelyn gathered her bags and turned to look up at the house. 'So, here I am. The Coach House.'

The garden gate was framed by two stone pillars, and steps led up to a path to the front door. They made their way up the steps; Jocelyn leading, and Max following with the suitcase. The path through the front garden was bordered by vegetation that curled over the flagstones and brushed Jocelyn's ankles. Not manicured flowerbeds, like those in parks of London that she was used to, but a sea of soft, waving grasses, pocked with delicate colours and teeming with insects that crawled and buzzed on the flowerheads.

Max placed the case down under the porch and turned to Jocelyn. 'Right, Miss Jocelyn. Doreen will be here now in a minute, I should think.'

'Now, or in a minute?'

'Yes.'

'Which?'

'In a minute.'

'Right.' She really needed to get a grip on the nuances of this language. She reached to take her purse from her handbag.

'Don't worry about that now,' Max gestured to put the purse away, 'Get settled in first, and I'll be round at ten thirty in the morning to drive you to the church for the funeral service. We can sort it then.'

'Well, if you are sure…'

Max smiled and nodded.

'Oh, and Max, can you tell me of a place where I can get takeout food?'

'Takeout food? Hmm. There's a café up in the town centre,' he offered.

'Do they deliver?'

'I don't know about that. Perhaps you could ask Doreen when she comes. I'm sorry, miss, I'm going to have to leave you now - I've got another job waiting for me. I'm sure she won't be long.'

'Yes, of course.'

Max turned to leave, touching his flat cap in farewell and as he did so, the sun shone on the side of his face. Jocelyn noticed a few stray whiskers peeking from beneath his cravat and she felt a pang of something. What was it? Pity? She instantly felt guilty for feeling sorry for a man she knew nothing about - and who appeared perfectly cheerful!

Max hopped back into his car, started it up, and with another crunch of gears he did a three-point-turn in front of the house and then rumbled off around the corner.

In front of one of the windows was an area of neatly mowed lawn and a square of yellow gravel. On it stood a wrought iron garden table surrounded by chairs. Leaving the baggage on the path, Jocelyn walked across and took a seat at one of the chairs. There was a clear view of the street immediately below her, dusty and quiet, and beyond it, a wide valley of stone wall-lined pastures, and a scattering of huge trees with broad boughs.

'The Dragon's Valley,' Kate teased, as she tucked in the bedcovers. 'Go to sleep now, or he will hear you, and stir…'

'Oh!' The flashback was sudden and vivid. Then the front door behind her opened and a soft Welsh voice brought her back to the present.

'Ah, Jocelyn, is it?' A short woman, with black hair streaked with silver held back in a loose bun, was standing under the porch. She was wearing a plain t-shirt and knee-length skirt, and comfortable-looking shoes. Over her clothes was a green-and-white pinafore, like one a shopkeeper might wear.

Jocelyn stood up and spun around. 'Yes, hello. Mrs. Hughes?'

'Doreen, it is,' Doreen Hughes spoke quietly, and her dark eyes were framed by tanned wrinkles. She walked over as Jocelyn stood up.

'Good afternoon,' Jocelyn held out a hand. 'I hadn't realised you were already here.'

Doreen looked down at the extended hand, as if unsure what to do with it. Then she gently met it with her own, weathered one. 'Oh, I usually clean for Kate on a Friday, you know… and Max said earlier that he was heading off to collect you, so I waited.' Doreen pushed some wisps of hair back from her face and quietly clasped her hands in front of her.

'Right, good,' Jocelyn said. 'So, then - shall we go inside?'

'Oh yes, there we are.'

They walked over to the porch, Doreen leading the way and Jocelyn following, with her luggage in her hands.

'We've been keeping an eye on the place,' Doreen said. 'Alan went in yesterday and turned the water supply back on and the electricity has been on throughout - to keep the appliances running, you know.' She pushed the door open and stepped back, to allow Jocelyn into the dark hallway.

'Oh, that's very much appreciated.' Jocelyn stepped inside. After the brightness of the day, it took her eyes a few seconds to adjust. From her position in the doorway, she could see down the hall, and into the sitting room on the left and the dining room on right, all at the same time. She drew a breath. 'Oh, Aunt Kate!'

The house was still, and cool. The only sound was the steady tick of the grandfather clock, at the far end of the hall by the kitchen door. A rose-patterned carpet runner ran the full length of the hall, covering the dark polished parquet flooring beneath it. The walls were hung with black-and-white photographs, in ornate wooden frames.

Through the open doors to the rooms on each side, shafts of sunlight shone through the front windows, lighting up specks of dust in the air that had been stirred by their arrival. By the door stood a shoe rack, holding two neat rows of well-worn but polished leather shoes. Next to it was a terracotta pot with an umbrella propped in it and above it on the wall, a row of hooks still loaded with Kate's jackets.

'It's all as it was.' Doreen spoke quietly behind her.

Jocelyn stood still, looking to her left. There was the lace-clothed table, still under the sitting room window. The deep armchair still rested by the fireplace, cushions plumped and inviting. The shelves in the chimney alcoves were still laden with ornaments and books. The sitting room was filled to the brim with Kate's treasured things, but it didn't feel cluttered. It felt… *loved.*

Jocelyn slowly put down her case and bags and laid her mac on top of them; all the while, her gaze held fast by the serenity around her.

Doreen waited quietly for a moment, before speaking aloud what she knew Jocelyn must be thinking, 'Kate liked her antiques - and the memorabilia.'

'She did.' Jocelyn moved into the sitting room slowly. It's... oh! I'm sorry, it's just that it's been so many years since I was last here.' She walked to the mantelpiece above the fire and ran her fingers slowly along the front of it. 'Too many years,' she whispered, 'And yet, nothing has changed. It's exactly how I remembered it.' There were more photographs hanging from the wall above the fireplace. She listened with a smile to the grandfather clock. 'I'm not sure what I was expecting - but not *this*.' She turned to face Doreen.

'Kate was very house proud,' said Doreen. 'She loved her home - took great care of it. She asked me to start cleaning when she couldn't manage it herself anymore. I think I know the history of every ornament, every treasure. She loved telling her stories, Kate did, and I loved listening to them. Such a character.'

'She was.' Jocelyn sighed, and gently picked up a porcelain figurine and studied it.

Doreen and she were silent for a moment - until they sensed, simultaneously, the awkward heaviness that was starting to fill the atmosphere and moved to break it with a shrugged smile, and a change of conversation to one filled with efficiencies.

'So, the heating is an oil-fired system...'

Jocelyn frowned. 'What does that mean?'

'There's an oil tank around the back of the house. Don't worry; Alan has made sure the tanker carries on visiting, until you decide, you know, what you want… Anyway, so all you have to do is switch it on at the wall in the hallway. And we've laid the fire ready for you in case you feel chilly.' She gestured to the fireplace and Jocelyn glanced down at the grate, which she now saw was filled with scrunched up newspaper, topped with a neat criss-cross of firewood. She decided immediately that she wouldn't be attempting to light that!

'And hot water?' Jocelyn sounded worried now.

'Plenty of hot water; it's a combi boiler. And I popped a few essentials in the fridge for you. I thought you might not feel up to grocery shopping, after your journey.'

'Oh, that was thoughtful, thank you.'

'Well, I do a few hours at the farm shop, behind the school, you see,' Doreen explained.

'Ah, that's very handy. I was rather hoping there would be a place that I could get takeout food nearby?'

'A place to get takeout food…' Doreen repeated slowly, as if thinking, 'Ooo, now, I don't know about that.'

Jocelyn waited for her to continue, but she didn't. Instead, she stood expressionless, and Jocelyn wondered if the woman wanted anything else. 'Well, Mrs Hughes, if that's all…'

'Oh yes, that's all.' She placed the housekeys on the table, along with a scrap of notepaper. 'Well then, I'll leave you to get settled in. Here's my phone number, just in case you need anything.'

'Right. I can't imagine I'll need anything else but thank you all the same.' She moved to the door to escort Doreen Hughes out, as politely as she could.

The woman nodded, bowed her head and made her way out of the door.

'But will you want me to still come on a Friday?' she asked quietly.

'Oh, well, yes - why not. Thank you.' It wouldn't hurt to have someone keep the place tidy until it was sold. 'And I'll arrange to set up the weekly payments to you and Mr. Hughes from my own account.'

Doreen left and Jocelyn closed the door after her, leaned back against it, and exhaled slowly. The house was not merely habitable, it was welcoming. She laughed to herself, and her laughter rang down the hallway and around the empty rooms.

Then she frowned. Now what? The clock in the hallway ticked slowly. 'Jocelyn Anderson, you expected the worst. That might be an appropriate survival strategy in London, but it's done you no favours this trip!' She allowed her shoulders to fall with relief. 'Phew!' She went to explore the little kitchen at the end of the hallway.

This room was also as she remembered it. The house had been built on ground that had been levelled into the hillside, so the kitchen window looked out onto a steep face of rock - which you could touch if you reached out. The rock was damp and moss-covered, and delicate ferns sprung out of the crevices, and the kitchen was shaded and cool.

Kate had painted the wooden cupboards blue and white, and there was a deep white rectangular sink with two brass taps and a hook with a striped tea towel above it. Jocelyn wandered around the room, opening the cupboard doors and scanning the mismatch of pots, pans and crockery jammed inside them; chunky hand thrown holiday-souvenir mugs and plates, a stack of seaside-blue-and-white striped cereal bowls, and an elegant Wedgwood porcelain dinner set all on equal par in the same space.

The solid wood counters held a kettle, a tiny microwave and an assortment of colourful tin storage pots with lids. The room also had a small Formica drop-leaf table with a chair pushed under, a free-standing gas cooker and a modest sized fridge.

Jocelyn opened the fridge. Doreen had indeed stocked it with essentials. A glass bottle of milk stood in the door. On the shelves were a tray with six eggs, a jar with a handwritten label: 'Strawberry Jam', and a block of cheese wrapped in film. On the counter was a paper bag containing a loaf, a porcelain butter dish with a block of real butter, and a glass fruit bowl filled with apples and pears.

Jocelyn took an apple from the bowl. She rarely ate fruit, unless it was a component of a ready meal, but she was feeling hungry, and she had noticed a feint warning throb looming at her temple. She washed the apple in the sink, dried it on the tea towel, and took a bite.

'Oh, blast it; I forgot to give her something for the groceries!'

Now she owed Max *and* Doreen Hughes money - and it was unlike her to be indebted to anyone - whether it was money she owed them, or favours. Jocelyn was fiercely independent. It was way out of her comfort zone to owe money or favours to people, because then you had to remember to return them someday, and life was just too busy to be worrying about things like that.

Eating the apple, she walked through to the sitting room and sat down in the armchair. The patterned carpet was the same one that had always been here; you could play a game of Stepping Stones on the leafy bits… She sighed and finished the apple.

Now, was there a still a telephone in the old house? It used to be in the dining room. Was it too much to expect that there was one, and that it had been left connected? She got up from the chair and went on the hunt into the dining room across the hall.

The room still held the big walnut dining table she remembered as a child, its dark polished surface reflecting the trees outside. Eight chairs with burgundy and cream striped seats were pushed neatly under it. Long burgundy velvet curtains hung from the window in this room, tied back by gold tasselled cords that were looped onto decorative gold hooks in the wall. The room smelled of furniture polish.

There was a small table under the dining room window, with a red velvet stool beside it, and upon it - the same old, black rotary dial telephone. She walked across, lifted the receiver and closed her eyes in silent thanks at the hum of a dial tone. It was only four thirty though, too early to ring Jonathan. There was enough time to unpack and have some food, first.

She took the apple core to the kitchen and dropped it into the waste bin, then went to her luggage still piled in the hallway by the front door and hung up her mac on one of the coat hooks. Then she picked up her briefcase and handbag and whisked them up to the top of the stairs, before returning for the heavier suitcase.

The stairs were dark wood, and they had creaked in a welcoming way when stepped on. As she began to lift her suitcase up though, one awkward step at a time, they creaked in objection instead. She paused to rest between each step, wondering to herself whether she would really need the smart outfits she had brought with her, and then consoling herself that it was always better to be over-prepared.

She grappled with the case until she had manoeuvred it to the top of the stairs and laid it down on the landing above the hall. She stood up, massaged the back of her neck with one hand, and rolled her shoulders a couple of times.

Now, where to sleep? She remembered the house had two, very large bedrooms directly above the sitting and dining rooms, and a third, smaller bedroom - which Kate had used as a sewing room - at the back of the house, next to the bathroom. Kate's bedroom was above the dining room, she recalled, and the second room was the guest room where she had slept as a child. Not feeling quite ready to face Kate's room yet, she opted for the guest room and, leaving the bags where they were for the moment, walked around the landing to it. Kate's bedroom door, on the opposite side of the landing, was closed, and she left it that way.

The wooden door of the guest room was also closed, and Jocelyn turned the round porcelain knob and pushed it slowly open. The subtle scent of lavender greeted her, and the late afternoon sun was shielded behind delicate floral curtains, which had been drawn across the window by Doreen, she assumed, to keep the room cool for her. She stepped inside and glanced around. The double bed had been made up ready, and she wondered if the woman had changed the sheets especially. Kate hadn't used duvets. Instead, there were two pale striped cotton sheets - one tucked into the mattress and one laid above it, a thick woollen blanket with satin edging, and then a light, rose-printed quilt, on the top. One of Kate's hand-crocheted blankets was spread across the foot end of the bed. The top edge of the bedding had been folded down and the pillows plumped, ready for its guest.

Jocelyn smiled and turned to the rest of the room. It had an open fireplace, which was clearly unused because it had a vase of dried flowers standing in it. Between the fireplace and the window was a little wardrobe; empty, apart from an array of wire clothes hangers. Then was a small set of drawers, also empty, and a chair with an old, rather worn teddy bear perched on it.

She remembered the teddy. He had been Kate's when she was a young girl, and she had allowed Jocelyn to play with him. He had lost his original clothing decades ago, and so Kate had knitted replacement coat and trousers for him, with red wool left over from one of her crocheting projects. Jocelyn recalled sitting on a cushion on the slate shelf beside the fireplace, watching Kate knitting in the armchair.

The guest room would be pleasant to sleep in.

She walked back to the top of the stairs to retrieve her suitcase, popping her head around the bathroom door as she passed to have a look in, and the sewing room, empty apart from the old black Singer sewing machine still in the corner on its wrought iron stand, and three shelves stuffed with balls of wool, jars of buttons and haberdashery baskets overflowing with ribbon and lace. She picked up the suitcase and bags and carried them to the bedroom, and then heaved the suitcase onto the bed, unzipped it and began to take out the clothes she had so carefully folded back in London two days before. She hung the trouser suits and skirts in the wardrobe and placed the silk blouses and cashmere cardigans in the drawers. There was no dressing table for her cosmetics, and so she left those in their leather zip bag on the bedside cabinet. Finally, she laid her silk nightdress under one of the two pillows on the bed.

Satisfied, she plopped the lid back down on the empty suitcase and slid it under the bed, out of the way. That was better. It felt good to be on top of things. She took her towel and bathroom toiletries into the bathroom.

Downstairs, the grandfather clock chimed once, to mark five thirty. Jocelyn thought about the fresh bread and cheese in the kitchen. She usually ate late in the evening, but the smell of the bread had made her hungry and there was nothing else to do now, apart from wait for Jonathan to get home from work so that she could speak to him.

She made her way downstairs to the kitchen and took a plate from the cupboard above the counter. Then she made herself a cheese sandwich. It was a decidedly unglamorous supper compared to the food Jonathan and she usually ordered in, but it would have to do for this evening. She sat at the table under the window in the sitting room and chewed slowly on the sandwich, strumming her fingers on the wooden surface, and reflecting on the day so far. It had all gone to plan; there was nothing that could have been improved upon.

Jonathan usually arrived home from his office at seven. It was his turn on a Friday night to pick up food on his way home and she always arrived home a couple of hours after him, so it would be a nice change to be able to chat with him earlier tonight. Thinking about him and their Friday night routine brought on a pang of homesickness. She got up from the table and washed and put away her plate.

Eventually, the clock began chiming seven, and she went into the dining room to make the phone call home.

'Hello?' Jonathan answered immediately.

'Hello darling, it's me.'

'Sweetheart! Phew! I was wondering how you were. All OK?'

'Yes, all is fine, Jonathan. Very fine! I've arrived safely.'

'Are you calling from Kate's house?'

'I am; her phone was still connected.'

'Well, that's a very good start to your trip! I was wondering where on earth you might be able to call from, or whether I would hear from you at all tonight. I left the office early, so I wouldn't miss you if you tried early for whatever reason.'

'Well, thank goodness I don't have to find a smelly phone box on a dark street corner!' she laughed.

'That's great. And dare I ask, were you indeed faced with a ramshackle house and a jungle garden?' he queried carefully.

'Well, no - it's not like that. Not at all.' Jocelyn paused for words, 'It's rather more… captivating.'

'Oh?'

'Yes, it's perfect. The Hughes' had prepared the place for me. It's clean and welcoming and… oh I don't know Jonathan, it's…' she paused. 'It's Kate through and through.'

'Well, there we go then,' he said softly. 'And what's more, there's a lesson in not making assumptions.'

'I couldn't agree more.

'So, the house is fit for you to stay in?'

'Absolutely.'

And the journey? Was it dreadfully long?'

'Well, yes it was long of course, but it wasn't so bad. Certainly not the ordeal I had worked myself up to expect. The trains and the taxi ride were… uneventful.' She decided not to mention the trivial incident of Max's brakes failing on the downward journey from the common.

'Superb. Have you managed to source some food? I don't expect there are many takeaways up there.'

'I don't know about takeaways yet, but can you believe that Mrs. Hughes - Doreen - stocked the fridge for me! The food's a bit basic… Still, you wouldn't get a gesture like that in London, I doubt. I'm not used to it.

'That's very reassuring for me to hear, I must say. They do say that the Welsh are a friendly bunch.'

'Mm. Well, the people I've met so far, they seem decent enough,' she lowered her voice playfully, 'But there doesn't seem to be much rush about them. I suspect things work on a different timescale over here.'

'Well, that's guaranteed to drive *you* to distraction in, oh, a couple of days! You might have to put your patient pants on.'

'I'll do my best.'

'Well, good luck with that!' he laughed. 'Seriously though - I *am* relieved your day has gone without hitch. How do you feel?'

'Oh, on top of things I think - except that I forgot to pay Doreen for the groceries.'

'Well, there's plenty of time to return the favour.'

'Yes. The Hughes' are just across the road.'

'Fabulous. So, you are safe and nicely settled in?'

'I am. There are two jolly good bolts on the front door, and there's a streetlight outside the house - as well as a lovely row of cottages opposite, which…,' she pulled back the dining room curtain and peered across the street at the tidy row of dwellings, 'All appear to be occupied.'

'Then, do you want to hear about my day?'

'I do! We don't usually get the chance to chat like this!'

They chatted for over an hour, Jocelyn talking about the journey; the characters on the train and the changing scenery, and Jonathan filling her in on the cases he was working on and the meal he'd picked up from the Indian. Eventually, the daylight started to fade.

Jocelyn stood up to flick on the light and checked her watch. 'Right, I'm going to settle down for the evening, darling. There is a lot to sort out over the next three weeks and I want to get cracking straight away.'

'Yes, me too, although it will be terribly strange without you tonight.'

'Well, I have Kate's teddy for company. Oh, would you be able to speak to the solicitor tomorrow? It would be really helpful it they arranged to leave the phone connected; I'll be able to call Trudy, and any clients if necessary.'

'And me?'

'Of course, and you!' I'll call you every night.'

'All right, I'll contact them first thing Monday morning.'

'Thank you.'

'Take care sweetheart. Try to get some sleep.'

'I will. I miss you.'

'Miss you too. Goodnight, Jocelyn.'

The wave of tiredness hit without warning and Jocelyn realised she'd been running on adrenaline for most of the day. She had felt hungry again at nine, her usual mealtime at home, and so she had made toast with jam and was munching on the strawberry blobs, watching from the sitting room window as the sun's rays lowered on the big oak trees on the opposite side of the street.

Yawning, she heaved herself out of the armchair, tidied the kitchen and then prepared to retire, first checking that the windows downstairs were all closed, and then switching off lights. She turned the key in the front door and drew across the bolts at the top and bottom. They resisted at first - Kate had clearly never used them - but Jocelyn wriggled and ground at them, until they finally shot into place.

Far from home, but feeling safer knowing the house was secure and that there was a working telephone at hand, she wearily climbed the stairs. Her neck and shoulders had begun to ache, and there was still the feint pulsing at her temples.

She always preferred to shower in the evening rather than in the morning, to rinse away the grime of the city. She turned on the shower, playing with the dial for a while to get the temperature right, and undressed wearily in the tiny bathroom. The shower was over the little pink bath, with a plain white shower curtain hanging from a dainty chrome rail. She stepped in and pulled the curtain across the bath. The stream of hot water raining down on her face and shoulders brought a welcome relief to the aches. She stood with her eyes closed, breathing deliberately - in through the nose, out through the mouth. 'There isn't anything you can't handle, Jocelyn.'

After ten minutes standing almost asleep under the caressing stream, she switched the flow off, climbed out steadily and dried herself off. Her skin felt warm and soft as she slipped on her satin nightdress.

The bedroom door didn't have a lock and so she moved the teddy from the chair and sat him in one side of the bed, and then moved the chair over to the closed door and jammed the back of it under the doorknob. Probably unnecessary, but you could never be too careful in a strange place.

Jocelyn finally slid into the quilted bed at nine o'clock. It felt delicious. She lay with the covers pulled up to her chin - just as she had done twenty-five years ago. The bedside lamp threw shapes across the uneven plaster on the ceiling. She felt her eyes growing heavy. She reached out to the bedside table, flicked off the lamp and then turned on her other side to cuddle the teddy. Sleep came within minutes.

Day 2 - Saturday

The following day, the day of Kate's funeral, went without hitch. It was appropriately grey and drizzly, and a persistent wind was blowing from across the moor and whipping loose leaves in little whirlwinds in the nooks and crannies of the street. The valley was shrouded in mist and everywhere was silent except for the dripping of water from the porch and the guttering onto the path around the house.

Max had arrived in the morning, dressed in a pale grey suit and with his thick hair combed neatly over one side, to pick up Jocelyn as promised and accompany her to the church and afterwards, to the tidy little hillside graveyard for the burial. The previous day’s travel had taken a toll on Jocelyn, and she felt weary and low in spirit. It was a relief that one was not expected to be cheerful or sociable at a funeral.

She hadn't worn a black suit - she didn't own one - but she had brought with her a tailored charcoal skirt suit to wear that she thought Kate would have approved of, and she had teamed it with a black suede clutch bag and matching stiletto heels, and pearl earrings. She had worn her hair up in its usual style, and chosen a lipstick that was pale and subtle, so as not to attract too much attention.

Get up, dress up, show up. Her motto when she really wanted to be anyplace else. If she could just get the funeral over with, she could make up some of the work time she had lost yesterday, in the afternoon.

Kate hadn't wanted a fuss. In her will she had instructed her solicitor to organise and pay for the church service and the burial from her estate, but she had requested that there be no wake, and certainly no flowers. Donations were to go to the local wildlife hospital instead. She hadn't wanted people to 'get all morbid over an old bird like me', Mr. Daniel Rhys had explained to Jocelyn on the telephone, two weeks previously. That sounded like Kate.

The only thing of note was the sheer volume of people who attended the service. The church was tiny in comparison to places of worship Jocelyn had attended in London. A narrow, mossy path led off the main street in the town centre, through the grounds dotted with old, tilting gravestones with the carvings worn almost completely away, and a gnarled yew tree growing against the church's stone walls.

Through the hinged wooden door, the church interior had eight rows of pews on each side of an aisle paved with stone slabs and with a wrought iron grid running down the centre. Six stained glass windows showed scenes from the bible and the world wars. The sills housed flower arrangements in summer colours. At the front was a dark wooden altar with a colourful tapestry covering it, a modest-sized organ and seats for a small choir. The vaulted roof was crossed with old wooden beams and in the centre hung a chandelier filled with half-burned candles, dripping with wax.

Every pew of the little church was filled, and guests were standing against the walls and at the back, too. People of all ages had turned up to pay their respects to Kate - lowering their heads in thoughtful prayer or lifting their chins and filling their chests to sing magnificent tributes to a woman they clearly admired.

The morning passed in a blur. In the new graveyard on the hillside just outside of town, Kate was laid to rest. Despite the weather, Jocelyn's hair stayed in place for most of the service thanks to a good dousing of hair lacquer, and only began to surrender to the elements towards the end of the day. The shoes did not fare so well on the long damp grass, but those could be replaced easily enough with a phone call to Harvey Nicholls when she got home.

She nodded out of politeness afterwards to a few people with whom she had made unintentional eye contact, but she didn't stop to talk and was thankful that Max didn't delay in driving her back to the Coach House when she dropped the subtle hints that she'd had enough of the ceremony. Presumably, Mr Rhys the solicitor had been at the service, but she hadn't been in the mood for introducing herself to him; he represented the enormousness of her duty here.

Back at the Coach House, she had changed out of the charcoal suit and hung it up on the sitting room door frame, to dry. She had placed the earrings carefully in their box in her vanity case and thrown the ruined shoes into the bin. Then, still shivering from the effects of the soaking drizzle on the hillside, she went into the hallway and flicked on the switch for the heating, listening with relief as the system started up and the radiators around the house began to creak into life. Feeling slightly sorry for herself at the lack of substantial food in the house but not wanting to dwell on it, she made two pieces of toast with butter, and collapsed to devour them in the armchair in the warming room.

The taste of the warm bread and cool, salty butter on her tongue was soothing. She finished the slice and then sat back in the armchair and listened to the ticking clock.

***

The plate slid with a little bump onto the carpet and spilled crumbs around Jocelyn's feet, waking her with a start, wondering for a minute where she was. The light outside the sitting room window was fading, and she sat up in the chair, stiff and irritated. She checked her watch: six fifteen. She cursed silently. She had planned to catch up on work after the funeral, and now the afternoon was lost. There was no point trying to do any now. Her head felt thick - and anyway, Kate's lights were too dim to see without straining her eyes and bringing on a full-scale headache.

Oh, to be back at home!

She got up, went to the kitchen to find a dustpan to tidy up the spilled toast crumbs, and after some hunting around found one in the small cupboard under the stairs. Fighting the frustration that was causing her chest to tighten, she swept up the crumbs as well as she could, then decided that it wouldn't have been good enough for Kate and returned to the stair cupboard to wrestle out the little vacuum cleaner stored in the bottom.

Kate might have loved her antiques but thank goodness she had kept her household appliances up to date. Jocelyn carried the vacuum cleaner into the sitting room and plugged it into the socket behind the armchair. Then she pushed the nozzle back and forth over the crumb-covered rug, thinking that if only her cleaner Sandra had been here to do this job for her, she could at least have made a start on something more productive.

Eventually, the room was returned to its former neatness, and Jocelyn sat down feeling annoyed and thrown because her plans had been messed up. Her expensive suit hung soggy in the doorway, and her hair, already dishevelled by the rain, was now flattened by an unplanned doze in the chair too.

Don't start feeling sorry for yourself, Jocelyn. Find something else to focus on.

What was it Kate used to make for them both, on those drizzly days when outdoor play had been out of the question and the mood was threatening to dip? Milky coffee. She had watched Kate make steaming mugs of milky coffee for them both, from a stool that Kate had pulled up for her to stand on beside the hob. Could she remember how to make one herself?

She went to the kitchen and took the milk bottle from the fridge door, then opened the cupboard doors along the wall in search of a suitable mug. Over on the right side, she found an assortment of novelty mugs, and it made her smile. These must be ones that Kate had collected - or been gifted, perhaps - on her world travels. 'Genius at Work', 'I Love Madrid' 'Head Gardener', 'Ageing like a Mighty Oak'; it was amusing the things that Kate kept as memorabilia. She chose a plain white mug and measured out the correct quantity of milk into it, before pouring it into a little, slightly battered old saucepan that she had unhooked from the wall above the cooker. She turned on a gas ring and stood in the dim light, stirring the liquid to stop it from sticking to the pan, with a wooden spoon she'd picked from the utensil jar on the counter. When it began to simmer around the edges, she added a spoonful of coffee, stirred it in vigorously to whip up the surface into a froth, and then carefully poured it, steaming and full of comforting aroma, back into the mug.

It wasn't good to be cross about the weak instant coffee; she must do better to appreciate Doreen Hughes' gesture to her. She took a first sip the velvety drink with a sigh, just as the phone in the dining room began to ring.

'Hello sweetheart.' It was Jonathan.

'Hello darling.' With the drink in one hand, she took a seat beside the telephone and fought to keep her voice steady. 'It's wonderful to hear your voice.'

'How are you? How did the day go? I couldn't stop thinking about you today.'

'Oh, as well as could be expected.'

'The funeral?'

'Yes, all without hitch.'

'Are you sure you're all right?'

She sighed, 'I didn't manage to do any work today. I had planned to this afternoon, and now I feel behind.' Her voice started to rise.

'Well, perhaps you can do a bit tomorrow,' Jonathan spoke calmly. 'Don't be too hard on yourself; you have had a long journey and a funeral to deal with.'

'Yes, it's Sunday tomorrow, I can work then. Do you think it would be all right if I call Trudy at home?' she said.

'Do you really need to? I think it could wait until Monday, sweetheart.'

'I suppose.'

'Look, you've had a busy couple of days. Why don't you go to bed early tonight? Perhaps you could read a book?'

'A book?' It was rare that Jocelyn read for entertainment. When she had first met Jonathan, they both had a love of reading and their idea of a perfect weekend was curled up in their rented one-bed flat with the window open, listening to the hum of the city outside but lost in a John Steinbeck or Nevile Shute novel.

'Yes. Are there any books of Kate's there? She struck me as a big reader.'

Jocelyn blew out her cheeks. 'There are a few shelves of wildlife books. Not the most appealing of reads.'

'Nothing else to pique your interest?'

'Biographies of actors I've never heard of.'

'Well, go for a wildlife book, then. Come on - you used to love it up there when you were young. You told me so just yesterday morning!'

'We'll see.'

He didn't press her further. Instead, they chatted for the next half an hour about his own day, which had been spent, Jocelyn was surprised to learn, at the Tate. She was careful not to concern him any more than she already had by talking of bland food and unsatisfactory coffee. As always, a conversation with him buoyed her and when they ended the call at eight, she had agreed to have an early night.

She showered in the bathroom, rinsing away the musty smells of the church from her hair and a few grass seeds that had stuck to her damp legs. She yawned and watched the water stream down the plug hole. *It's okay, it's only Saturday. You can work all day tomorrow to make up for Friday.* She towelled herself off slowly, slipped into her nightdress and opened the tiny window to let the steam out of the bathroom. The night air was cool, and a fine rain drummed on the tiles, and made the rock face outside the window glisten.

Perhaps Jonathan was right - a book might help her relax, ease the tightness in her chest. She hurried back downstairs to the sitting room and scanned Kate's bookshelves. Illustrated British Wildlife; that should be enough to send anyone to sleep. She slid the heavy hardback down from the shelf and made her way back upstairs, checking that the windows were closed, the sockets off and the front door securely bolted on the way. Once in bed, with the sheets pulled up and the teddy tucked in next to her, she opened the pages of the big book and spent half an hour flicking absently through it, until her mind was calmer and she was ready to sleep.

Day 3 - Sunday

On Sunday morning, the sun returned. It shone through a slit in the curtains and fell in a pool across the end of the bed. Outside the window, birds chattered on the guttering and a pigeon sat on the top of the chimney cooing, its call echoing down into the fireplace as if the bird were inside the bedroom. The dawn chorus woke Jocelyn slowly. She opened her eyes, wondering for a moment where she was. She looked at her wristwatch; five o'clock. She breathed out; thank goodness she hadn't overslept. She really needed to get on with some work this morning, then she could devote the afternoon to having a sort through Kate's things.

Jocelyn was always well-presented. Without fail. This morning, the outfit would be her signature combination of navy tapered trousers and cream tailored blouse with a lace collar. She brushed her hair and clipped it up from her face and neck as usual, then added some gold earrings, a bracelet and a touch of red lipstick to complete the look. She picked up her briefcase from beside the wardrobe and, after checking her appearance once more in the bathroom mirror on the way past, she headed downstairs.

Working hard to drum up the enthusiasm, she boiled the kettle and made a cup of instant coffee. The first coffee of Jocelyn's mornings was crucial in getting the brain functioning; getting hold of some proper filter coffee was a priority.

She set up her workspace on the sitting room table. The placemats with pictures of Welsh castles on them and the little crystal vase from the centre were put away in the alcove cupboard. The textured lace tablecloth was exchanged for a cotton one that would be easier to press on when writing. Finally, she replaced the chair with one from the dining room with armrests and a padded seat. Satisfied, she sat down, opened her briefcase and began to spread its contents in organised piles - alphabetically by client surname, from left to right - on the table. By six am, she was immersed in her work, chic tortoiseshell-framed glasses perched on her nose and a frown wrinkling her forehead as she scanned lines of text. It was a relief to be an hour ahead of her usual start time - and on a Sunday, too. Gained hours. She'd make up for Friday's inferior performance today.

The grandfather clock ticked loudly in the hall. Out of the window, a blanket of white mist lay over the valley, with trees emerging from it like shadowy forms. The mist was shifting and changing in the breeze. Jocelyn rubbed her eyes, readjusted her glasses, and re-read the paragraph she had just completed.

A cow mooed from somewhere. A few seconds later, another cow mooed a reply. Jocelyn paused, listening. Her office in Mayfair was on the third floor of a Georgian building and was double-glazed, so street noise was always at a minimum. Here, the glass panes were thin, and the wooden frames had gaps in places that let a whistling draft through - and street noises.

She waited. Silence, apart from the tick of the clock. Had they finished mooing? She started on the passage of text again; the third read through, and it still hadn't sunk in. She removed her glasses and strummed the table with her fingers. This whole setup was too… *relaxing*! Was it possible to stop the ticking, somehow? It was making it hard to stay alert. Perhaps it would be better with the curtains closed - and the door to the hallway too, to block out the clock's noise.

She stood up and tugged the lace curtains together. They didn't quite close all the way but even a restricted view was less distracting than a panoramic one. She closed the sitting room door too, which worked in muffling the sound of the clock.

She wished it were Monday and not Sunday, because she desperately wanted to call Trudy and check in on things in the office. Trudy had been Jocelyn's secretary and right-hand woman for over ten years. She was punctual and reliable, with a can-do attitude and not too many family commitments to distract her from her job; Jocelyn approved of everything about Trudy. She checked her watch. Monday was an eternity away. She got up and went to the kitchen, made another coffee and forced it down, knowing that there would be no rewarding caffeine hit for the effort.

Just after seven, faint voices floated from the street through the curtains. She peered through the gap. The sun had risen high enough now to clear the hills, and it shone down in shafts on the lane and across the valley. Max was across the street. He was dressed in a crisp shirt, a pair of dark grey trousers and boots that had dried mud around the soles. A neckerchief covered his neck from the sun, and he had left off the waistcoat today. He had stopped to talk to someone in one of the cottage gardens, and now he was looking up at The Coach House.

Jocelyn quickly looked back down and resumed writing, hoping he hadn't seen. The next time she glanced up, he had gone.

The next few hours passed without interruption, until ten thirty, when her stomach rumbled a protest at the lack of breakfast. In London, the first nourishment of the day was a strong filter coffee and a cheese toastie on the way to work, from the deli near the tube station manned by Giovanni, the efficient Italian with greying hair and a white apron. This morning's two weak beverages were no match. She got up from the table, stretched her back and made her way to the kitchen. She opened the doors of the floor cupboards and hunted for a toastie maker.

It didn't appear that Kate owned any such device and even if she had, Jocelyn hadn't made a toastie for years. The ingredients were all there in Kate's kitchen, though, thanks to Doreen: bread, butter, cheese. It was amazing really that three simple ingredients, so bland on their own, could be combined using a bit of heat into a tasty snack.

She cut two pieces of bread and three slices of cheese, buttered the bread thickly and laid it all on a plate. It was a primitive breakfast by comparison to the usual, but it would have to do. With a pang of homesickness for Giovanni and his deli, she sat back down to the paperwork and continued without further interruption until noon.

Convenience shopping is something that city dwellers take for granted. Jocelyn realised this when it was too late, when she had gone beyond hunger and into the zone of utter grumpiness. There was no Trudy to send out for lunchtime sandwiches. No supermarket nearby. And no takeaway restaurant around the corner to hurry to the rescue this, or any other, evening. She sat in the armchair and breathed.

Stop and think, Jocelyn; it's what you are good at.

Doreen's farm shop would have some ready meals, surely. If not, she would just have to live on the basics. It would be fine; it was only for three weeks. She grabbed her purse and keys, slipped on her shoes by the door and headed out of the house.

Jocelyn never ventured out of the office during a workday because it interrupted the flow of her productivity. It was difficult to get back into the swing of work once you had tasted the fresh air and vibrance out on the streets. After the cool darkness of the Coach House interior, the sunlight was bright and the air warm. She put her head down and hurried down the garden path, sending a family of chaffinches fleeing into the bushes. She didn't notice. She strode around the corner, onto main the street towards town.

The entrance to the lane leading to the farm shop was just beyond the school. Three hand-painted signs at the end of it read 'Llanfairyn Farm Shop', 'New Potatoes' and 'Free-Range Eggs'. The lane was hot and dusty, with thick hedges on either side and a few muddy patches where yesterday's rain was still drying. She walked down it carefully in her high heeled sandals, until she came to a low, green corrugated tin building, with a rough gravel parking area, big enough for two or three cars, in front of it. Two full-height double doors on the front of the shop were propped wide open and she went inside.

The shop was small but seemed well stocked. There were three aisles that held wooden crates of fruit and vegetables. Shelves on the outside walls were filled with an assortment of jars and packets. A pair of refrigerators with glass-fronted doors gave out a dim hum at the back, against the rear wall.

Jocelyn looked around but didn't see Doreen. Instead, a young girl with a long red ponytail tied back with a green scrunchie was standing at the checkout desk, reading a magazine. She glanced up and smiled a greeting but didn't speak. Jocelyn collected a basket and moved swiftly around the shop, filling the basket with goods she figured she could create some simple meals with - eggs and bread, cheese, jam; more of what Doreen had already stocked her with.

There were no ready meals though, and no filter coffee that she could see. She headed for the checkout and deposited the basket on the dusty counter. 'Do you sell filter coffee?'

The girl looked up and, smiling, she put the magazine aside. 'Filter? Aw, sorry, we only have what's on the shelf.' She rolled her r's softly when she spoke, and her freckled face wore an open and pleasant expression.

'Well then, are there any supermarkets nearby?'

'There's one on the other side of town.'

'Any takeaways nearby?'

'Aw, I don't know, sorry,' the girl's cheeks flushed slightly, and she concentrated on the shopping basket. 'Do you have your own bags?'

'No, I don't. Don't you have plastic bags?' Jocelyn replied, feeling herself growing hot. She knew they did;

she could see them hanging on the wall behind the counter.

'We do, it's just that most people bring their own basket.' The girl reached behind her, pulled off two plastic bags from the bunch and then started typing into the till, popping each item into a bag as she went.

'Oh, wait, there *is* a fish and chip shop on the other side of town,' she offered helpfully.

'I was thinking something more… well, not fish and chips.'

The girl frowned, but then immediately resumed her smile, 'Aww. Then no, I don't think there's anywhere. Sorry,' and then she added, 'But we're the only place open on a Sunday, anyway.'

Stifling a sigh, because she didn't want to make the young girl feel any more awkward than she already had, Jocelyn paid for the goods, gathered up the bags and made for home.

She ate a late lunch of boiled eggs and toast, cut into soldiers in the way Kate had done. To her surprise, the free-range eggs were tasty, the yolk rich and warm as it soaked into the warm buttery bread. Afterwards, she sat for a moment in the armchair to think.

She had inherited all of this - this old house and all Kate's belongings in this backward town with its instant coffee and absence of delis. The personal belongings didn't mean much - Jocelyn wasn't a sentimental type - and the modest amount of money that would be remaining in Kate's savings account after the solicitor's fees for the funeral and for tying up the estate, well, it wouldn't be enough to break into a sweat over.

She was to live here for three weeks and after that, she simply had to instruct the solicitors what to do with it all. Was it worth it? Why not just go home now and tell Daniel Rhys to sell everything? And she could return home, where she could get filter coffee and takeaway food on a Sunday.

But Kate had asked her to come. Why?

She leaned back against the cushions of the armchair to ponder it; legs stretched out over the leaf-patterned rug next to the fireplace. From the hallway, the clock ticked its lullaby. At least she'd managed to do a few hours' work today. This afternoon, she would make a start at sorting through Kate's bookshelves.

***

The grandfather clock chimed five. Jocelyn sat up in the armchair with a start. Had she fallen asleep in the chair *again*? Three weeks was going to fly by at this rate.

This was why she rarely took holidays; it took three days to wind down enough to relax; the rest of the time was spent trying to stay awake in the absence of a regular routine. With the time it took to get back up to speed once back in the office, it just wasn't worth the interruption.

And yet, other people seemed to enjoy their vacations. Trudy always came back from Malta tanned and revitalised, didn't she?

She hauled herself out of the chair, went to the kitchen and poured a cool glass of water. After drinking it, she went upstairs to clean her teeth and tidy her hair and face.

Right, it was time to get on with sifting through Kate's things and the bookshelves in the sitting room were surely a good starting point. Jocelyn had enjoyed reading when she was younger, but nowadays, by the time she'd lifted her head from client paperwork at nine at night, the last thing she felt like doing was burying it in a novel. It shouldn't take long to scan Kate's bookshelves and determine that there was nothing among the musty realms that she wanted to keep.

She carried a chair from the table over to the alcove and climbed carefully onto it. The top shelf was devoted to Kate's profession; paperback novels, play scripts, and celebrity biographies. The lower shelves - those easier to reach, were filled with manuals on British and local flora and fauna; garden birds, butterflies, and numerous other topics to do with the natural world that Kate had so loved.

On the lowest shelf, above the alcove cupboard, was a row of eight navy hardbacks, with 'The Children's Encyclopaedia' embossed in gold on the spine. Jocelyn leaned over, slid the first one out and opened it. The pages were brittle and had a smell… and in an instant, she was 12 years old again.

How funny that a scent can transport you in a flash, from the present moment to one thirty years earlier. She remembered that Kate used to let her look at these books - but only under her careful supervision.

'They are very precious,' she had explained to the young girl.

Jocelyn closed the book carefully, then sat down slowly beside the fireplace and laid the book on her knees. She opened it again, this time at the front page. On the inside cover was an ink inscription - 'Dearest Kathryn, from Samuel' and a small hand-drawn flower. Jocelyn paused, frowning. Samuel had been Kate's older brother. She remembered Kate mentioning him briefly when she had asked about a photograph in the hallway; he had been killed when he was quite young. Kate had never elaborated.

She put the book down, reached behind her and pulled out another from the shelf. There was a bookmark in this one, and she remembered reading the marked pages with Kate. She sat down and began to read through the chapter - 'The Literature of Italy'. The language so formal, it was hard to believe it had been written for a young audience. She started reading and found it quite interesting. She read that chapter, and then pulled out further books from the collection and started to read chapters from those. From The Ancient Egyptians and The Great Composers to How to Make a Bag from a Glove, Kate's generation of children could find the answers to all their worldly questions in these volumes.

Jocelyn sighed and checked her watch; seven o'clock. She felt weary and really needed caffeine. She put all the books away and went to the kitchen. Among the storage tins on the counter, she found one with teabags in. She wasn't a tea drinker - she couldn't remember last drinking tea - but, where needs must…

She ignored the oversized china teapot next to the kettle - wondering momentarily why a woman who lived alone needed such a big one; another souvenir, perhaps - and plonked the teabag directly into the cup, adding a splash of milk and half a spoon of sugar. She then returned to the armchair. Something had stirred in her when looking through the encyclopaedias - an unfamiliar feeling. She wondered how many hours she had spent at Kate's as a child, and why it had been so easy to forget and move on when she reached her late teens.

Jocelyn's parents had divorced when she was eighteen. The news hadn't affected her as much as they feared it would; it had been obvious to her that they were drifting apart. She sympathised with her father. It must have been hard for him, being married to a touring musician. He was left for long stretches, holding the fort at home with a young child. Only Kate, his wife's aunt, offered to help care for Jocelyn.

Even so, Jocelyn believed that he would have tried to make the marriage work. In the end, he agreed to the separation and they managed to keep it civilised. The material evidence of their marriage was dispatched with minimum fuss. Her mother had never been one for drama, and she quickly moved on with her life. Her father withdrew into his office, to bury himself in his books.

Luckily by then, Jocelyn had the distraction of her law degree at a lively city university, and a handsome fellow student by the name of Jonathan Anderson.

Jocelyn's own workload was so demanding that working mornings-only for the duration of the three-week visit was not going to be enough to stay on top of cases. She'd been a fool to think it was - it had been that way for seventeen years. She suddenly wasn't sure how she'd be able to sort through Kate's clutter before the three-week period was up. The house and its contents were resurrecting old memories and it felt uncomfortable; they had been safely buried for too many years. She needed to work to keep her mind focused on the present day.

What was this nonsense, having to come and stay at Kate's? She ran her hands over her hair a few times. It was so untidy! She went upstairs to where she'd left her comb in the bathroom, removed the clips and restyled it. Then she applied the bold red lipstick usually reserved for the toughest of her clients. That was better. She went downstairs to the dining room, took a quick look out across the street, then sat down and picked up the telephone receiver. She dialled her home number and played with the gold tassel on the end of the curtain cord as she waited for Jonathan's reply.

'Hello darling, it's me.'

'Jocelyn! How are you? How was your day?' he sounded cheerful, which irritated her for some reason.

'Oh, fine.' Be reasonable, Jocelyn.

'How did you spend your Sunday?' he asked.

'Well, I didn't achieve as much as I had planned…' She bit her tongue. It wouldn't help to be negative. 'But I did go through some of Kate's books. Oh, and I found the farm shop that Doreen Hughes works at, so I'll be all right for food.'

'Oh, that's good. Was there anything worth reading?'

'Plenty of wildlife books.' She exhaled, 'Oh, look Jonathan, I'm sorry, but it's a bit difficult right now to get excited about The Great Outdoors.'

'Fair enough. So, you went out for a bit?'

'Out?'

'Yes - you left the house?' he asked.

'Well, only briefly, to go to the farm shop, as I said.'

'Is it nice?'

'Is what nice?' It was becoming difficult not to snap at him.

'Well, the town.'

'I suppose. I wasn't paying much attention, to tell you the truth.'

'Have you seen anyone today? Spoken to anyone?'

'No. Why would I?'

'I was just wondering if any of Kate's friends had called round…' He tailed off.

'Well, I must confess, I kept a low profile. The thing is, I really need to get on with things. I'm so fearful of falling behind with my own work and as for the house, well, I could have done without having to sort out someone else's possessions.'

'All right, Jocelyn sweetheart. I just thought it might do you good to have a bit of social contact…'

'Oh, for goodness' sakes Jonathan!' she cut in, 'Llanfairyn is full of old people! I need to work.' She stopped herself from saying anything further.

'All right sweetheart, whatever you feel is best.'

She sighed. 'I'm sorry darling. I'm in such a grumpy mood tonight and I'm taking it out on you, and on the people of Llanfairyn, which isn't fair of me.'

'Would you like me to come to you?' he offered. 'I can probably be there by Tuesday.'

'No, it's fine. Really.' For the rest of the conversation, she tried to be upbeat, describing to him the house, the garden and what little detail she could remember of the farm shop - which wasn't much because her mind had been full of other things. At nine, they ended the call and Jocelyn made herself a cup of tea. The curtains in the sitting room were still closed but it was light outside, and she could hear voices and laughter. She finished the tea, and then returned to her paperwork spread on the table. She sat down. It was always a relief to lose herself in British Law.

Eventually, the sky outside turned navy and the streetlight flickered on. At eleven, she began her evening routine: check windows and doors, turn off sockets, remove makeup, shower, fold clothes neatly, brush teeth. It was past midnight when she finally collapsed into bed.

Day 4 - Monday

On Monday morning, the fourth day in Llanfairyn, Jocelyn was roused from sleep at five-thirty by pain throbbing at her temples. She rolled onto her side and noticed the ache across her shoulders.

Fighting the nausea that always accompanied the headaches, and with eyes squinting against the daylight, she peeled herself out of bed, chose a fresh outfit from the drawers and fumbled into it. She reached down the side of the bedside table for her handbag and dug around in it for her migraine tablets. Where were they? She couldn't find the packet, and it was always in the inside pocket.

Except… She remembered clearing out her handbag on the bed in London, to re-pack it for the trip. And now, the tablets were missing. She took out a container of paracetamol from her cosmetic bag instead, and opened it, to find only two tablets remaining inside.

A tight feeling rose in her throat. Why hadn't she checked that she was carrying all the tablets she might need for the trip? Of all things she should have been sure to pack, those were the most important. She might have guessed that the trip would trigger a migraine!

She went downstairs and into the kitchen, swallowed the paracetamol with a glass of water, then, against the wishes of the nausea, forced herself to eat some bread to stop the headache from progressing further. Cursing silently, she raked the kitchen cupboards for any type of pain relief medication. There was none.

Stay calm - you'll only make things worse. Eat, drink and do the breathing exercise.

She sat down in the armchair, eating the bread and sipping a second glass of water, then holding the cool glass against her forehead. She massaged the back of her neck with a hand, trying to knead some life into the blood vessels there. When she had finished the bread and water, she made a mug of sweet tea, and slowly drank that too. Then she waited. After half an hour the paracetamol began to work, and to her relief the headache regressed to a dull throb. It was six thirty. She moved to the sitting room table, sat down and opened one of her files.

She'd been working for ten minutes when female voices echoed from the street outside. Relaxed conversation floated through the closed curtains, followed by light laughter and a dog bark. She ignored it and stared at the document in front of her.

Another few minutes and she heard a male voice now, the old man from the cottage opposite. He called a greeting to the women. The woman must have stopped, because the three of them were chatting. More quiet laughter.

Irritation filled Jocelyn's chest. She glanced through the gap in the net curtains. The two women were walking off with the dog, and the old man had disappeared. She reached over and pulled at the curtains, but she couldn't make them meet in the middle. Did they even fit the window, or were they just there for decoration? Kate probably left them open, so that she could see out onto the street. Why would anyone want people looking right into their sitting room window? Privacy was something Jocelyn had taken for granted in the city. She carried on reading.

Seven o'clock. Another voice now, male. Familiar guffaws. She peeked through the curtains. Max had arrived and was leaning on the garden wall, conversing with the old man. He threw back his head in laughter. The old man had mirrored Max's stance, one hand on the wall, one hand resting on a hip, and they looked settled for the duration.

This was ridiculous. She might as well make another cup of tea until the distractions had passed. She got up and went to the kitchen to boil the kettle, then made the drink with a whole spoonful of sugar and sat drinking it in the seclusion of the dark little room. The tea tasted good, and the warmth filled her stomach and spread to her aching shoulder muscles. There was no point rushing back to the sitting room; the two men across the road were probably still putting the world to rights.

She crossed her ankles in the chair and studied the kitchen. The white walls were rough and uneven, where paint had been layered on over the decades. More lacy curtains framed the little window in here, too. How long would she be a fugitive in here? She did her breathing exercises and allowed her shoulders to drop. It would be all right; the work would get done. She finished the tea slowly and checked her watch.

Trudy would be in the office now. She decided to give her a call.

She crept down the hallway to the dining room, mindful that the curtains in there were not closed. Max and the man would see her if she wasn't careful. She sidled over to the telephone and dialled the office number, being careful to stay behind the wall as she waited for an answer.

Trudy picked up the phone at the other end and Jocelyn could have hugged her. It was wonderful to hear her voice, as calm and efficient as ever. They discussed documents and clients for three-quarters of an hour. Trudy reassured Jocelyn that she had everything under control and there was no need to worry - and would Jocelyn please remember to eat some lunch?

When Jocelyn returned to her paperwork at the window table, Max had gone and so had the old man. She pulled her attention back to the open file on the table in front of her and tried to ignore the creeping return of the headache.

***

The tap at the door at noon was soft, but it still startled Jocelyn. Could she ignore it? She decided that a brief interruption wouldn't hurt. Despite her efforts to ignore it, the ache in her shoulders was resuming. She got up stiffly from the table, straightened her clothes and hair, and made for the door. The bolts were still across, and she slid them back and opened the door - not fully, but just enough to be able to converse with the caller.

'Good afternoon, Jocelyn.' A short man with check shirt and khaki trousers stood in the doorway. A ring of fine white hair protruded from around the base of his cap, and it appeared brilliantly translucent against his tanned skin. He lifted his eyes and then lowered them again, as if making eye contact pained him.

'Yes, hello?'

'I'm Alan Hughes; my wife Doreen let you in.'

Ah yes, Mr. Hughes.'

'I'm sorry I wasn't here to welcome you. I was working in the community garden, you see.' Alan removed his cap and held it in front of him.

Jocelyn waited. Was she supposed to invite him in?

'I hope I didn't disturb you,' he continued.

'Well, I was working, but it is lunchtime…' She stopped herself, deciding against mentioning taking a lunchbreak, in case it encouraged the man to linger. Instead, she asked politely, 'No Mrs. Hughes this afternoon?'

'No, no - not this afternoon. I thought I'd, you know, come round for an hour and keep on top of things in Kate's garden.'

'Ah yes!' it dawned on Jocelyn, 'You've been gardening for Kate. Sorry, I…'

'It's all right, we all know you've come from London, and that you must be very busy.' He said 'London' with an emphasis more suitable for 'Outer Space'.

They *all* knew? Who knew? She didn't want to appear hostile to Kate's former neighbours. 'Mr Hughes, Alan. The garden is looking beautiful, I must say. It really is something else.'

'Yes well, it's a good time of year to be enjoying it.'

'I'm sure it is. And I do appreciate that you and Mrs. Hughes - Doreen - were taking care of the house for Kate.'

He looked at his feet. 'All right then. So, I'll just get on then, is it? If it doesn't affect your work.'

'That's fine Alan.'

'There we are, then.'

She went to close the door, but Alan was still looking at her. 'Are you feeling all right?' he asked, 'Only, you *do* look pale.'

'Oh, I seem to have come down with a bit of a headache,' she dismissed, 'Very annoying, I'm not usually ill. I'll be fine, I just need to buy paracetamol later.'

'Oh dear. I'm sorry to hear that.'

She waved away any concern with her hand and made one last effort to display some manners, while still gently encouraging him on his way. 'Righty-ho. Must get back to work. Thank you again, Alan.'

Alan ambled off to where he had parked a rather battered green metal wheelbarrow in the middle of the lawn and picked out a rake and a shovel from the jumble of other tools in it. Jocelyn closed the door and went to make a cup of tea. Now it was on her mind that she might have appeared impolite. Why was this trip proving so complicated? Go to Kate's for three weeks, do some work and perhaps a bit of packing, return home. What was so hard about that? In the anonymity of London, you can ignore people at your will, and it does not result in a judgement of your manners.

Perhaps it would be easier to work in the bedroom. She would have to carry up the little table from the dining room, that was all - moving the telephone into the windowsill first. The grandfather clock would be dull and there would be no distractions from outside.

Within ten minutes, Jocelyn had relocated to the upstairs room. She didn't need to sort through Kate's possessions; after three weeks, she would instruct the solicitors to pack and sell everything. No more aggravations. Between now and then, she would eat, work and sleep.

She willed the hours to pass.

***

At five in the evening, there came three soft raps on the front door, a pause, and then three more raps. Jocelyn sat silent at the table in the bedroom. The headache of the morning had fully returned, and she was feeling too unwell to share any further pleasantries with strangers today. She held her breath and listened. After five minutes and no more noise from downstairs, she was confident the caller had left.

She pushed aside the guilt she felt at ignoring the person at the door. The headache was too established to continue working; she could barely concentrate on the text. Perhaps a cool shower would ease the tension in her neck and shoulders, or maybe a bath - not too hot, for that would make the throbbing worse, but at least then she could lie down. Without her tablets to ease the headache, she needed to do whatever it took to stop it progressing into a migraine.

Jocelyn never took baths. They were a waste of precious time - all that filling of the tub and then lying around - and she had only had one installed in their London apartment to preserve its resale value. Of course, that one was a cast iron rolltop one on legs, in keeping with the apartment's period style.

She left her work spread on the table in the bedroom and walked around the landing to the bathroom, pulled the shower curtain out of the way and looked down at Kate's tiny pink bath. It wasn't inviting, but she put in the plug and turned on the two taps. On the side was an ornate glass bottle, labelled 'Lavender Bath Oil'. She tipped a glug of the oil under the stream of water. Soon, the soothing scent filled the room.

When the bath was filled, she slipped out of her clothes and folded them on the stool, then unbuckled her watch and lay it in the windowsill, with the face propped up so she could keep an eye on the time. Then, dipping first a toe in, and then a foot, she eased herself slowly into the water. She settled down and lay back, resting her aching shoulders and ignoring the occasional drip of cold water onto her head from the shower above, as tendrils of lavender-scented steam swirled around the room.

***

She awoke with a start. What on earth…? The bathwater was cold. The light outside of the small window was turning orange and the room had grown cool. She sat up and squinted at the watch on the windowsill; eight o'clock. Llanfairyn was a black hole! The days were passing, and she was achieving nothing! What an awful trip this was turning out to be.

Disorientated from sleep, she scrambled out of the bath and, feeling quite miserable form the cold, towelled herself vigorously and dressed. Her stomach was rumbling indignantly; it had received only liquid since breakfast time. Well, there was only cheese and bread on the menu.

She made her way downstairs intending to go the kitchen but stopped at the front door. It was hours since the mystery caller had left. Had Alan left now, too? Something urged her to look outside. She opened the door. The evening breeze that met her was cool and soothing. The garden was empty; Alan had gone, and the street beyond silent apart from a lone bird calling a stern 'Pink, pink,' from the branches of a tree on the opposite side of the road.

She went to close the door, and as she did so, she noticed a bag on the doorstep at her feet - a square hessian shopping bag with a sturdy flat base and two handles. It was half-full of something, but the contents were obscured by a tea towel. Hesitantly - because Londoners are terribly afraid of ownerless bags - she stooped down beside it, pulled the handles apart and lifted the tea towel.

Inside, there was a round, orange-and-white Pyrex casserole dish with a lid on it. Next to it, wedged in the side, were two thick slices of crusty bread wrapped in film. Finally, tucked away in the bottom corner, was a box of paracetamol.

After looking around one last time to make sure the mystery caller hadn't waited for three hours in the garden, for a response they justly deserved from the rude Londoner, Jocelyn took the bag inside and closed the door. She locked it, slid the bolts across and then carried it into the kitchen.

The casserole dish contained a rich, dark stew of beef cubes, chunks of carrot and potato, and whole button mushrooms. It had all been roasted in a rich caramelised onion gravy and the aroma that wafted out when she opened the lid made her stomach weep with joy. Jocelyn sat down on the kitchen chair with a plonk, her head hung down, not knowing how she felt - but certainly not proud of her behaviour. Kate would have been disappointed at her attitude towards her neighbours, she knew. She remembered Kate had made time for everyone who called at the Coach House.

The next hour was spent seated under the soft glow of the sitting room lamp, with a tray on her lap, spooning the mouth-watering casserole from a deep bowl, dunking in the bread to soak up the gravy and willing the paracetamol she had taken to start working. Afterwards, she picked a book from the shelf, 'Cottage Garden Flowers', figuring that Kate would have approved of this choice, at least. She turned the pages, flicking past colourful images of plants she'd never heard of nor cared for: hollyhock, lupin, phlox.

At nine, Jonathan called. 'How are you, Jocelyn?' his voice was gentle but concerned.

'Oh, I'm fine.' The automatic answer.

'It's late, I was worried about you.'

She closed her eyes and let the words continue, 'I'm fine, honestly. Just a little headache today. I've managed to get some work done. And I've eaten some stew. All fine.'

'Well, that's good.' He didn't sound convinced.

'Do you mind if we chat tomorrow darling? I'm just rather tired tonight. I'll have a good night's sleep and then I'll be back on top form tomorrow.'

'Of course. Whatever you wish. Just remember I'm happy to come to you, if necessary. I don't want to push, but…'

'No need for that. Right then, I'll go to bed now. Goodnight.' She fought to keep her eyes open as she ended the call in the most 'I'm-fine' voice she could summons.

She deposited the tray of dirty dishes on the counter in the kitchen and then made her way upstairs. 'Please let me feel better tomorrow,' she stared at the pale reflection in the bathroom mirror. 'I have so much to do.'

Too tired for the bedtime routine, she changed into her nightdress, leaving her expensive outfit in a crumpled heap on the floor, then crawled into bed and closed her eyes, thankful to shut out the world.

Days 5 & 6 - Tuesday & Wednesday

The headache persisted the following morning. Jocelyn woke with a tight band of pain around her forehead. Something was different. The sun filled the room and instead of birdsong, there were the sounds of people talking in the street. She looked at her watch. Seven thirty! She'd slept two hours longer than usual.

In a little over two weeks' time, Jocelyn would be utterly ashamed of her attitude and behaviour in that first week in Llanfairyn, but right at this very moment, five days into the trip, she cursed the unfamiliar place, her three-week assignment in it, and the aches and pains that the whole fiasco had triggered. She crashed out of bed, head immediately flooded with thoughts of work deadlines and the phone call she needed to make to Trudy. The pain throbbed harder in response, and her mind was thick. The box of paracetamol lay on the bedside table, and she fished for it and popped two pills out of their blisters into her hand. The water glass was empty. She fumbled into a robe of Kate's that was hanging on the back of the bedroom door and crept down to the kitchen to refill it, her bare feet unpleasantly cold on the quarry tiles. Then she returned to the bedroom to dress. Her back ached with the effort so she sat on the bed for a few minutes, willing her brain to engage her body. Nothing. Heavy limbs, a foggy brain, and this awful headache. She finished the glass of water - that should help, surely - and crawled back under the sheets. Just another hour's sleep.

Jocelyn slept almost all of Tuesday, only struggling downstairs in the evening to make phone calls to Trudy and Jonathan - who both insisted that she should eat something and rest. When Jonathan heard her feeble tone, he had said that he was going to catch a taxi to Wales immediately. She insisted that he should not; it would only add to her anxiety if he fell behind with his projects. Only the distress in her voice at the idea of his coming stopped him from opening his front door and hailing a cab there and then. Then he proposed to call the Hughes' to see if they could be of assistance, and again Jocelyn insisted that the fuss would upset her more than if she were just allowed to recover privately and quietly.

Feeling helpless at her refusals of support, but not wanting to go against his wife's wishes, Jonathan gave in. Instead, they agreed that he would post the emergency supply of migraine tablets she kept in the bathroom cabinet first thing in the morning; it was unlikely that a pharmacy in Llanfairyn stocked the strength she would need.

Had she eaten? His tone was worried. She told him she'd managed bread and water - although she couldn't really remember when she had eaten, or what. The four days since arriving were a blur.

Jonathan urged her to fetch something more substantial from the kitchen. She promised to eat something and to spend a couple of days resting, and then ended the call. She shuffled shakily into the kitchen and opened the fridge to look for something to eat. There on the shelf was the remainder of the cheese and the casserole dish. She took the dish out and placed it onto the counter. There was still enough stew left in it for two meals, so she ladled half into a china bowl and returned the rest to the fridge. Her hands were trembling as she lifted the bowl. She put the dish into the microwave and set it to two minutes, leaning weakly against the counter as she willed the appliance to hurry up and finish heating.

She sat at the kitchen table in the gloom of the evening, heavy head resting on one hand and eyes closed, spooning down the stew. Afterwards, she dragged her heavy limbs up the stairs and, too tired and weak to think about cleaning her teeth, climbed under the covers and went to sleep.

Wednesday also passed in a haze of illness. Unaware of birdsong, or sunlight, or people going about their day in the street, she slept and woke and slept again. In the afternoon, as the sun moved around the house and the room fell into shade, the noise of a lawnmower in Kate's garden brought on a dream; Jonathan was mowing their lounge carpet and she was frantically trying to stop him from chewing up the expensive Axminster pile - waving her arms and shouting above the engine noise. Jonathan didn't respond; he smiled and kept on mowing. Later, the pigeon on the roof cooed down the chimney and she dreamed it was sitting on the end of the bed, with a casserole spoon in its beak.

She woke at one point, disorientated and thirsty, and her watch said five, but she didn't know if that was five in the morning or the evening. She crawled weakly out of bed, tugged the robe around her and went downstairs, knowing that she must keep forcing herself to eat and drink to get better. She finished the last of the casserole, then filled a glass of water at the kitchen sink, catching sight of herself in the window as she did so.

How pathetic she looked!

She took two paracetamols, drank the whole glass of water and then refilled it to take back to the bedroom. Passing the dining room, she stopped to make a phone call home, leaving a message on the answerphone, 'Jonathan, I'm still feeling a little under the weather. Don't worry about me darling, I'll be fine. I'll be resting this evening though, so don't worry if I don't answer your call.'

She climbed the stairs and summoned up the strength to clean her teeth, before flopping back into bed. The next time she woke, the house was in darkness. At least the door was bolted. She grappled with the paracetamol packet and took two more - hoping that four hours had passed since her last dose - and then fell back into a deep sleep.

Day 7 - Thursday

Why had people wallpapered their ceilings in times gone by?

Jocelyn lay on her back under the soft warm folds of the bedcovers, studying the ceiling. Pale light was filtering in through the curtains. She had woken feeling fragile, but confident that the illness had broken. It was Thursday; she had spent almost one week in this town, and what had been achieved? She curled her toes under the covers and felt the warmth of the sun across her legs. What was it that Trudy and Jonathan had both said, in separate conversations on Tuesday night? That she shouldn't get upset because her work would get done; Jocelyn's work always got done. And what else had they each said, that had surprised her at the time? That they couldn't understand why someone as intelligent as she didn't see this.

Her wristwatch read six o'clock. Life was a daily battle against the clock. This morning though, her senses were dulled. It was nice just lying here.

Once she was sure that the headache had gone, she slowly got out of bed, went downstairs and called Jonathan. She wanted to catch him before he left for work and reassure him that she was on the mend. She couldn't imagine anything worse than him trekking all the way over to Llanfairyn, just for a pesky headache. After the call, she showered. The water running down her back was warm and lovely. Then she dressed in Tuesday's clothes that still lay crumpled on the floor, because she'd worked her way through everything she'd brought with her and hadn't had time to do any laundry. She didn't bother with jewellery or makeup - that she was out of bed and dressed was enough of an achievement.

On the phone on Tuesday night, Trudy had insisted: Jocelyn must eat properly. These motherly instructions rang in her ears. Not wanting to disappoint the woman she respected so, Jocelyn went to the kitchen and made toast, spreading a generous layer of butter on the warm bread, and a mug of tea with plenty of sugar.

Perhaps it would be sensible to spend ten minutes in the fresh, outdoor air. After all, on a usual morning at six forty-five, she would be on the tube at Lancaster Gate, face pressed into the armpits of some or other Very Important Businessman. She found a tray, propped upright in the gap between the fridge and the cupboard, placed the tea and toast onto it, then grabbed her cushion on her way past the sitting room. Someone had thoughtfully pushed a local newspaper through the letterbox, and she collected that too. There was a side-table next to the front door, with a basket containing a collection of crocheted blankets underneath it. She balanced the tray on the table - it seemed positioned for that purpose, while she unbolted and unlocked the door. She opened it gently and stepped outside.

The morning air was cool and still and smelled of cut grass. A couple of birds bounced off across the lawn at the sight of her, into the undergrowth. She headed for the garden seats and placed the tray onto the broad iron table. There was a film of dew on the metal chairs and it was a little too chilly for the light summer clothing she was wearing, so she headed back inside to fetch a blanket from the basket. She chose one of cream and blue tartan wool, and took it with her back to the seat, wrapping it around her waist a couple of times and tucking it under her armpits, before sitting down.

Food tastes better outdoors. How Jonathan and she had enjoyed dining at the little harbourfront taverna in Pythagorion, on the Greek island of Samos… how many years ago? Cobbled streets, warm smells, candlelight and melt-in-the-mouth moussaka; it had been more than three years since they had dined like that.

She sipped the tea and chewed the toast, sitting back against the cushion. A handful of small birds quarrelled in a nearby bush; otherwise, the street beyond the garden wall was still. It was hard to slow down a morning pace that had become established over seventeen years, but the mouthfuls of the buttery toast did well at keeping Jocelyn's thoughts in the present. Two ponies whinnied to each other somewhere in the distance on the common. She looked down and began to absent-mindedly thumb through the newspaper.

'Morning!' Two teenage girls were striding arm-in-arm along the pavement on the other side of the street. They were clad in bootcut denim jeans, long-sleeved t-shirts with images on the fronts and identical Dr.

Marten boots that looked like they should belong to workmen. The girls were heading away from town towards the river, and they each had a rolled-up towel under their arm.

Jocelyn looked up briefly but didn't reply. The greeting *appeared* to have been directed at her, but she hadn't been expecting it. Where on earth were they going, at seven in the morning?

They turned instead to the old man who had come out of his cottage on their side of the road and was pottering in his garden. 'Bore da, Bob.'

'Bore da.' The man stood up from the patch of earth he'd been surveying and smiled at them as they walked on, engrossed in conversation and comparing each other's outfits. Bob looked across at Jocelyn and raised a hand to her in a cautious half-wave.

Jocelyn responded with a small nod and then buried her face back in her mug of tea. She checked her watch. Just a few more minutes - then she'd call the office to let Trudy know she was still alive, and to catch up on what she'd missed.

A familiar voice from the other side of the garden wall made her jump. 'Well, here she is!' It was Max. 'And good morning to you! We haven't seen you for a few days; we were starting to worry!'.

Oh no, not a visitor now. 'Ah, Max, hello.'

'Everything dandy this morning?' he stood in the gateway, awaiting her invitation to enter the garden.

'Well, I think so. The house is comfortable.' She began to clear the crockery onto the tray.

He wandered up the path and stood by the table, 'Are you sleeping well in the old house?'

'Yes, fine thank you.' She pushed her chair out to stand up.

'Alan mentioned that you were feeling rough when he called round on Monday.'

'Yes, I was a little under the weather. I'm fine now.' Jocelyn looked up at the man. He still stood over the table, his whiskers silver in the sunshine and his waistcoat looking like it could have used a hot iron over it.

'Did you find the paracetamol?' he went on. 'I knocked once, but I didn't want to disturb you if you were sleeping.'

Jocelyn blinked. *Max* had brought round the paracetamol and casserole? She suddenly felt ashamed. 'Would you like to sit down, Max? I have a few minutes before I need to start working.'

'Don't mind if I do! Ah, there we are then.' Max pulled out a chair on the opposite side of the table and sat down with a thud. Then he noticed Bob across the road and raised his hand, 'Bore da Bob.'

Bob raised a hand back in reply and continued gardening.

Jocelyn sat back down next to Max and put her hands on her lap. 'I really appreciated it all. I can't seem to shift my headaches nowadays without tablets, and I'd forgotten to bring my usual medication. And the casserole, that was delicious.'

'Well, it's a pleasure. Can't have you up here on your own, feeling ill and without anyone to look after you!'

'I'll return the dish to you once I've washed it. I haven't gotten around to it yet…'

'There's no rush,' Max interrupted, 'You still look pale.'

'As I said, it was just a headache - I get them from time to time. I have no idea what causes them.'

'You don't?' he cocked an eyebrow.

'No, but I've slept for two days, so I'm sure I'm over the worst of it now.'

'There we are, then.'

They sat back and looked out across the street below. Two women dressed in outdoor clothes were walking past. They each had a dog, which were straining at their leads with tongues lolling. The women and the dogs all had the same happy expressions. They waved to Max and Jocelyn and looked as if they were about to stop when Max waved back. Jocelyn merely nodded and looked away and was relieved to see that they continued walking instead. Her mind was turning to her workload again.

'There are a lot of people around in the mornings.'

'Ah yes.'

'Are there usually so many people around at such an unearthly hour, or is there something going on down that lane that I should be party to?'

'Unearthly?' Max sat back in his seat and let out a hearty guffaw, then scratched his head, 'Surely someone from London doesn't consider seven o'clock early?'

'Not for London, no, but out here in the… you know, these rural parts… where on earth are people heading? And youngsters, too - a couple of teenagers sauntered past looking like they were on the way to a nightclub - except that they were carrying towels.'

'It's hardly an 'unearthly hour'. It's daylight. The sun has been up for well over an hour. He spread his arms and gestured around the garden, 'What better time to bathe in Nature's glory than first thing in the morning, with all her unspoiled promise of the coming day?'

'So, where are they going?'

'For a paddle, perhaps!' he laughed.

'But don't these people have to go to work, or to school?'

'Of course they have to go to work and to school. But if they head off by eight forty-five, which is in...' he looked at his watch, '...Almost two hours' time, they'll be there by nine. He nudged Jocelyn and grinned, 'As long as there are no sheep on the Main Road; then it might be ten-past.' He laughed loudly.

'Well, I just... I see.'

'What's puzzling you?'

'Everyone calling 'Good Morning' to me, and...'

'Yes?'

'It's just - I was minding my own business. Ouch, I know how hostile I just sounded...'

'Ah, I see,' Max raised a finger and smiled at her. 'They weren't meaning to interrupt your reading.'

'No, I know, of course. Sorry Max; please excuse me - introspection is a legacy of too many years in the city.'

'Well, I've heard this about city folk, and now I've seen it with my own eyes,' he let out another hearty laugh, which brought a curious robin out from the hedgerow onto the gatepost. 'Sit back. Relax. Enjoy your tea and the view. And just say '*Good Morning*' back.'

'But what if I - gosh I don't want to say this; what if I can't get rid of them?'

Max threw back his head and laughed. 'Now I've heard it all.'

As Max sat chuckling, a man in a waterproof coat and lace-up boots strolled past the house. He noticed Max laughing and waved. Max turned to Jocelyn and said playfully under his voice, 'Look, here's your chance. Say 'hello.'

It had to be past eight o'clock now. The only way to end Max's game would be to humour him. 'Good morning,' she called.

Their eyes met, and the man threw her a wide smile.

'You're doing grand! Next time, try '*Bore da*'.'

She laughed at the absurdity of the situation, 'Oh, behave Max!'

'How does that feel?'

It was her turn to tease, 'Oh, it feels - unusual. A warm feeling in one's stomach that spreads all over one's body.'

'I think you are describing the pleasure of 'interacting with people".

'I'd better take it steady. I feel a bit dizzy!' She reached for the tray and went to stand up again. 'Well Max, now I really must…'

Max stayed seated. He patted her arm. 'You enjoy your morning. There is no rush hour here. Make time for people. You see how different it makes you feel.'

Jocelyn looked at him. Country people just didn't understand. 'Trudy, my secretary, would agree with you there.'

'Trudy sounds like a very sensible woman,' he said.

She's incredible. We've worked together for ten years. She is more like an aunt than a colleague! I'm just going to call her now; she'll be waiting.'

Max looked at his watch, 'It's quarter past seven in the morning!'

'I know, I'm late - and I've barely spoken to her these last few days as it is.'

'What time do you normally call her?'

'Oh well, we usually arrive at the office at the same time, seven on the dot, and then we have our morning briefing straight away.'

He scratched his head, 'And was that her idea, this seven on the dot morning briefing, or yours?'

Jocelyn was taken aback. 'Well, mine.'

'Perhaps now you are away, you could have your briefing or whatever it is, at a different time?'

'Trudy likes routine.'

'*Trudy* likes routine?'

'Max, what are you getting at?'

'Nothing!' his eyes twinkled, 'I'm just playing with you.' He grinned, then went to stand up. 'Ah well, I can see you want to get on with your work now. I'll go.' He put his cap on and adjusted it, then pushed the chair under. 'Just look after yourself, missy.'

Something shifted inside Jocelyn. She was far from home and yet, here was someone who cared. She smiled up at him. 'Max - thank you for the casserole.'

'It's a pleasure.' Max ambled off down the path, looking at the trees and the skittering birds, and waving again to Bob as he went.

Max had been right; Trudy welcomed the suggestion they change their daily briefing to nine, at least while Jocelyn was in Wales. It would make Trudy's commute from Acton in the West London outskirts less frantic. She reassured Jocelyn that everything was under control and reminded her that no matter what pressures they had faced in the past, the firm had always delivered. The company's clients had remained loyal over decades and were never disappointed. Jocelyn could ease her foot off the accelerator; the work would not suffer.

Trudy had been worried about Jocelyn. Her headaches had been getting worse and she often skipped meals. She made Jocelyn promise: a ten-minute break outdoors, twice a day. After all, she was no use to anyone unwell in bed.

Jocelyn agreed on the strength of this last comment. Ten minutes in the morning, ten minutes at lunchtime. It was a reasonable enough request.

After she had cleared away the breakfast dishes, she sat at the sitting room table and eased herself back into work. At noon, she made more tea and a cheese sandwich and ate them in the garden. She was prepared to acknowledge passers-by, but this time, no one passed, and the street was quiet. Only the robin joined her, flying down to watch her from the gatepost. She threw him a crust and he bobbed down to grab it, then flew back to his perch and watched her finish her food.

She forced herself to pack up the documents at six - feeling that she could have continued but wanting to behave sensibly. She made toast for supper, and then decided to eat in the garden. Her heart rate felt normal, and her head still clear - common sense told her that another trip outside would surely preserve her current calm state.

She stepped outside with the tartan blanket around her shoulders, wandered over to the table and sat down. Her eyes were bleary after a day of squinting at text, but they slowly adjusted. The evening air had a delicious warmth and across the road, the light in the valley was turning orange. A herd of brown cows stood beneath a large tree in the middle of the field, munching slowly and swishing their tails. Above them, some large birds - crows or something, she thought - were hopping noisily among the branches, occasionally flying to the ground to wander cockily amongst the legs of the cattle and peck at the bare earth at the base of the tree.

She turned away from the valley, took a bite of toast and looked around the garden - at the wild borders, the tumble of different coloured foliage, and the contrasting neat patch of lawn, which had clearly been recently mown. To the side of where she sat, a rosemary bush with a covering of soft lilac flowers was alive with foraging insects, buzzing gleefully. She leaned across and picked a leaf from it, pinching the silver leaves to squeeze out the sap. The aroma on her fingertips was warm and herby.

A bird flew from the densest part of the honeysuckle by the porch and landed in the centre of the lawn. It was plump and brown with speckled markings all over its cream breast. It paused to survey her; its dark round eyes were fixed on her. Jocelyn held her breath and sat motionless. Deciding she was harmless, the bird commenced stabbing into the grass with its beak, bobbing its head up every now and then to check she still posed no threat to its harvesting. It hopped back and forth across the lawn, cocking its head to the side to listen for movement in the soil, then stabbing at the ground to pluck out a fat worm. Eventually, with a beak-full of wriggling grubs, it flew up and disappeared with a rustle back into the vine.

Aunt Kate lifted her up, so that she could peer into the dense greenery. A nest, built with twigs and dry grass and lined into a perfect half-sphere with mud. And to her joy, four smooth, blue speckled eggs! Oh, how she wanted to hold one of those eggs - just for a moment!

'We must leave well alone,' whispered Kate firmly, 'Or the mother will abandon them, and then they will never hatch. Learn patience my girl. What comes later brings longer lasting joy.'

Jocelyn sat in silence and watched the bird gather food for its chicks. Every few minutes it reappeared on the lawn, working. She watched the bird's devoted labour until the light across the valley turned from orange to pink, and it was time to make the nightly call home.

***

'Hello darling.'

'Jocelyn! How have you been today? You sound much better.'

'I'm well - really well. I've been improving all day and the headache is completely gone. Sorry I'm a bit late calling; I was watching a thrush on the lawn, gathering worms for its chicks.

'Well, that's interesting.'

'Yes, I think its nest is in the honeysuckle over the porch. Do you know, a thrush used to nest there when I was young; I remember Kate showing me.'

'Perhaps it's a descendant!'

'Ha, imagine that. I don't have much else interesting to tell you Jonathan, I'm afraid.'

'It doesn't matter, it's just lovely to hear your voice and I'm relieved you feel better.'

'Gosh, me too. I promise I'll take it steady from now on; well, a little.'

'That would be sensible - unless you want me landing unannounced on your doorstep!'

After talking for a while with Jonathan about London and work, Jocelyn returned to the garden for a little longer, to watch the last of the sun's light disappear from the cloudless sky and the stars begin to appear in the navy expanse. Then the air grew cool, and she gathered up her things from the table and returned to the house for the night.

Day 8 - Friday

Jocelyn stretched and eased herself into a sitting position in the big old bed. Friday morning - one week after arriving in Llanfairyn and she was waking later; it was six thirty. She lifted the covers and swung her legs around, dangling them towards the floor that she couldn't quite reach, and thought about getting dressed. Her outfits were feeling… *uncomfortable.* Where the tailored clothes brought confidence and composure in London, here, well, they were just scratchy. Plus, she still hadn't gotten around to doing any laundry and anyway, most of her wardrobe was dry-clean only - fine in London, but in Llanfairyn? Mrs Organised-Anderson hadn't thought *that* through fully, had she?

Kate was bound to have some sensible clothes she could borrow; well, they were all hers, now, anyway. She hadn't been into Kate's room yet; it had felt too invasive, but now it looked as if she'd have to venture in there. She got up, slipped on her robe and made her way to the opposite side of the landing. The bedroom door had been closed since she arrived. She turned the handle and slowly pushed it open with a creak.

Kate's bedroom was as she remembered it; a big space with high ceilings and lots of natural light. The walls were covered in pale pink wallpaper with a tiny floral pattern running vertically up it. The wide, uneven floorboards were polished dark ebony and almost completely covered by a large, patterned rug, on which the bed stood. The bed itself was a four poster, and like the guest room, it had a colourful patchwork quilt and a crocheted blanket covering it, with an array of plump pillows.

All the furniture in the room was of dark wood. Under the window was a dressing table with a small drawer on each side with gold dangling handles, an oval mirror on top and a stool with a padded seat pushed underneath. Beside the dressing table was a matching set of five drawers with the same gold handles. In the corner was a gold-framed, full-length mirror on a stand, and in the opposite corner, a changing screen with Chinese images painted on it.

The back wall of the room was filled entirely with dark wood fitted wardrobes; in all there were five pairs of ceiling-to-floor doors with round knobs. Jocelyn remembered that they housed Kate's evening gowns and theatre costumes. She wasn't ready to look in there, yet.

She stepped fully inside the bedroom and stood by the bed. The rug looked old - parts of it were faded and the wool had worn away - but it was clean and the room, although filled to the brim with Kate's possessions, was neat and smelled of rose and lavender. Jocelyn went to the drawers and opened them in turn. Piles of folded clothes, in light summer colours and cool fabrics, lined each one. She began to pull out items, unfolding them and holding them up to check for size and style. Kate had been so quirky! Jocelyn's own style felt conservative by comparison. Smart, but boring, she thought with a sigh. Feeling daring, she chose a pair of ankle-length baggy trousers in lime-green, an embroidered cotton shirt with wide cuffs and rather long tails - presumably meant to be left untucked, she reasoned - and a cropped, chunky-knit cardigan with three big buttons. She looked in the mirror. Wow! The clothes were flattering, and with her brunette waves left loose, the look was, well, it was different. Sort of Continental.

Beside the bed was a pair of red leather loafers, and Jocelyn slipped them on. A touch of lipstick from her own bedroom and she felt fresh and comfortable, and ready to start the day.

In the kitchen, she made tea and toast. Two hours until she made the morning call to Trudy. Smiling, she spread butter on the bread and cut it into two pieces. By seven fifteen, she was settling at the garden table, blanket on her knees. She closed her eyes, face lifted to the sun.

'Now that's what I like to see!'

Jocelyn opened her eyes again abruptly, looked down and smiled. 'Good morning Max, and yes, I am taking the time to enjoy the morning.'

'I'm impressed!'

'Well, Trudy and I have rearranged our daily call for nine.'

'Very good.'

'And she's insisted I spend time outdoors twice a day.'

'And you are listening to her! She must be some woman.' he laughed and tucked his thumbs in the arm holes of his waistcoat.

'Would you like to join me for a drink?' She gestured to the tea tray.

'I never say no!'

'I'll just fetch you a cup.'

Max walked slowly up the garden path and took a seat, smoothing back his hair with a paint-splattered hand and making himself comfortable in the morning's rays. Jocelyn popped back into the house and emerged two minutes later with a cup and saucer, and the sugar bowl.

She poured Max some tea and passed it to him. 'I was watching a bird last night,' she said, sitting down, 'Coming from the vines around the porch and gathering worms or something from the lawn.' She poured her own tea.

'Ah yes. Was it the thrush? She nests in the honeysuckle.' He scooped up a spoonful of sugar, plopped it into the drink and stirred it slowly.

'I think so; have you seen it, too?'

'I have. Kate and I used to sit and watch her in the evenings. This must be her second clutch this summer. She's a busy lady, isn't she?' He leaned forward and gingerly took a sip, the delicate china teacup dwarfed in his huge hands.

'The honeysuckle smells beautiful in the evening,' Jocelyn said.

'To attract the moths.'

'Really?' She looked at Max, interested to learn more, but he still had a mouthful of tea. She took another slice of toast from her plate, bit into it and glanced across the street. A woman was crossing the street at the far end of the row of cottages and heading towards them. At first glance, she looked around the same age as Jocelyn, and was wearing a long, tiered tie-dye skirt that reached her ankles, and an orange strappy top, eye-catching against her smooth olive skin. Her thick dark curls were held back by a red bandana. It was clear from her smile that she was coming over to talk.

'Hello, Max,' she said as she reached the garden wall. Her voice was soft and had a warm European accent.

'Morning, love,' Max replied.

'And is it… Jocelyn?' she turned her liquid brown eyes.

Jocelyn was transfixed. 'Yes, that's right.'

'I'm Rosa,' she lifted a bangled arm to run her hand through her hair, which Jocelyn now noticed was greying slightly at the temples, so she was probably in her fifties - and the assorted bracelets jangled around her wrist. 'I live in Heather Cottage, the little white one on the end there, with my children Will and Emily.' She pointed across the street.

Another of Kate's neighbours. 'Hello Rosa.' Jocelyn smiled.

'Kate was very dear to us; we're so sorry about her passing.'

'Thank you.'

'And you have come all this way from your home to sort Kate's house out.'

'Just for three weeks.'

Well, I hope your stay is a comfortable one. Are you visiting by yourself?'

'Yes, I am. My husband is a lawyer and, well, work is very busy for him.'

'Ah.' Rosa smiled at them both and folded her arms across her chest. 'Well, if you want something to do while you're here, you can join me for a walk sometime.'

'Oh,' Jocelyn was taken aback by the invitation from the stranger, 'I didn't bring any clothing suitable for off-road hiking.'

Rosa smiled and showed perfect white teeth. 'You only need trainers. Look!' She hitched up her flowing skirt and revealed a pair of feet clad in men's ankle socks and well-worn shoes hiding beneath it.

A woman who could make fun of herself; Jocelyn decided in an instant that she liked Rosa.

'So come on, join me!' Rosa grinned, 'The walks are fabulous. You can walk a long way and not see another soul. And all the pine forest on the hills there,' She pointed up to the hills above the town, 'There are footpaths through it to the top.'

'I don't know,' Jocelyn pulled a face, 'It sounds a bit rugged for me. Although it's obviously the pastime of choice around here.'

'Well, enjoy your day.' She turned to Max. 'See you later.'

'Bye love.'

Rosa turned and walked off down the lane, hair bouncing, skirt flowing and bracelets jangling. Max and Jocelyn watched her and when she was out of earshot, Max leaned forwards and gave Jocelyn a nudge, 'There you go! Making friends already.'

'I hope I haven't come across as stuffy.'

'Not at all. I'm teasing.' He adjusted his cravat. 'But you really should take up Rosa's invitation to go for a walk with her, while you are here. If you like, I can drive you into town to buy some trainers or whatever.'

'Oh goodness, definitely not!'

'It would be a shame to stay in Llanfairyn and not go up onto the common.'

'Driving over it was enough,' she said - then stopped herself before she said something offensive. She began to tidy the breakfast dishes from the table. She looked at her watch. 'Well Max…'

'Ah, yes.' Max took the hint. He stood up. 'Well, it's the weekend tomorrow. You might be able to find some time to relax.'

'I will do my best.'

Perhaps I'll see you having breakfast outside every morning, then?'

'Who knows! You might just,' she smiled.

'And remember, if anyone says hello to you, here we say *Bore da.*' He bowed, and as he wandered away, he pretended to greet people on each side of the path, lifting his cap and bowing in a sweeping gesture, 'Bore da!'

Jocelyn watched him leave, shaking her head in bemusement as she collected up the breakfast tray and headed indoors.

She had her call with Trudy at nine, then - after moving the workspace back downstairs into the sitting room because it was silly to be so fearful of disturbances - she worked until noon. She sprinted easily through the morning's documents. At lunchtime, she had boiled two eggs, watching absent-mindedly as the water bubbled in the pan and clunked the eggs gently together, and eaten them in the cool of the sitting room.

After lunch, Doreen had arrived to clean Kate's house. She had said a brief 'hello' and then busied herself in all the rooms, except the sitting room where Jocelyn was working; she hadn't wanted to disturb her.

Jocelyn had left the woman to her job. The rest of the afternoon sailed by and by six, the stack of documents to-do had become a stack done.

She stretched her arms in the air and her legs under the table. It was incredible; more had been achieved today than on a regular day in the office.

Supper had been the last of the bread and cheese. She ate outdoors and watched, again, the thrush flit back and forth between the honeysuckle and lawn, as it fed its hungry babies. At one point, another bird had landed with a bounce on the lawn - a proud male blackbird with a sleek dark plumage and a rich orange beak. He spotted the thrush and for a minute the two birds sized each other up, puffing out their chests and hopping aggressively towards each other in a display that said, 'This is *my* territory!'. Then, because the thrush was unwilling to back down, the blackbird gave in and retreated into the undergrowth. He noticed Jocelyn sitting motionless in the chair and stared at her for a moment, before flying away across the lane, calling in annoyance, 'Pink, pink, pink!'.

Jocelyn had slowly let out the breath she had, without realising, been holding. It was a privilege to have spent a moment in the private world of the two birds.

There had been several ornithology books on Kate's bookshelves, she remembered. She got up and went indoors to find one, chose a small hardback book and took it back outside. The street was growing quiet. She leafed slowly through the book, stopping at each page and reading - about this bird's habitat, that one's plumage, the feeding behaviour of another… The evening flew by.

After a while, she took off her glasses and laid them on the table and rubbed her eyes. It was approaching ten o'clock and the street was almost dark.

The breaks she'd taken in the garden these past couple of days had been a tonic, there was no doubt about it. As for work; well, Trudy had confirmed that everything was under control. Should she accept Rosa's offer of a walk on the common? She didn't even know the woman! But she had seemed genuine enough - and the drive over the common from the station *had* been beautiful. Perhaps a short stroll; something manageable for a city person who seldom walks anywhere?

But she'd have to pick up some walking shoes from somewhere, and a trip into the town centre was not appealing. No, walking with Rosa would be an unnecessary extravagance. Time in the garden would be enough of the Outdoors. Why, before this week, she hadn't eaten outdoors since… Jocelyn tried to remember the last time she and Jonathan had taken a stroll in Hyde Park, which was on their doorstep. Was it last autumn, or the summer before? She couldn't remember.

The night air had dropped by a few degrees and a breeze was playing in the leaves at the top of the trees in the street. She wondered if Jonathan had enjoyed his evening at the bar. She gathered up the things and left the table to go indoors and prepare for bed. At eleven, she climbed under the warm covers and fell into a deep sleep.

Day 9 - Saturday

Wasn't it the standing joke that it always rained in Wales? Apart from the day of Kate's funeral, the sun had shone almost every day so far.

It was Saturday; there was no need to call the office this morning, no need to rush. Jocelyn sat on the edge of the bed and rolled her shoulders a few times, then massaged the muscles in her neck with her hand. They felt relaxed.

In Kate's room, she chose an outfit and slipped into it, and then went downstairs into the cool kitchen to make breakfast. She made a pot of tea and placed it onto the tray with her usual teacup and then, as an afterthought, reached for an additional cup too - just in case someone else arrived. Max had struggled with the delicate teacup though. Was there anything bigger in the cupboards more suitable for him? Something with a big handle, perhaps in Kate's memorabilia collection? She opened the cupboard door, picked out the mug with the chunkiest handle - *Genius at Work* - and placed it onto the tray. Then she went down the hallway. The grandfather clock seemed to know it was Saturday; it's tick seemed slow and steady today. She rolled her eyes at the clock as she passed.

It was delicious to sip hot tea outdoors with the sun on your face and a gentle breeze on your skin. The longest day of the year was approaching and now that sunrise was earlier, the morning air was already warm. Flies were buzzing in little swarms above the long grasses, and the whole scene was backlit by the sun's rays.

At the far end of the lawn, a little yellow bird with a red and white face was clinging precariously to dandelion seed heads and pulling the seeds out with its beak. It was eating the seed and spitting out the feathery head with little jerks. When it had flown away, Jocelyn shielded her eyes from the sun with her hand and looked down the valley. Across the road, the old man was bent over his vegetable patch. He was tinkering with a row of canes with leafy shoots growing up them, adjusting them for the sake of it, it seemed. He noticed Jocelyn and straightened up, shielding his own eyes with his earthy hand. They locked eyes.

She would usually have looked away by now, her mind filled with client deadlines and meeting schedules and having no space to spare for strangers. Instead, she raised a hand to the old man. 'Good morning.'

He waved back, and a wide grin spread across his face. He went back to his tinkering. When Jocelyn snuck a look at him a while later, he was still beaming.

'Bore da!' a familiar voice boomed cheerfully over the wall.

'Good morning, Max. Are you joining me?'

'I never say no.' He waved across to Bob, then came through the gate and pottered up the path to where Jocelyn was sitting.

Jocelyn poured tea from the pot into the mug, filling it up before moving on to the cup. Max pulled out a chair and shifted it around slightly, so that like Jocelyn's, it was facing down the valley. He sat down, 'Ah, that's better!'

Jocelyn handed the mug to him, and he turned it around on the table to read the inscription - *Genius at Work* - and then laughed.

She poured milk into her own cup and stirred it - the metal spoon tinkling against the china. Then they sat back and stretched out, and watched Bob in his garden.

'So,' Max started, 'Did you think any more about Rosa's offer?'

She looked back at him. 'You are persistent, aren't you?'

He laughed loudly, and a handful of small birds fled from the bushes behind him. Jocelyn brushed a fly away from her face and re-folded her arms. 'I suppose a short walk wouldn't hurt - but I don't know if I can face a shopping trip to buy shoes, on top of everything else.'

'Why don't you call the shop in town and get them to put a pair aside? I'll collect them for you this afternoon.'

Jocelyn thought for a minute. 'I suppose that would work. Would you mind doing that?'

'Not at all. I'm going into town later, anyway.'

She looked at her watch and Max did the same. 'Almost nine,' he said, 'Call them in a minute, before I leave and then we'll know where we are.'

It seemed there was no backing out. She smiled, shaking her head. 'I don't know the telephone number of a shop that might sell...'

'It's here,' Max handed her a number scrawled on a piece of paper, 'I just thought you might need it.'

She looked into the man's playful eyes, then sighed. 'All right Max. I'll phone them now.'

'Right we are.' Max looked across the valley, smiling to himself.

In the dining room, Jocelyn called the number and was connected to an outdoor equipment shop on the town's high street. They had been expecting Jocelyn's call and yes, absolutely, they had the perfect pair of shoes in a size 4 - already put aside for her, in fact. They understood that Max Griffiths would be calling round mid-morning to collect them.

She returned to the garden. Max had finished his drink and was sunning his face, smiling serenely.

'Thank you, Max. They do have a pair, in my size, put aside ready to collect, funnily enough.'

'Oh, that's lucky!

'*Lucky*, yes, isn't it?' she raised an eyebrow and grinned.

'I'll be on my way, then. I'll drop them off later.' He reached over and placed his empty mug onto the tray, pushed the chair back from the table and stood up slowly. 'And what is on the cards for you today?'

Jocelyn thought. 'Well, I need to pop over to the farm shop now, to replenish the cupboards. Oh, that reminds me - your casserole dish.'

'And then?'

'Then a little bit of work…' She pulled a face and Max laughed.

'You can take the girl out of the city…' He chuckled and put the chair tidily under the table. 'Remember it's the weekend.'

'I know, I know,' she said, 'I will just feel happier if I keep things ticking over. But I promise, I will make time over the weekend for other things, too!'

Max waited while Jocelyn went into the house for her purse and keys. She picked up the casserole dish from the kitchen and as she did so, spotted a wicker shopping basket on the floor under the kitchen table. She remembered the girl in the farm shop and decided to take the basket with her to the shop.

She locked up the house and handed the dish to Max. 'There you are - and thank you again. Now, I'll walk across the street with you.'

They walked down the path - Jocelyn striding off at first, then pulling herself up to wait for Max, who was ambling behind, surveying the flowerbeds. In the street, Max crossed the road to speak with Bob, and so Jocelyn bade him farewell and then continued around the corner and towards the school. A figure was walking on the other side of the road - a woman with her head down, deep in thought, and as Jocelyn crossed, she recognised Doreen Hughes.

'Doreen?'

Doreen looked up, startled, 'Oh! Hello.'

'How are you?'

'Ah, fine,' Doreen smiled, but the smile didn't reach her eyes. 'I'm on my way to open the store.'

'And that is where I am headed, too. Can I walk with you?'

'Of course.'

'How is Alan?'

'Fine, fine.'

'Ah.'

They walked on; the atmosphere a little awkward, although Doreen did her best to make it less so. 'Is everything all right in the house for you?'

'Oh yes, it's lovely. I must pay you for the groceries, Doreen. I kept forgetting and I haven't seen you all week.'

'It doesn't matter about that.'.

'Well, I insist.' Jocelyn looked at the woman walking alongside her. Doreen didn't look back; instead, she watched the ground. They reached the school and turned into the dusty lane to the farm. Small birds skittered through the hedgerow as they wandered down it towards the building.

'You know, I don't mind dropping round any groceries that you want. I'm passing the Coach House almost every day, on my way home.'

'That would be helpful, thank you.'

Doreen reached in her pocket for the keys. She fumbled for a minute with the lock, then swung open the big metal doors. They scraped along a worn groove in the gravel. She hooked each one back, using two big metal hooks that hung from the wall behind each door, then reached inside the dark building to flick on the lights. The neon strips blinked a few times and then came on. They stepped inside.

'Well then, you show me now what sort of things you like, and I can bring them round. You only have to phone.'

'Splendid!'

Apart from the hum of a fly around the ceiling, it was cool and quiet in the shop. An earthy aroma of fruit and vegetables hung in the air. It was exciting to be the first inside, let loose into the produce-laden aisles. The supermarkets in Bayswater didn't have this effect on her! Doreen walked across to open a window in the rear of the shop, and a gentle breeze drew through the building. Then she walked over to the counter, deposited her handbag safely behind it and began fumbling with the cash register.

Jocelyn wandered over to the first of the aisles, treading quietly on the smooth concrete floor. The aisle was lined with wooden crates, and she walked along it, running her hands over the produce: bunches of carrots, crisp and bright with feathery green tops, a jumble of turnips of various sizes loose in a tray, and spring onions tied in together in clumps with elastic bands. Jocelyn picked up a clear packet from one crate, filled with huge green leaves with red veins running through them, and inspected it.

'It's chard,' said Doreen, looking over from the counter. 'It's very good for you.'

Jocelyn pulled a face, put the leaves back and carried on browsing. At the end of the aisles, on the floor, stood a large brown sack with the top rolled down, filled with soil-caked potatoes.

'I wouldn't know where to start…' Jocelyn said under her breath.

Doreen appeared to have heard. 'Did you enjoy the casserole that Max made you?'

'I did! Did you know about that?'

Doreen nodded, 'He came in for the vegetables.'

'It was probably the healthiest thing I've eaten in… well, years.'

'Is it? You could make yourself one.'

'I don't cook, Doreen! I've never needed to.'

Doreen looked at Jocelyn in surprise, then quickly looked down.

In the second aisle, there were trays of loose apples, oranges and pears, strings of garlic hanging from nails in the shelf frames, and little hand-filled packets of herbs with written labels: 'Rosemary', 'Thyme' and 'Sage'. Jocelyn surveyed it all, then walked on. The last aisle contained shelves stocked with jars of homemade strawberry and damson jam, which, according to their labels had been made the previous year, as well as 'local wildflower honey' and a range of chutneys. Two refrigerators at the back of the shop held bottles of milk, tubs of cream, a few blocks of film-wrapped cheeses, and ham. There was also a small variety of household brand produce that Jocelyn recognised - presumably to make up for anything the farm could not supply.

Jocelyn perused the refrigerators and then wandered over to the checkout. On the counter was a tray with a handful of freshly baked loaves with dark brown crusts, and an assortment of homemade cakes. 'Does the farm make all of this produce?' she asked, as she eyed a block of carrot cake.

'No, no; some of comes in from other farms in the area, and some is made by people in Llanfairyn - like the bread and the jams. A little bit has to be brought in, too - you know, like fruit and things we can't get at this time of year - but most of it is local.' She lifted her chin proudly, 'We're the first shop like this in the area - you know, selling all local artisan goods! People love it, especially the tourists, so I expect more will pop up in the future.'

Jocelyn eyed the rows of chutney and pickle and wondered how any tourists even found their way to Llanfairyn, let alone to its tiny farm shop down a discreet dusty track behind a school. Still, there was no denying, the little store was a jewel in the town's crown. She selected a jar of apple chutney and a jar of honey and put them in her basket. Then she meandered around the aisles again, from the start, adding to her basket cheese, eggs and a loaf. She took the basket to the till, where Doreen was checking the petty cash.

'I actually have my own basket today!' Jocelyn put Kate's wicker basket on the counter.

Doreen smiled. 'Ah, yes.' She looked moved by the sight of it. She began ringing the items through the till and placing them carefully into the basket. 'Is this all you want?'

'Well, I've been eating the toast, and cheese sandwiches. Occasionally boiled eggs…'

'A casserole is straightforward,' Doreen offered, keeping her voice casual, 'I could give you the recipe.'

Jocelyn looked down at the meagre supply of provisions she'd selected. 'Well, perhaps if it's straightforward, as you say…'

Doreen smiled. 'Come.' She picked up the basket and gestured for Jocelyn to follow her around the shop.

First, she went over to the veg aisle and chose some carrots, a couple of potatoes, three sticks of crispy celery and a fat white onion and placed them in the basket. Then she went to the refrigerators and took a packet of diced beef from the lower shelf and placed that in the basket, too. With a box of stock cubes from the dried food shelf, and thyme and bay leaves from the herb section, the shopping list for Jocelyn's first casserole was complete.

They returned to the till. 'And the instructions?' Jocelyn queried, feeling silly.

'I'll write it down.' Doreen reached for a biro and a sheet of paper - which, Jocelyn noticed, was an old flyer for the Llanfairyn Mountain Rescue Team Annual Fundraiser - from under the counter. 'You'll find Kate's casserole dish in the oven - that's where she stores, sorry, stored it.' She turned red, and quickly put her head down to scribble down the recipe, mumbling aloud as she wrote, 'Chop everything into small chunks… into the casserole dish on the hob… heat it… couple of tablespoons of flour… cover it with water… stock cubes… handful of thyme and two bay leaves, salt and pepper…' She looked up, 'Oh, that's in Kate's cupboard with the jars of spices - and cook at one hundred degrees for about five hours. There!' She finished writing and handed the sheet over.

'*Five* hours?!' said Jocelyn.

'Nothing like a slow-cooked casserole. You can cook it in the day and eat it for your supper! And if you do a big one, it'll last a few days in the fridge and you won't have to worry about cooking every night.'

'Or worry about *not* cooking every night, in my case.' Jocelyn quipped drily. 'Can't I cook it any faster than five hours?'

'A couple of hours at one-eighty then, if you're in a rush,' said Dorren.

Jocelyn puffed out her cheeks and then exhaled slowly. 'Well, let's give this a shot, then. Otherwise, I'm going to waste away without a takeout around the corner.'

'I can pop groceries over any time, as I said. How about every couple of days? This will do you now until Wednesday, I would think. So how about I bring you another bag around on Wednesday morning?

'Doreen, I'd really appreciate that.'

'There we are then! Oh, one last thing…' The woman trotted off to the refrigerator and came back with a packet of something. 'If you're going to be surviving on jam, eggs and cheese, at least try something local this time. Welsh cheese,' she whispered with a wink. 'And here - treat yourself,' she popped a block of cake into the bag too, 'That's on me. Now, let's get you on your way.'

She rung the rest of the items through the till and Jocelyn paid and put her arm through the laden wicker basket. 'I feel like I'm straight out of some Country Life magazine,' she grinned.

"You look good!' Doreen smiled. Jocelyn saw her glance down briefly at the high heels she was wearing, and then quickly look away, embarrassed that Jocelyn had followed her gaze.

She joked to Doreen, 'Well, Country perhaps down as far as the shoes!' She bade Doreen farewell, picked up the shopping basket and left the shop. The birds were singing in the bright morning sunlight as she walked smiling back to the Coach House.

***

The casserole dish was indeed hiding inside the oven. Jocelyn took it out and put it on the counter and found a wooden chopping board and a sharp knife in the drawers. Then she set to work. It was strangely therapeutic to stand in the little quiet room and concentrate on chopping the vegetables into similar-sized chunks. When the pile was done, she stood back and put down the knife, feeling very satisfied. She scooped everything into the casserole dish, covered it in the stock liquid and then put on the lid. Then she slid the heavy dish onto the middle shelf of the oven and set her wristwatch alarm for later that afternoon.

This would be interesting. She hadn't cooked a proper meal from scratch since she was a student. The last thing she needed was a visit from Llanfairyn's fire brigade - if Llanfairyn had a fire brigade. Oh goodness, it *did* have one, didn't it?

She steadied her breathing and to distract herself, turned her attention to other things: finding a suitable tin for the cake - which had turned out to be homemade carrot cake - and then making a cheese sandwich for lunch. She unwrapped and cut a wedge of the cheese - which was a creamy white-and-blue variety, buttered a thick crust of bread and blobbed a dollop of the chutney on a side plate. Popping it all onto the tray with a pot of tea, she wandered outside.

A figure was kneeling in the corner of the garden, busy tending to the flowerbed. Alan stopped weeding and sat back on his heels, pushing his cap back on his hot forehead. 'Hello.'

'Oh hello, Alan.' Here was an opportunity to be more civilised to the man. She placed the tray down on the table and wandered over to where Alan was getting up. 'Have you been gardening for Kate for many years? It all looks - what's the expression - mature?'

'Oh, around ten years now,' He brushed his trousers down and wiped his brow. 'You know Kate; she enjoyed being outside. Her two great passions were the theatre and her insect garden. She had a love affair with both.' He gestured at the border, teeming with insects. 'She had me plant all this up with particular specimens - lavender, thyme, hebe - to attract butterflies and bees. Then she'd sit out here all morning - at the seat there, with a pot of tea - and watch them working away.'

Jocelyn laughed apologetically, 'I'm afraid I haven't inherited those genes.'

'Oh? You're not green-fingered yourself, then?'

'Well, it's not that, really.' She looked at Alan. His eyes were sweeping over the flowerbeds, a gentle smile on his lips. She paused, thinking, then said, 'Listen, would you like a cup of tea with me?'

'No, no,' he mumbled.

'Please? I've made a huge pot. I'm practicing the art of relaxing more and making time for people. Max has set me upon it!'

'Ah, well, I don't want to interrupt you.'

'Not at all. I have just put a casserole in the oven - under Doreen's instruction!' She noticed his shoulders drop a little. 'I'm due a break Alan, so please join me. I've discovered that the front garden is the perfect spot for people-watching.'

'Well, lovely then, thank you. Milk and one sugar.'

Alan wandered over to the table and sat down, while Jocelyn went into the kitchen to fetch another cup. Without a thought, she selected the mug from Kate's collection with 'Head Gardener' on it. Back outside, she poured tea into the mug and handed it to Alan. He sat fiddling with his cap and didn't speak apart from to say thank you, and Jocelyn found herself in an unfamiliar position of having to make idle conversation.

'So, I was saying, we don't have a garden where we live. We're in an apartment - a wonderful old Georgian apartment that I love dearly - but there's no garden. There are plenty of parks nearby and I spend time in those, on the occasions that I am home from work in the daylight. Just one street back from the hustle and bustle and you can be immersed in the most tranquil of settings.'

'Yes, parks are nice, for city folk. Somewhere to go and just… be.' He sipped his tea.

'And of course properties are very expensive in the South East and life is so… busy, so you'd really have to want a garden to stretch yourself and buy a house with one, and then of course you'd be working so hard to pay the mortgage, you'd barely have time to maintain it! Perhaps I'm wrong, but that's how it seems.' Gosh, did she sound like a chatterbox?

'Oh. That's a real shame. So, what is it that people are working for?'

'What do you mean?'

'If you don't have time for things.'

She squinted at the man. 'It's important to throw all of one's heart into one's career, isn't it?'

'I suppose not everyone wants the hassle of a garden. There are plenty of attractions to visit in the city.' He studied his hands for a while, as if wondering what to say.

'People have window boxes in our building,' she offered.

'You can get plenty of joy out of a window box. Many plants will grow happily in a window box.'

'Yes, it seems so. My neighbour's is colourful.'

'Or if you have a balcony, you can do all sorts of creative things with balcony space - while doing your bit for wildlife too, you know.'

'Hmm. Plants need to be very resilient if they are dependent upon me for survival.' Jocelyn laughed, encouraging him to continue.

'Well, herbs are the best bet for the amateur gardener. You can't go wrong with herbs. There are some very resilient ones and it's useful to grow something you can eat. They are very good for your health and the insects love them, too.'

'Oh really?' Jocelyn sipped her tea and thought about the delicious aroma of herbs in the farm shop. 'Which herbs would you recommend I start with, then?'

Alan thought for a minute. 'Well, oregano would be a good one. It likes a sunny spot and won't mind if you forget to water it.'

'Well, we'll see. I might dip a toe in, at some point in the future!'

Alan sipped his tea.

'Do Doreen and you have a garden, Alan? I imagine it's fabulous.'

'Oh yes, we do. I couldn't manage without one. We grow a lot of things; ornamentals, vegetables, legumes. Doreen grows a few exotics, too.

'It sounds homely!'

'We used to spend a lot of our time together in the garden.'

'Used to? You don't anymore?'

'Oh, well, things...' He picked at the soil caked in the creases of his palms. 'Anyway, as I was saying - start off with a few herbs in a window box. See if it takes your fancy.'

'I might just do that. While I'm here though, I suppose I should make use of some of Kate's produce - well, I should say *your* produce. I'll pick some oregano, if you can show me the correct plant Alan, and I'll buy some tomatoes from the grocery.'

'Doreen can sort you out with some fresh tomatoes.'

'Ah yes, Doreen is bringing groceries around on Tuesday.'

'There we are then; I'll leave a note for her to add tomatoes to the order.'

Jocelyn looked at the man. 'Leave a note? Are you going away?'

'No, no I just, you know, I might not see her to speak to.' He focused on his hands.

'There's no rush,' she laughed, 'You will see her over the next few days, I'm sure!'

'All the same. I'll see that you get your tomatoes.'

Jocelyn hid her puzzlement. 'Very well.'

'We leave each other notes a lot.' He laughed, but it sounded hollow. He put his cup down, 'Well, I'll leave you to get on with your afternoon; I'm sure you have a lot more to sort out.'

He stood up and pushed the chair under, and Jocelyn stood up too.

'Will you send Doreen my regards?'

'Yes, yes. Goodbye.'

She watched Alan shuffle off to gather his gardening tools. He put them into his wheelbarrow and then, with a smile and a nod back at her, he wheeled it around the side of the house to Kate's shed.

***

The rest of the day was spent indoors scrutinising documents, with the aroma of casserole taunting her from the kitchen. At six, she was disturbed by the telephone ringing from the dining room. Jonathan's voice was a welcome distraction. 'Hello sweetheart, how are you?'

'Oh Jonathan, it is lovely to hear your voice!'

'Well, I'm very glad to hear it, because I am missing you dreadfully! How do you feel today?'

'I'm fine, darling. I took things steady again and yes, I feel extremely well.'

'I'm glad to hear it.'

'How has your Saturday been?'

'Well, I must say it's rather boring in London without you. How was yours?'

'Mine was certainly different to usual! I went to the farm shop this morning. You wouldn't believe the things they sell Jonathan, and it's almost all produced locally. And best of all, it's just around the corner - well, up a dusty lane that my heels would have objected to, could they talk - but still...'

'Sounds convenient.'

'It is. You walk down a little track beside the school - oh did I tell you about the singing? The schoolchildren sing so beautifully - and in Welsh, too.'

'Wonderful.'

'Oh, and I had tea with Max Griffiths and Alan Hughes. Separately, not at the same time - but Max had told me I needed to take time for people, so I tried to be hospitable. Jonathan, do you think I need to make more time for people?'

'Like whom?'

'Like, well, I don't know. Who do we see…? Our friends? Neighbours?'

'Well, we don't really know our neighbours.'

'Mmm,' she chewed her lip, and then changed the subject. 'Well anyway, what about you? How was Saturday in beautiful London?'

'It wasn't the same without you. I did a spot of work, then went out for food by myself.'

'Oh goodness, you just reminded me; I have a casserole in the oven.'

'A what?'

'I need to take it out, it's been slow cooking since lunchtime. Why hasn't my alarm gone off?'

'Sorry? I thought you said you had a casserole slow cooking in the oven, but I must be mistaken. Who are you and what have you done with my wife?'

'Oh, don't tease! I must go.'

'Oh, really? Already?'

'Sorry! I cannot mess up this dish, Doreen will be disappointed. Speak to you soon darling. Goodbye!'

'Jocelyn?'

Jonathan waited for a reply, but Jocelyn had already hung up the telephone and dashed into the kitchen.

***

The raindrops were pattering gently on the sitting room window and making little wet circles on the garden path outside. Jocelyn blew gently on the spoonful of stew to cool it, then put it into her mouth. It was warm and tender, and her stomach urged her to spoon in more. She ate the bowlful, and then filled it again and finished that, too. The rain fell harder, drumming on the roof. She went over to the armchair, flicked on the lamp to light the room and then sat down, trying to keep her eyelids open.

Kate, why am I here? You want me to stay in your home for three weeks- but you haven't left me any further instruction. Is there something hidden here, that you want me to find? If so, where on earth do I begin looking?'

The grandfather clock ticked.

No, it was not going to send her to sleep this early! She heaved herself back out of the chair, grabbed the tartan blanket and wandered outside to watch the rain.

It was dry and cosy under the porch, behind the curtain of water that dripped off the tiles. The garden was still, apart from the shudder of leaves being strummed by raindrops. Jocelyn stood in silence.

Suddenly, through the mist of the downpour a scurrying, wet figure appeared from the direction of the common, holding a jumper over its head to shield against the rain. 'Hello Jocelyn!' It was Rosa.

'Rosa, hello,' Jocelyn replied with a tired smile. 'Come and shelter under here.' She pulled the blanket tighter around herself and moved over to make space, as Rosa dashed up the Coach House path and squeezed alongside her under the porch. She took the jumper down from her head and shook the water droplets from it, then ran a hand through the tight ringlets of her soaked hair. 'Eugh! I got caught; I wasn't expecting a monsoon!'

Jocelyn looked at her. 'You're sopping.'

'I'll be all right; I'm almost home.' She took a minute to regain her breath, and then the two women watched the rain in silence. 'You really are a committed walker,' said Jocelyn finally.

'Walking clears my head.'

'Does it? It sounds useful then.'

'It really is, you know. How about coming with me tomorrow?'

Jocelyn carried on watching the rain. 'I still don't have any walking shoes - but Max should have collected them today.'

After a few minutes, the rain eased to a drizzle. Rosa shivered and folded her arms across her chest. 'Well, that was invigorating! Thanks for the shelter. How about I call round tomorrow after lunch, to see if you fancy coming with me.'

Jocelyn was too tired to resist. 'Sure.'

'Well then, enjoy your evening!' Rosa dashed out from under the porch, then turned back as she reached the gate. 'Oh, is it all right if I send Will over tomorrow morning? He has something of Kate's that he needs to give to you.'

'That's fine; I shall be here.'

After Rosa had gone, Jocelyn returned to the house and locked the door. It was only seven thirty, but she was struggling to stay awake. She tidied the kitchen quickly, then went upstairs and showered. By eight fifteen, she had crawled under the covers, exhausted from the effort of the day's numerous social interactions - which she had always found more draining than the most intense professional ones.

For a while, she couldn't get Doreen off her mind. Perhaps the woman was missing her visits to Kate's house; what was it she had said - that she used to go there weekly to clean and to chat? Jocelyn fell asleep before she could think any more about it.

Day 10 - Sunday

'Hi!' The young man smiling from the other side of the garden wall had long blonde hair protruding from beneath a colourful beanie. He was wearing an oversized t-shirt with 'Nirvana' scrawled across it and ripped blue denim jeans. A cluster of colourful woven bands was knotted around his wrist. 'I'm Will,' he said.

A black bike with a basket on the front was propped against the wall in front of him. Jocelyn frowned, and then realised who the visitor was. 'Ah, yes! Rosa's Will.'

'Well, my full name is Wilson Joseph Brown Junior - I was named after my dad and grandad - but everyone just calls me Will.'

Jocelyn raised an eyebrow, 'I see! Then I shall call you Will, too.'

Jocelyn had awoken earlier that morning to a room full of sunlight. She had shot up out of bed and looked at her wrist for the time. Where was her watch? It must still be in the bathroom window. Oh no, Trudy would be waiting, and... Then she remembered, it was Sunday. Remember Sundays, Jocelyn? Lazy Sundays with Jonathan, in those early years…? She had lain back on the pillows and slowly let out a breath, allowing her heart to stop thudding in her chest.

She had vowed to take the rest of the morning slowly, only venturing outside at nine, when the street was empty. She was still having breakfast when Will arrived at nine thirty.

'And you're Jocelyn,' Will said now, 'But I'm going to call you Josey.'

'Oh! All right then; that's different. And how are you?'

Will's face dropped, and he kicked at the ground with the toe of a scruffy Converse shoe. 'Well, I'm all right.'

'Are you sure? You don't seem it.'

He looked up at her again, 'Well, I'm not all right really. I wanted to go fishing today, but I broke my rod last week reeling in a lively trout and now I need to wait for the store to call and say that my new one has arrived.' He kicked a stone. 'I'm a bit disappointed, that's all. Mum said I had to go and find something useful to do, before *she* finds me a job!'

Jocelyn looked at Will, not quite able to work out how old he was. 'Ah, I see. So, have you identified a useful errand?'

His face broke into a smile again, and he rang the silver bell on the bike's handlebars. 'Yes. I'm just returning this bike.'

'That is a fine bike. With a basket and a bell - it's the perfect bike. Who are you returning it to?'

Will laughed and pointed to her, 'I'm returning it to *you*, Josey!'

'Me?' Jocelyn was taken aback.

'Yes! It's Kate's bike. I've been keeping it safe since she went. I used to fix it for her, see. She was always getting punctures, flying around the lanes and with the thorns and all that… and I'd always fix them for her and she would repay me with cake and stories. Kate had so many stories to tell.'

'Yes, I remember when I used to stay with her; she had many a tale. Such an enviable life…' She turned back to Will, 'I hadn't realised she bicycled, though.'

'Oh yes. She said she 'loved the freedom'. And now, her bike, it's yours.'

'Oh. Well, thank you very much.'

Will lifted the bike up the garden steps and wheeled it to where Jocelyn was sitting. 'The perfect bike is now your perfect bike. Here.'

'Oh, OK. Hmm.' Jocelyn stood up and took hold of the handlebars.

'Don't you like it?'

'Oh, yes I love it. It's…' She frowned. 'I'm just not sure what I'm going to do with it.'

'Won't you ride it, like Kate?'

She laughed and shook her head. 'Goodness, no! I don't cycle. I did as a child, but I don't in London. I suppose I'll have to find a new home for it.' She leaned the bicycle against the house.

'Oh wow. Really? You won't keep it? I've always had a bike. When I was little, I had a red Chopper, and after that I had a Grifter, a green one and then I had a Raleigh Mag Burner with stunt pegs. That was blue and yellow.'

'Oh.' Jocelyn was well out of her depth in a conversation about bicycles.

'Now I've got a mountain bike.' Will stated proudly. 'I love my bike; I'm always riding it. I don't know what I'd do without it to get around on. Can you ride a bike?'

Jocelyn folded her arms, 'Well, you never forget how to ride - or so the saying goes. But I'm unlikely to take it up again, especially not on the London streets. I'd end up with a broken wrist or something. Possibly around Hyde Park…? Anyway, I feel far too old to start trying now!'

Will pulled out a chair and sat down. Jocelyn raised an eyebrow at his familiarity. She uncrossed her arms and sat down next to him.

'Would you like some tea, Will?

'No thanks, but I'll have a piece of toast.' He reached for some toast and took a bite. 'So,' He mumbled, leaning forwards to fix his eyes on her, 'Do people *feel* older in the city, then? I mean, this is Kate's bike…' he gestured to the bicycle, 'and I'm pretty sure that Kate was older than you. She was more than ninety-five; I know because I can remember her party - I don't know how long ago it was because I'm not very good with time and things like that, but she was definitely more than ninety-five.'

'She was ninety-seven.' Jocelyn spoke between sips of tea.

'She was a great lady, she was - she rode her bike all over the place, every day!'

Jocelyn put down her cup and looked at him, surprised. 'What, you mean recently? She was still riding it up until…'

'Yeah. Why wouldn't she be? Kate always went whizzing round. In fact, it's unbelievable really that you don't ever ride a bike; I mean, you're an adult. I've never met an adult who can't ride a bike.' He laughed and shook his head to himself. 'Wow.'

'I suppose that is quite tragic; thank you for pointing that out. It's just that… there isn't much room in my life for cycling. I guess maybe it's something I need to address at some point, when my life isn't quite so chaotic.'

Will was concentrating on finishing the toast.

'Well, anyway, thank you so much for repairing the bike and taking such good care of it.'

'I always did.'

'Ah, of course, and I must also repay you. If you can call around the house one evening in the week, I am sure we can have some tea and cake.'

'How about now? I don't like tea, but I will eat the cake.'

'I have things to do today, Will. How about Tuesday, at six thirty?'

'Six thirty, 'he repeated, 'You mean half past six. Right, I'll knock-on for you. Lemon drizzle is my favourite - and perhaps you have some interesting stories about the city to tell me!'

'I'm not sure that my stories would compare to Kate's, I'm afraid! And I only have carrot cake - is that all right?' She was starting to feel that her hosting was substandard to Kate's.

Will got up and shrugged with a smile. 'I'm going home now. Tuesday, half past six. I'll tell mum to remind me.'

'Well, I look forward to seeing you then.'

He nodded and then, tucking his hands into his jeans pockets, padded off down the path.

'Have a good day now. I hope your rod arrives,' she called after him.

He turned at the gate. 'I hope it does, too. And I hope that you'll have a go on Kate's bike.'

She waved her hand, 'Yes, yes.'

'I'll come with you! I can show you some fab roads right on top of the common, with hardly any cars. And if you look over the edge… arghhh!' He circled both arms as if falling, laughing loudly as he did so. A cow in the valley opposite raised a curious head, then returned to grazing.

'Oh my goodness! Well, we'll see.'

'Eugh, I hate it when people say *that*.'

'I'm just a bit busy…'

'And *that*.'

'Truthfully Will, I can't afford any injuries right now. Cake, Tuesday; we can discuss it then.'

'Yes! Result! Ok, Josey. See you.' He waved, then cleared the steps in one leap and sprinted across the street towards Heather Cottage.

Jocelyn turned back to her now-cold tea and the remaining piece of toast. She smiled to herself.

'*Josey*? Ha!'

***

Just after lunchtime, there was a knock at the front door and when Jocelyn opened it, Rosa was standing holding a shoe box.

'Rosa?'

'Hi Jocelyn,' she held out the box, 'Our walk, remember?'

Jocelyn had forgotten. She had been so tired the evening before, when Rosa had suggested it and she had agreed.

'Max gave me these to pass on to you,' she handed the shoe box to Jocelyn.

There was no getting out of it. 'Rosa, of course. Come in.'

In the sitting room, Jocelyn sat down and opened the box and took out a trainer. She noticed that Rosa was keeping her eyes on the floor. She slipped the shoe on. The laces needed a bit of adjustment, but once they were tied, it was a perfect fit. She took the other shoe out of the box and put that on too, then stood up and walked back and forth, wiggling her toes. 'They are prefect.'

Rosa smiled, but still stared at the ground. 'You just need a jacket,' she said.

Jocelyn rummaged around on the coat hooks in the hallway and found a lightweight rain mac. She put it on, then looked at Rosa with a shrug. 'I'm ready.'

'Kate's clothes fit you well.' Her eyes remained lowered, as she led the way back outside.

They agreed to walk to the top of the nearest hill overlooking their side of town. From the Coach House, they turned left and headed away from town and towards the common. Within a hundred metres the houses ended, and the tarred street narrowed to a gravelly track with patches of grass down the middle. Further down the lane they came to a stone wall, which marked the boundary of the common. There was a rusty cattle grid across the lane, with a wooden five-barred gate propped open at the side, and a stile in the wall next to it. They climbed over the stile one after the other, and jumped down the other side, sending a pair of rabbits bolting away into the undergrowth.

Beyond the cattle grid, the lane disappeared and there were only tyre tracks in the earth, which continued up into the distance. A group of sheep were lying each side of the track and they eyed the two women, but only the one nearest got up, with an irritated heave, and ambled to safety behind its comrades while they passed. They followed the track for a hundred metres or so, before turning off onto a narrow path on that wound upwards through the bracken.

The women walked at a steady pace and in silence - Rosa looking ahead and pointing at two brown butterflies dancing among the fronds, and Jocelyn concentrating on each step on the rugged terrain. She felt a little breathless, but surprisingly, not so unfit as to feel humiliated. A little further and the path cut through thick thorny bushes covered in yellow flowers. A noisy little brown bird escorted them along it, hopping from one prickly perch to another and chattering at them crossly. Rosa smiled and continued to watch her step, holding back branches so Jocelyn could squeeze through.

'Just mind the thorns through here.'

Jocelyn stopped and inhaled deeply. 'It smells divine! It's like… warm coconut.'

'It's gorse. Isn't it lovely? I always think the flowers are like a yellow carpet stretching across to the skyline. And this noisy little fellow is a stonechat.' The bird eyed them curiously.

It took about half an hour to weave through the gorse to the top of the hill. At the summit, they came across a herd of around ten small ponies, dotted among the bushes so that only their furry backs were visible, and snatching hungrily at shoots of succulent grass among the scrub. Two ponies stood separate from the herd, dozing while their leggy foals suckled milk and shook their bristly tails in delight.

Upon seeing the herd, Rosa had stopped, but with a whisper she pointed and guided Jocelyn around them. A beige pony with a dark brown mane saw them and lifted his head to stare with big dark eyes. He gave a small whinny and took a few steps towards them in youthful curiosity.

Jocelyn stepped back, closer to Rosa. At the back of the herd, a jet-black pony raised his head to see what the fuss was. He was bigger than the other ponies and his long mane flowed around powerful shoulders, bold eyes blinking at them from beneath a thick forelock.

'He's the stallion,' explained Rosa in a low voice, 'We'll give his mares a wide berth.'

The stallion's nostrils flared as he smelled the air, and his sides heaved sleek and muscular in the sunlight. The women quietly moved away from the herd and walked on.

'The beige pony seemed tame.' Jocelyn said when they were farther along the path. 'I thought they were wild.'

'They are semi-wild; they do belong to someone - one of the farms that has grazing rights on the common - and they are used to hikers. The little beige pony is a Dun, and he's a yearling, so he's inquisitive. We don't want to worry the stallion by stopping, though.'

They moved away from the ponies and, with Rosa leading the way, continued along the side of the hill, following a narrow sheep track through the thick gorse, which then ended and gave way to a thick mat of purple heather, until they came to a rocky lookout point above the town.

Rosa was a quiet companion. She didn't need to fill the silence with conversation and didn't talk much unless it was to point out a landmark or the local wildlife. She stopped a few times so that they could 'enjoy the view'; but Jocelyn suspected that the thoughtful guide was in fact giving her city companion a break from hiking.

At the top of the hill, they stopped beside a fallen tree, and Jocelyn was once again able to take in the vastness of the sky she had been struck by on her arrival. It stretched across the miles, pale and clear above them, but with a little band of cloud gathered over the hills in the distance towards the west.

'See how the clouds gather on the mountains there, when the air from the Atlantic first hits the land,' said Rosa, pointing. 'This is why we have our rain! The weather can change quickly up here. And over there,' she swung around now and pointed northwards across the common, to a dramatic and jagged mountain range far in the distance, 'That ridge is Cefn y Ddraig - the Dragon's Back. You should see it in the winter when the snow covers the summit.' She stared in silence across the miles, and Jocelyn did the same.

After a while, they turned around and sat down on the tree trunk, which was perfectly positioned for looking down upon the town below; the bridge with its two arches and the frothing river spilling away down the valley. There they sat for a while, watching skylarks singing in the sky above them. Rosa had brought two blocks of cake wrapped in tinfoil, and she handed one to Jocelyn. They munched in silence.

The way back down was easier, and Jocelyn made polite conversation. She learned that Rosa had been born in Madrid but had lived in Wales for twenty-eight years, and that she owned the café on the High Street.

'But I've lived in England since I was fifteen.' Rosa said. 'My father was a diplomat.'

'Ah. So, do you still have family in the U.K.?'

'Yes, in London. My father and brother and his family live near to each other. What about you?'

'My father lives in Ealing,' said Jocelyn, 'In our former family home. My mother - Kate's niece - passed away a few years ago. I live in Bayswater with Jonathan, my husband. We've been married for fifteen years next month. That's it - apart from a few distant cousins on my father's side that we don't see very often.'

Eventually, they arrived back at the stile and Jocelyn climbed over it first. 'Oh, that view from the common! It was like being on the top of the world.' She jumped down into the lane.

'Isn't it amazing?'

'It is! There was nothing higher than us for as far as the eye could see.'

Rosa jumped down beside her and they carried on walking. The sun's rays were warm, and ahead of them, flies danced among the tall stems of cow parsley lining the verges.

'I've really enjoyed it, thanks Rosa. It was just the tonic I needed - as you said it would be.'

'Well, then I will look forward to our next walk,' Rosa smiled. They made their way back up the street towards the Coach House and stopped when they reached the garden gate. 'If you would like to come again, I usually go at around seven in the morning, before work.'

Max was on the opposite side of the street, leaning on the wall of Bob's garden and talking over the wall to Bob. He saw the women arrive and nodded to them, then looked each way along the street, before crossing and wandering over. 'Been for a walk, have you?' he said, winking at Jocelyn. 'How are those feet?'

'We have - and my feet are just fine; the shoes are perfect.'

'Good, good. Where did you go?

'Up onto the hillside, there,' she pointed. 'There was a herd of darling ponies - although one came a little too close for my liking, and we saw birds - oh, and butterflies that I must be sure to identify from Kate's Lepidoptera manuals. And the view, goodness, it was breath-taking.'

'That's the spirit; you're becoming a Country Girl,' he teased.

She let out a laugh and then pulled a face back at him. The three of them chatted for a while longer and then Jocelyn made her excuses because she wanted to go and eat and take a shower. She watched Rosa and Max wander towards Heather Cottage, before climbing the steps to the garden heading indoors.

Inside, she removed her shoes and mac and put them away. Her legs were aching, but in a pleasant way - as if for once, the muscles had been used in the way they were intended. She felt ravenous, so she went to the kitchen, took the dish of stew from the fridge and a bowl from the cupboard, and spooned out a generous portion. She leaned on the counter as she waited for the stew to finish heating, traced her finger along the wooden grains. The microwave finally stopped, and she carefully carried the steaming bowl with a plate of buttered bread into the sitting room.

She ate it at the window table, watching the valley grow pink as the sun dropped behind the hills. A horse and rider jogged past the house, and two walkers heading home with dogs - one with a stick in its mouth that was so long the dog could hardly walk straight.

At eight thirty, Jonathan called. She got up with a tired sigh and plodded into the dining room, to answer. 'Jonathan, hello darling. I'm sorry, I forgot to call earlier.'

'That's all right, as long as you are well.'

'I am. I've had such a busy day though. I met Will and he brought round Kate's bike, then I went hiking with Rosa on the common…'

'Hiking?'

'Yes, and now I really want to shower. Do you mind if we chat tomorrow? I might fall asleep sat here, otherwise.'

'Oh, yes, all right then. I can't wait to hear more; I'm intrigued!'

Jocelyn laughed tiredly, 'I can't wait to tell you, but I'm just so drowsy. It must be all the fresh air. Let's speak more tomorrow when my mind is alert.'

She had rung off, tidied away the dishes, then dragged herself upstairs and showered, the water running in delicious rivulets over her tingling muscles. She put on her nightdress, climbed into bed and looked at her watch. Nine thirty; she'd usually be turning off her office light now - and here she was, two hundred miles away, tucked up in bed and flicking off Kate's lamp. She lay back on the pillow and gazed at the shadowy ceiling, smiling at the thought of the foals on the common - legs too long, ridge of fine hair along their short necks and wide-eyed faces.

Sleeping in until eight, breakfasting in the garden, hiking up mountains… who am I becoming? I don't recognise myself! But Kate, I still don't understand why you wanted me to come here.

She fell asleep; her mind as empty as the common she'd walked upon.

Day 11 - Monday

Monday morning - the beginning of her second week in Llanfairyn. Jocelyn roused to the soft sound of rain drumming on the roof tiles and dripping from the fascia above the bedroom window. Outside was silent, apart from its gentle strum. She lay for a moment, enjoying the peaceful rhythm. Then she checked her watch - eight o'clock. An hour before she needed to call Trudy. She was relieved that it was raining. It was Monday morning and she really wanted to tackle some paperwork, uninterrupted yet without appearing hostile. Rain was the perfect excuse to have to stay indoors.

Within twenty minutes she was downstairs at the window table, cup of tea steaming on the windowsill and the contents of a client file spread in front of her. She left the curtains closed - not wanting to have to interact with Max or Bob or anyone else, but at the same time, not wanting them to *know* that she was hiding from them.

Why was this so complicated? In London, you could just ignore people; it was normal, no one cared!

And yet now, here, alone, she felt something; a slight…emptiness.

She worked for a few minutes on the documents, then sighed and looked up. She pulled the net back a touch to peek out of the window. The rain trickled down the windowpanes. There was no Bob to hide from this morning, after all, and no Max either. Had Rosa walked past already? She said she walked at seven. And the women with the dogs - where were they?

The street was empty. The birds were somewhere else and the cows were far away down the fields. She rested her chin on a hand and gazed down the valley. Jonathan used to say, 'Be careful what you wish for.'

He was right.

She looked back down at the table. Ah well, at least with no distractions she'd be able to fly through today's workload. She picked up a sheaf of papers and began thumbing through them. She read a paragraph, and then reread it. On the third attempt, she cursed herself and slapped her cheek lightly, 'Come on, concentrate!'

It was no use. She folded her arms on the table, blew through pursed lips and looked around her. A pair of binoculars stood in the corner of the windowsill, tucked behind the curtain. She stared at them. Is this where Kate sat, on rainy days; watching the world from the warmth of the sitting room? She picked the binoculars up. They were old, but free from dust. Beneath them was a soft piece of fabric, the kind for cleaning spectacles. She took the cloth and shook it to used it to carefully wipe the binocular lenses. Then she put them to her eyes and fiddled with the focusing wheel in the centre.

In an instant, the hedge at the far end of the garden rolled into focus; so clear it seemed if she reached out, she would be able to touch the leaves. She slowly scanned around the undergrowth, and then the stone wall, investigating the nooks and crannies.

There wasn't a lot of movement in the garden and then she spotted the little red-faced bird, hopping around at the base of the hedgerow.

She lowered the binoculars, placed them on the table and quietly moved over to the bookshelf - not wanting to disturb the tiny visitor and forgetting that it was in fact quite a distance away. She drew out a book on garden birds, brought it back to the table and began scanning, page by page.

There it was; a goldfinch.

Kate was kneeling by the border, weeding and Jocelyn was lying on her back on a check blanket in the middle of the lawn, watching the clouds drift overhead.

'Look, Jocelyn,' Kate whispered, 'A goldfinch. He loves the dandelions. That's why I leave them grow!'

Jocelyn rolled over on her front and propped herself up on her elbows, but the bird had been startled by the movement and flown away.

She watched the bird, holding her breath despite the distance between them. Unaware of her, it hopped around among the long grass. The binoculars were a window into the creature's world, and she accompanied him in his foraging for several minutes, until he reached the end of the hedge and then flitted away.

She returned the binoculars to the sill and checked her watch. Eight-fifty; ten minutes until she needed to call Trudy. She picked up the documents again and began reading. The rest of the morning passed quietly.

It stopped raining just before noon. The vegetation outside appeared a brighter green than usual - as if it had *enjoyed* the rainfall. Jocelyn removed her glasses and rubbed her eyes. Then she picked up the binoculars again, unable to resist, and went into the dining room to sit quietly at the window there - elbows on the table, focusing the wheel, and then scanning the garden.

The dining room looked out onto the front lawn on the left side of the path. She hadn't paid much attention to this side of the garden because the seating area was on the other side. It was planted with the same thick borders of long grasses and flowers, except that now, Jocelyn could see that it wasn't only grass growing, but a variety of plants and shrubs she couldn't identify. Through the binoculars she could make out various forms - slender silver leaves, dark leathery ones, clusters of tiny purple flowers swaying alongside bright pink ones. And now that the rain had stopped, the insects were returning. A wasp, no, not a wasp but something similar but smaller, hovering and dipping above the swaying lavender stems. And bees; one, two, three bees, each rummaging in a separate flowerhead. She watched the insects - oblivious to each other except when their tiny paths crossed, and then they gave an irritated little dance before moving out of each other's way.

Jocelyn chuckled to herself, and then swept the binoculars from the borders and up to the dense shrubbery at the end of the lawn. Here, a tall bush was growing; many slender arcing branches that fanned out from the base, each tipped with a long cream conical flowerhead. She paused and studied the blossoms; each one was in fact comprised of numerous tiny flowers, clustered tightly together.

She saw movement and searched through the binoculars until she found the source; a dark butterfly with a bold red stripe across the tips of its wings had landed on one of the cream blossoms. It slowly opened and closed its wings, manoeuvring itself into position and probing the tiny flowers, before pausing to feed. A few short seconds and it was off, fluttering to the next flowerhead.

'Where can you find admirals mixing with painted ladies and peacocks?' Kate chuckled. 'Here, on my Butterfly Tree!'

Jocelyn put the binoculars down and sighed. She looked down at her hands. They were pale and showing the first signs of wrinkles despite the daily application of the expensive hand cream she'd treated herself to - and the fingernails were in dire need of a manicure. She looked up and sighed. Oh well, that would have to wait.

She moved to the kitchen to make lunch and ate it in armchair in the sitting room. There was no sound apart from the subdued ticking of the clock. Aware that her mood might begin to fall, she shook off the thoughts of Kate. She replaced the binoculars on the windowsill and busied herself with work for the rest of the afternoon. The rain started again; a persistent drizzle swathed the valley in mist. All bird- and insect-life disappeared, leaving the garden still except for the nodding of leaves as rain pattered onto them. Jocelyn felt alone.

She worked uninterrupted until the evening, then called Jonathan - trying not to concern him unnecessarily, but instead, conversing about his and her work day and interesting elements of their legal cases. Afterwards, she showered and retired to bed; glad that she had achieved so much workwise, but less so that she now had a heart filled with strange emotions. It took a while for her feelings to settle and for sleep to come.

Day 12 - Tuesday

Tuesday dawned much the same as the day before. A low mist hung over the valley and the rainfall continued throughout the day. Jocelyn hadn't seen anyone again in the morning, despite being up a little earlier than the previous day and making sure she was peering through the net curtains by eight o'clock. She avoided the binoculars on the windowsill - not keen to revisit the emotions they had aroused - and instead she buried herself in her work. She pored over folders, frowning as she read, and scratching hurried notes onto her pad. By three in the afternoon, the headache was threatening to make a return.

Jocelyn treasured the seclusion of her private office in London. She realised now that the subtle presence of Trudy, working at her own desk outside the door, and her two colleagues in their own personal offices on the opposite side of the foyer, obviously brought comfort and made the work environment conducive to peaceful concentration. Alone in a big house, held hostage by the rain, she was finding it difficult to focus. There was nothing for it; she needed to take a break.

Under the porch was a rack with a pair of upside-down wellington boots, and Jocelyn gave them a knock to dislodge whatever might have crawled inside, before cautiously sliding them on. It was warmer outdoors than she expected, the rain had stopped and the air was rich with the scent of wet earth and vegetation. Up on the hillside, low rainclouds drifted along, obscuring the view of the summit and the sky was a flat carpet of grey. She inhaled slowly and listened to the sound of her own breathing and studied the droplets on the blades of grass on the lawn in front of her. Then she wandered absently around the lawn - picking a few stems of lavender, pinching and rolling the leaves between her first finger and thumb, and inhaling the soothing aroma left behind.

The thrush flew down, unaware, from the honeysuckle and landed on the lawn almost at her feet - then realised its blunder and scooted back in again. A few bees had ventured out and were seizing the opportunity to feed before another downpour.

After a couple of circuits of the soggy garden and a very brief and casual glance up and down the street - to avoid appearing too lonely or needy - she returned indoors and took the lavender stems into the kitchen, found a drinking glass and half-filled it with water, and placed the dainty stems on the windowsill in the sitting room. Then she returned to the kitchen and gathered herself some bread, cheese and chutney.

She sat in the armchair, feeling tiny in this huge house, but better with a plate of food in front of her. She chewed slowly on the soft bread slathered in creamy cheese, delighting in the contrasting tang of the chutney; then sipped the tea with her feet stretched out across the hearthrug and her toes wriggling contentedly. That felt better; the focus had returned. Time to get back to work.

The rest of the afternoon passed without incident. At six thirty, there was a cheerful rapping at the front door. Jocelyn frowned for a moment and then walked over to answer it.

'Hi!' Will was standing there.

'Oh Will, hello.'

'You said half past six on Tuesday.'

'I did.' Jocelyn remembered.

'Shall I come in then?' Will stepped inside, kicked off his trainers and walked past Jocelyn into the house.

She closed the door and followed him into the sitting room. She had forgotten the arrangement, but she was pleased, after two days alone, to see another person.

Will stood over the window table, hands on hips, scanning the array of folders and papers. 'Is this your work?'

'Yes, it is.'

'It looks really boring.'

'Oh!' Jocelyn didn't know whether to laugh or feel offended, 'Well…'

He looked up. 'What do you do?'

'I'm a lawyer.'

'Yuk! Looks like too much reading.'

'Well…'

'I definitely prefer my job,' he laughed. He moved to sit down on the hearth - lifting the cushion that was there and positioning it behind his back to lean against the stone fireplace. Jocelyn watched him. It was clear this seat was Will's place - next to Kate's armchair.

'Why haven't you lit the fire?' he asked.

'I don't want the room to get all smoky.'

'You mean you're too posh!' Will teased. 'Or don't you know how to light it?'

Jocelyn changed the subject. 'So, let us have cake then, shall we? And I'll make myself a cup of tea.'

She disappeared into the kitchen and made tea and carried it in on a tray along with the block of carrot cake, a knife and two small plates.

'So, you work, Will?' She sat down at the table, took a plate and cut a slice of cake she thought would be adequate for him.

''Course!'

'I just wasn't sure whether you were, well, at college or…'

'No, I didn't go to college. Anyway, now I'm twenty-six.' He took the plate that she was holding out, and happily tucked into the slice.

'What job do you do?' She cut herself a sliver of the cake.

'I help Max,' he mumbled.

'You drive taxis?' Jocelyn sat down in the armchair.

Will roared with laughter at this. 'No! Max does other things, you know. Today we were painting the windowsills in the church hall.'

Jocelyn glanced at Will's paint-spattered jeans and briefly worried about Kate's textiles. Will saw her expression. 'Don't worry, this is dry; it's from last week. I wore overalls today.'

'I see.' She took a bite of the cake. It was rich and moist, with sweet carroty bits.

'My job is great because we do different things every day, and we see different people.' He took another bite. 'Do you just have to read all the time?'

'Well, I write, too.'

'Reading and writing. Okaaay.' He'd heard enough about her job. 'Are you married?'

'Yes, I am.'

'What's your husband's name?'

'Jonathan.'

'Is he a lawyer too?'

'He is…'

'Wow, I bet the conversations in your house are really exciting!' He shoved some cake into his mouth.

Jocelyn didn't know how to answer. She didn't feel offended, though, but… *amused.*

Will carried on talking, between chews, 'We play scrabble in our house at night. Mum insists; she says it's good for us. What do you do at night?'

'Well, I am usually at work until nine,' she squinted and pulled a face. 'I suppose we are a pretty boring couple.'

'But I bet you were fun when you were younger.'

She almost choked on her cake. 'I'm only forty-two, Will!'

He shrugged.

'Jonathan and I do things….'

'Like what?'

'Well…' Jocelyn racked her brains. 'We go to the theatre.' She couldn't remember the last time they had gone to the theatre.

'Ooo, yes!' Will's eyes shone at this, 'Kate was an actress. What have you seen at the theatre?'

I'm just thinking…'

He watched her, waiting for an answer, and when one didn't come quickly enough, he moved on. 'Kate told me that the buses in London have two storeys, so they can fit loads of people in!'

'They do.'

'And their taxis are black and they all look the same.'

'I suppose they do.'

'Have you seen Big Ben?'

'Oh yes.'

'I saw him at New Year. On the TV.'

They both took another bite of cake and munched it, Will more slowly this time. His face turned solemn, and he frowned. 'I've never seen you before. I've known Kate since I was a baby, but I've never seen *you*. Where have you been?'

Jocelyn paused. 'I've been in London. Working.'

'Reading and writing?'

'Pretty much.'

'For twenty-six years?'

Jocelyn didn't know how answer. Will's face broke into a wide smile. 'Lucky you came here, then! You can have a break from reading and writing. Come on a bike ride. Please!'

'I...'

'Please.'

Jocelyn looked at Will's face, filled with hope. He pointed at her, grinning. 'You're going to say yes. I know it!'

Jocelyn sighed in submission. 'Only if you p*romise* me that we can go slowly.'

'Promise!' Will put down his empty plate, and looked around him. Then, changing the subject, 'Kate and me, we used to read after we'd had cake.' When Jocelyn didn't reply immediately, he gestured to the books on the shelves.

'Oh, I see. Would you like to read now? You're welcome to.'

'You have to read too, otherwise it's not the same. We both have to read, and we don't speak to each other or anything. And - we have to have a fire.'

Jocelyn made a noise through her lips, 'There isn't anything I really want to read….' She saw Will's face fall a little and stopped herself. 'Oh all right then; let's. How long must we read for?'

'Kate never got bored of reading with me!' He jumped up with a smile and drew out a large hardback book, *Illustrated British Wildlife*, then he sat back down and opened it eagerly. When Jocelyn didn't move, he added, 'Go on!' so that she ended up selecting herself a hardback too and settling in the armchair with it.

Will reached for a box of matches from around the corner of the shelves, took out a long match and struck it. He touched the flame to the white firelighter blocks nestled amongst the newspaper, and the newspaper and wood kindling caught immediately. Soon, the fire was crackling gently. Jocelyn watched, unsure how she felt about having an open fire burning in the house, but assuming it must be safe because Doreen had prepared it for her. The smell on her clothes she'd have to just deal with.

They read, in silence as Will had requested, for half an hour - although Jocelyn noticed that Will was not actually reading the text but looking through the images. The only sound was of the clock ticking, the turning of pages, and the occasional chuckle from Will as he came across an image he approved of.

Finally, satisfied with Jocelyn's company for one evening, he closed the book, returned it to the shelf and walked over to put on his shoes. Jocelyn followed him.

'So, our bike ride; how about tomorrow?' He opened the door.

'Thursday would be better, Will. If we could make it six thirty - half past six - again, I shall be finished work then.'

'I thought you said you worked until nine,'

'Well, I do - at least, I do usually.'

'Half past six the day after tomorrow. I'll come round.' He hopped over the doorstep and, without looking back, disappeared down the path.

Jocelyn closed the door and leaned back against it. She put her head back with a groan and lifted her eyes to the ceiling. Why did she have so little control here? Could she remember how to ride a bicycle? Surely she could.

But did she *want* to? No! Well… maybe.

Day 13 - Wednesday

The rain passed and Wednesday morning dawned cool and cloudless. After two days indoors feeling something… frustration, or loneliness? - Jocelyn was up by seven and at the garden table with her breakfast. She had already waved to Bob and given the ladies with dogs her cheeriest 'Hello'. Then Max had appeared and before he even made it to the gateway, Jocelyn had started pouring tea into his cup.

They were sipping and chatting and pointing to birds and insects, when Rosa strolled past the house. She stopped to chat with the pair. 'I didn't see you for a couple of days,' she smiled at Jocelyn.

'No, the rain kept me indoors. Did you walk past?'

'Oh yes. Every day.'

'I didn't see anyone,' said Jocelyn, 'Apart from Will, yesterday evening.'

'Well, I was thinking of calling on you, but I know you are trying to work,' Rosa explained. 'Do you fancy a walk again soon?'

'That would be lovely. Are you sure you don't want to join us now, for tea?'

'No, I have to do my walk before work. When are you free?'

Jocelyn thought for a moment. 'Friday evening would be good for me. I'm expecting Doreen sometime this morning - and I will probably enjoy myself more at the end of the working week.'

'All right then; Friday it is!'

Jocelyn smiled, 'Wonderful. Oh, I meant to mention; Will has offered to be my guide on a cycle trip tomorrow evening. I'm sure I'll make a terrible fool of myself - haven't ridden a bicycle in years - but he was quite persistent, so I agreed. I hope that's all right with you.'

'Yes, of course it is. Will is an expert around these country lanes. He knows his way very well; you won't get lost.'

'I was rather meaning that it might seem a little odd, you know, a twenty-six-year-old boy, I mean man, escorting a forty-two-year-old old woman for a cycle ride!'

'Odd? Not at all. You'll have a lovely time.' With that, Rosa said goodbye and carried on down the lane. Max made to leave too, and Jocelyn tidied up the crockery. She hadn't arranged a time for Doreen to drop off the groceries, and she wanted to get on with some work before the woman arrived.

The morning passed swiftly. Jocelyn felt relaxed and was pleased with her achievements as lunchtime approached. She looked out of the window and pulled the curtain aside. The sun was drying up the last of the previous day's puddles. Perhaps a little air in the house would be helpful, too.

The wood-framed sash windows were made of two halves, each with four panes. The bottom half slid up in front of the top half and stayed there due to tension from a rope-and-weight mechanism in the side of the frame. She unclipped the catch at the bottom and then slid it up a few inches. It opened easily; Kate must have opened it often.

She went upstairs to the bedroom. The window was the same sash design, and she opened that one too. The delicious breeze blew in and fanned the curtains. She moved over to the row of wardrobe doors, grasped the knobs of one set of doors and slowly pulled them open.

The wardrobe was packed with garments - the whole rail across the top filled, and the base too, so that there was not a spare inch of space. She moved along the wardrobes, opening each set of doors wide. Every rail was filled the same. She stood back in amazement at the sheer volume they held.

Jocelyn had a weak spot for fine clothes, and she took only a few brief moments to absorb the extent of Kate's clothing collection, which, it was now clear, was beyond anything she had ever imagined, before she moved forwards to delve into the Aladdin's cave.

Everything in the wardrobes was precisely organised, with blouses, skirts, dresses, ballgowns, two-piece suits and coats grouped together on the rails. Jocelyn ran her hand along them all. The fabrics felt exquisite, and the clothes were clearly valuable; many were in clear protective bags and looked very old - some a little faded in parts. Some of the styles were outrageous, evidence of Kate's time in London in the 1960's. Others looked even older, judging by their fabric, and cut, and their seams so neatly hand-stitched;

vintage garments collected by Kate for their sentimental value, or purely out of her love of clothes.

In the bottom of the wardrobes were stacks of shoe boxes, with yellowing labels on the ends: Bourne & Hollingsworth, Galeries Lafayette and Bruno Magli. Jocelyn judged there must have been almost fifty boxes in total, and many more loose pairs of shoes and boots on open racks in each wardrobe.

She glanced at her watch; twelve o'clock. Doreen hadn't been yet, and it was time for a lunch break. How could she resist a quick dressing-up session? She grinned, feeling like a child in a sweet shop. She peeled off her shirt and trousers, discarding them inside-out on the bed, then took the clip from her hair so it wouldn't catch in any of the clothes. Then she began to sift through the items on the rails. She started with the ballgowns, sifting through them in turn; velvet ones, satin ones, ones of lace, ones a cascade of sequins, ones without sleeves and daring plunging necklines…

She chose a long, dark green satin dress with a bead bodice, lifting it from the rail, removing the cover and hanger, and then easing the delicate zip open. Then she slipped the dress on - putting her arms into the armholes and unrolling it carefully down her body. It looked like it was going to fit. 'Now, if I can just get the zip up…' She reached under her left arm to slide the zip closed again, 'There!'

She stood back and turned to look in the mirror. The dress fit like a glove, the bodice following the small curve of her breast and the tuck of her tiny waist, and the skirt falling in soft loose folds onto the floor. She twisted to view the back, and then swung back again, watching with rapture the fabric move and shimmer around her legs.

Within fifteen minutes, there were three ballgowns on the bed, and Jocelyn was fastening herself into a fourth. This one was crimson, cut away at the back and with fine straps that crossed her shoulder blades. The colour of the dress was striking against her pale skin and dark hair. She looked in the dressing table mirror. This dress would look better with her hair up.

Kate sat Jocelyn on the stool in front of her. 'And now, you can pin your hair up, like this.' She reached a mother-of-pearl hair clip from the top drawer, then swept up the girl's long hair and fastened it loosely at the back.

She opened the dressing table drawers. The clip was still there, on the right. She sat on the stool and pinned up her hair as she had watched Kate do. The skin of her neck and shoulders was creamy and smooth and the dress straps emphasised the shape of her collar bones. Jonathan would love this look…

There was suddenly a cry from the garden; a shriek that didn't sound animal but couldn't be human. It was followed by a thump as something was dropped. Jocelyn jumped up from the stool, heart pounding, and peered out of the window in front of her nervously.

There was a figure slumped on the path below, face turned up at the bedroom window, eyes wide. A torn grocery bag dangled from one hand, and a pile of vegetables and a loaf were scattered on the ground. Three apples rolled away in different directions.

Jocelyn picked up the front of the gown and hurried down the stairs. She unlocked the door quickly and stepped outside.

Doreen was on her knees, with her hand on her chest, groaning. 'Oh, my life! Kate!'

Jocelyn crept over cautiously. 'Doreen. It's me, Jocelyn. Look. It's not Kate!'

Doreen was nodding and trying to smile, although her face was red. 'Oh my word. I can't breathe. I'm such a fool, just for a split second I thought…'

'Yes, I realise. I'm sorry.'

'It's just that you were the image of her - in the theatre photographs above the fireplace! Your hair, everything,'

'Oh dear. I've given you such a fright. I was just trying on Kate's dresses.'

Doreen glanced at Jocelyn in the dress, then still blushing, began to gather up the groceries.

'Are you injured? Do you feel ready to try to stand up?'

With Jocelyn's help, Doreen struggled to her feet and brushed off her knees. 'My heart is galloping like a herd of Welsh Mountain ponies in a storm. Oh, ouch.' There was a small graze on her left knee, with a smudge of blood around it.

'I think we need to sit you down for a moment,' said Jocelyn. 'Come inside and we'll bathe it, and I'll make us a cup of tea.'

'Oh, I don't want to intrude.'

'You're not. It's the least I can do, after giving you a fright like that.'

'No really, I must get back,' the woman pleaded.

'Doreen, I can't let you leave in this state. I insist. Just wait there a minute.' Jocelyn marched indoors, and returned with Kate's shopping basket to put the spilled groceries in. She hoisted the full basket onto one shoulder, put her other arm around Doreen and steered the shaken woman into the house. After a bit of hunting, she found a first aid kit under the kitchen sink with a few plasters and bandages in it, and then made a pot of tea while Doreen disappeared to the bathroom to clean and dress her wound.

She put the teapot and two cups onto a tray, along with the remainder of the carrot cake, and took it to the sitting room. Five minutes later, Doreen reappeared, looking less flushed and with a plaster across her knee cap. She had redone the bun in her hair. 'It was only a scratch,' she said, coming to the sitting room table and pulling out a chair. She sat down and smoothed her pinafore with hands that were still trembling.

'Here we go.' Jocelyn poured tea into the cups and handed one to Doreen. She took it, and then Jocelyn sat beside her, trying not to spill tea on, or crease, the gown she was still wearing. They drank a few sips in silence.

'I'm glad of a bit of company today,' Jocelyn admitted. 'This whole situation; Aunt Kates's death, being responsible for packing her possessions, finalising the estate, it's becoming more difficult than I expected.'

Doreen smiled gently and sipped her tea.

'Well, at least I've become an established tea-drinker since arriving in Llanfairyn,' Jocelyn continued. 'Doesn't it taste so much nicer in Kate's Staffordshire bone china?'

'It does. And when I was cleaning for Kate, I always used to marvel at the hand-painted flowers. Such skill.' Doreen admired the cup, then placed it down and turned to Jocelyn. 'I'm sorry I dropped your groceries onto the ground.'

'It doesn't matter at all. Nothing is broken. Such beautiful fresh food - I can't wait to try the tomatoes.'

'Those are from our greenhouse. You can't beat freshly picked fruit and veg.'

'Do you have chickens, too?'

'We don't; we have a resident fox who would enjoy that too much, I'm afraid,' said Doreen, 'but there are plenty of other folk in town who do.'

Jocelyn put her cup down and ran her fingers over the lace tablecloth. 'Tell me about the townsfolk, Doreen. I've met some generous friends of Kate's already: Max, Alan and you. Rosa and Will…'

Doreen shifted on her seat. 'Yes, all wonderful people.'

'Will still lives at home? He told me he was twenty-six.'

'Ah yes. Such a helpful lad. Wouldn't harm a fly.'

'He hasn't found a love yet, or anything?'

'No, no, not yet.' Doreen looked away and sipped her tea.

Jocelyn cut a slice of cake and passed it to her. 'And Rosa?'

'Thank you,' she said, taking the cake, 'Ah yes. A beautiful lady.'

'Is there a Mr. Rosa?'

'Joe. He was a lovely man. Sadly, he passed away.'

'Oh?'

'Yes, yes. A lovely couple.' Doreen broke off a piece of cake and filled her mouth with it.

'I see,' said Jocelyn. 'And Max?'

'Max is grand, too,' she mumbled. 'Goes out of his way to help folk. This cake is tasty, isn't it?'

Jocelyn cut herself a slice. 'And does Max have a family?'

'Never a happier chap than Max. There we are. Oh my goodness, what's the time?'

'Erm, oh, about one o'clock I think.'

Doreen nodded to Jocelyn's dress. 'Kate really did have exquisite taste, didn't she?'

Jocelyn looked down at the gown. 'She did. I remember her being glamorous - even in the daytime. But the photographs of her partying with the theatre set; those are something else.'

'She was glamorous for sure. Such an attractive lady, inside and out. I admired how she paid attention to her appearance.'

'I know! I remember watching her when I stayed here. Before she left the house, she made sure her presentation was immaculate.'

Doreen was nodding and smiling at Jocelyn now. 'But she never made you feel bad about your own inferior turn-out. She was sweet and kind and always had time to chat. She looked good for herself, not to intimidate anyone else. She simply loved clothes and jewels - and good for her, I say. I wish I could have taken a leaf from her book!'

The two women laughed in agreement. Doreen looked around the sitting room. 'I used to be in an amateur dramatics group - a local one, you know. In the church hall. Nothing like Kate used to do.'

'Oh! You don't still join in?'

'No, no.'

Jocelyn noticed the woman's shoulders sag a little. She thought for a minute, before asking, 'Do you want to come and try on some of Kate's dresses with me? Please! I was just in the middle of holding my own fashion show, and it's boring by myself.'

'Oh goodness. I don't know.'

'Come on! Let's dive into Kate's wonderful wardrobes. She would want us to - you know she would.'

'I don't think so, not today.' Doreen put her cup down, then stood up and smiled. 'I must be off now.'

'Oh, are you sure?' Jocelyn placed her own cup on the table, then stood up too and followed Doreen to the door.

'Yes, yes. Enjoy the tomatoes.' Doreen opened the door and stepped out into the porch.

'Wait a minute, I almost forgot.' Jocelyn walked over to the bookshelves and picked up an envelope lying on it, with a cheque inside. 'This should cover the groceries, and Alan's gardening fees.' She handed the envelope to Doreen.

Doreen took it and smiled. Then she looked down at Jocelyn. 'It *is* a lovely dress you're wearing.'

'Another time then, Doreen?'

'Perhaps,' she replied, looking at the ground. 'Thank you. Goodbye.'

'Yes, goodbye.' Jocelyn closed the door, frowning. She went upstairs and changed back into her clothes. Then, one by one, she carefully hung the ballgowns back in the closet, feeling deflated that Doreen hadn't wanted to join in the dressing up, and wondering if she had been insensitive in the first place for expecting her to. After all, the woman had recently lost her friend and here was a stranger from London rifling through the woman's wardrobes.

Jocelyn went back downstairs to the kitchen and busied herself with preparing a casserole, with the vegetables that Doreen had brought. She washed the earth from the carrots and potatoes under the tap, and then sat down at the kitchen table with the chopping board to dice them. All the while, her mind was on Doreen. Her warm eyes - and the smile which did not quite make them sparkle. The kind gestures she made - but refusing to accept any in return. Doreen stayed on Jocelyn's mind while she worked that afternoon, when she called Jonathan that evening and when she showered and went to bed at nine.

Day 14 - Thursday

Thursday was quiet and uneventful. At seven o'clock, rather than have breakfast in the garden Jocelyn had sat down to work, mindful that she had promised a cycle ride with Will that evening and wanting to get ahead of the workload. She heard Alan arrive at two and unload his tools, but she hadn't gone outside to chat with him because she was immersed in a case file and didn't want to interrupt her flow. She had an early supper at five, and then went upstairs to Kate's bedroom to hunt for some clothing that would be sensible for cycling.

Will came at six thirty and went straight round to Kate's shed to get the bike out for Jocelyn. Jocelyn had seen him arrive from the sitting room window. She picked up a bag, containing two apples and a bottle of water, and went outside to meet him. Alan was weeding in the far corner of the garden, and Will was bent over, examining one of the bike's chains.

Jocelyn waved to Alan, and then spoke to Will. 'I must confess, I'm nervous about this.'

He stood up. 'It's easy!'

'For you, perhaps.'

He handed the bike to her. 'You can have a practice in the road, first.'

She put the fruit and water in the basket. 'Oh dear. I'm having doubts.'

'Better get moving then. Mum says he who hesitates is lost.'

'This could indeed be a lost cause.' she muttered. 'All right, Will. Let's go.'

She wheeled the bike along the path and lifted it down the steps onto the pavement. Will followed.

'Put the bike in the middle of the road, facing down there. That's it. Now, just sit on for a min and check the seat height. Both feet down, like this.'

Jocelyn did everything he instructed.

'I think it's O.K. You are about as tall as Kate. Right, get your pedal ready to push off, like this.'

'Which pedal?'

'Whichever you want!'

Jocelyn took a breath. She brought the pedal round so it was under her right foot.

'Now check nothing's coming before you go.'

Jocelyn looked both ways down the street. No vehicles.

'Right, go!'

She pushed off. The bike was wobbly at first and the water and apples jiggled in the basket, but on the smooth surface she soon found her balance and was pedalling cautiously past the cottages. Will was whooping and applauding in the background.

Will had done a good job of keeping the bike maintained for Kate. After a few yards, Jocelyn pulled at the brakes steadily and the bike came to a smooth stop. She put her feet down and then walked in a loop, bike between her legs, to turn it to face back up the street.

She could feel a rather silly beam plastered across her face. Will waved and she waved back. 'I did it!' she said it to herself as much as to him.

'And come back again!'

'All right. Watch out!' She cycled back to him with just a little wobble.

Will was laughing. 'See? Easy.'

'More luck than ease, I think. Now, let me just have another couple of goes.'

She rode the bike back and forth several times, her brow becoming less furrowed and the bike becoming less wobbly with each successful pass of the Coach House. She brought the bike to a stop next to Will. 'I think I've got it.'

He nodded. 'Shall we go up onto the common, then?'

'Is it a proper road? I don't think I could ride up the dirt track.'

'Yes, we'll go up there.' He gestured further down the lane, where Jocelyn could see now that a narrow road - just about wide enough for a small car - forked left on the bend before the cattle grid.

'Oh, is that a public road? I walked past with Rosa the other day, but I hadn't realised.'

'It leads up to the top. There's never any traffic on it.' He set his foot on the pedal and pushed off. 'Follow me!'

'Go slow, then!' Jocelyn took off behind him, concentrating hard and hoping that Will was right about the lack of traffic.

With Will in the lead, they followed the road onto the common. It wound gradually upwards, snaking back and forth on itself, and Jocelyn managed to keep pedalling for most of the way. She only had to dismount and push the bike on each of the sharp turns, which were steeper than any road she had ever seen and had grooves scraped in them from the undersides of vehicles who had also struggled to navigate them. Will also dismounted, out of politeness she guessed.

They cycled up the road for half an hour, and then stopped at an outcrop of rocks off to their left, where they rested their bikes and walked over to look down on the town.

A large hawk circled the empty sky above them. 'A red kite,' pointed Will. 'Max says they're rare; he says when he was a boy and came up onto the common, there were none. But he says now, they're protected, so who knows - perhaps one day there will be loads!'

Jocelyn watched the bird. After a day at a desk, it felt good to focus her eyes into blue infinity. 'That sky! It stretches for ever. And the *space*! I haven't felt freedom like this since I was a child.

They stood for a while, Jocelyn looking over the town and Will occasionally asking if she was having fun. As the light began to change, they remounted their bikes and Will led the way again. This time, they were heading downhill and they freewheeled; Will went in front, calling behind him to encourage her to go faster, and Jocelyn behind, blinking the breeze-induced tears from her eyes and watching nervously for potholes.

They slowed the bikes as they reached the main road, then turned right and pedalled up the street to the Coach House. Will pulled on his brakes and came to a stop by the gate and Jocelyn pulled up alongside, laughing and breathless. She dismounted and leaned the bike against the wall, then picked bits from her mouth. 'Eugh, flies! Oh my gosh, I'm aching. But I haven't had that much fun in ages. Look at my silly grin; it certainly has brought out the youngster in me. That was the most exhilarating thing I've done in a long time.' She smoothed her hair and then walked around to stretch her legs. 'Phew! Thank you so much for encouraging me to give it a go. Although - ouch - I suspect I shall be dreadfully stiff in the morning!'

'You'll soon get used to it; it's just cycling. I do it every day. I feel sorry for a person who doesn't have the time.' Will climbed off his bike. 'Everybody cycles around here, it doesn't make a difference how old they are, or how busy they are - or whatever your excuse was.'

Jocelyn smiled. 'I can see why. It's a splendid feeling, pedalling along with the wind in your hair, the flies in your mouth; not the best moment but I loved it all the same.'

'I think you need to get out on your bike every day. It would be good for putting some good feelings into your heart.'

'I think it would.'

'When I'm up there, it always makes my heart feel really, like, *big*. Just me and the common and the birds singing. I just keep going and then when I'm hungry I come home. I don't worry about how far I go.'

Jocelyn stood with her hands on her hips, staring up at the hillside they had returned from. 'Everything that's on your mind, it dissolves. All of life's burdens carried off on the breeze.' She laughed to herself.

Will fiddled with his pedal. 'Oh yes, it does all of that. I told you the common was beautiful. This is my life every day. I don't know any different. If it can't be *your* life every day, well then as I said before, that's a shame - a real shame.'

She didn't reply.

'Shall we go riding again?' he asked.

'I think we must. When?'

'Now?'

'Now?' she laughed. 'No, not now.'

'Why not?'

'We've only just arrived back!'

'You said it was fun and you wanted to go again.'

'It's a good point, Will. I did. Do you mind if we go another day, though? I'm aching, and I have things to do at the house.'

'All right. I'll call on you.'

'It's fixed!' Will's face broke into a grin. He mounted his bike. 'It's really cool to have a new friend. See you, Josey.'

'Bye Will. Thanks for teaching me to ride again.' She watched him pedal off, and then lifted her bike up the steps and started to wheel it along the path to the shed.

A nervous cough from behind made her start, and she swung around. Alan was still in the corner of the lawn, forking at the earth with a hand trowel. 'Goodness Alan, are you still here?' Jocelyn looked at her watch. 'It's way past supper time.'

'Oh, is it? I was just finishing off,' he said.

'I feel terrible, keeping you from your own garden - and Doreen.'

'That's all right. I like to keep on top of things here.'

'I know, and you most certainly do keep on top of it.' Jocelyn looked around at the neat lawn and colourful borders. 'I'd feel awful though if I'd made you think you had to come so often. We must discuss increasing your payment.'

Alan looked at his feet. 'I enjoy it. The existing payment is enough, thank you.' He picked up the tools and headed for the shed.

'Oh, all right.' Jocelyn followed him. She waited for him to store the tools and come back outside, then wheeled the bike into the shed and leaned it beside the barrow. She closed and bolted the door. The bolt had two holes for a padlock, but she couldn't see one anywhere. People seemed casual with their belongings in Llanfairyn

'Is there a padlock, Alan?'.

'A padlock? No, no,' he shook his head. 'So, I'll see you on Saturday.'

'Not Saturday Alan; please, take a day with Doreen.'

'No need. As I said, I enjoy coming.' He shifted slightly.

She looked at him. 'Well, if you are sure.'

'I'm sure, thank you.'

She went into the house to shower - puzzling about Alan and Doreen and questioning once again why Kate had asked her to come to the Coach House - but the memories of her cycle ride with Will soon filled her mind and she went to bed at nine smiling.

Day 15 - Friday

Jocelyn stood in front of the open wardrobe doors in Kate's bedroom. Next to her, Doreen was surveying the laden rails with wide eyes.

'I'm glad you agreed to help me look through Kate's clothes, Doreen. It's daunting, and I only have a week left in Llanfairyn to figure out what to do with all this.'

'I know - you could clothe a Royal with this wardrobe.'

It was lunchtime and Jocelyn had taken a break at twelve when she had heard Doreen's gentle knock on the door. Instead of cleaning this week, Doreen had agreed to help sort through Kate's wardrobe of clothes and organise for the local charity shop to collect them. It would have been straightforward to simply bag up the clothes and send them off, but Jocelyn hadn't wanted to face it alone.

'Just look at all these dresses!' said Doreen now, her eyes sweeping the rails. She moved the hangers along the rail in turn, surveying each dress as she did so and stroking the soft fabrics between her fingers. 'Where do we start?'

'Alan spends a lot of time in Kate's garden,' Jocelyn said casually, running her fingers over the stitched detail of a halter neck gown. 'Has he always done so?'

'Yes.' Doreen lifted a protective bag from the rail and turned to the bed, her back to Jocelyn. She laid the bag down and unzipped it.

'I don't want him to feel obliged.'

'It's where he wants to be. He's happy when he's gardening. Oh, just look at this!' Doreen took a bold turquoise-and-pink flowered dress out of the bag and held it against herself. Her cheeks flushed red.

'Wow! I think it's a muumuu - a Hawaiian dress. It suits your colouring.' Jocelyn had knelt to look through the racks of shoes in the base of the wardrobes. 'And look at these shoes! I think they are from Paris. Harvey Nicks has nothing on this.'

Doreen put the turquoise dress back. 'Oh my, I feel wrong - guilty - poring through Kate's things like this.'

'Nonsense Doreen! We are appreciating the clothes in the same way she did. I'm sure she would want us to enjoy them.' She stood up. 'This would fit you. Here, try it on - use the changing screen.'

'Oh no, I couldn't…'

'Come on! You try that, and I will try… *this*! She pulled out the halter neck and held it up.

Doreen took the dress reluctantly and went behind the screen, while Jocelyn changed by the bed. For a few minutes, the room was quiet apart from the rustling of fabric.

'Ta daa! How do I look?' Jocelyn fastened her zip and twirled over to the mirror. 'I could be on stage, at the Palladium with my very dashing co-star by my side. I would bow and the audience would cheer...'

'I'm dressed,' Doreen's small voice came from behind the screen.

'Come out, then! Let me see.'

Doreen emerged wearing the colourful dress. Although she was a bigger size than Kate or Jocelyn, the loose fit was flattering, and the bold colours suited her dark skin.

'Oh, my, Doreen - it's breath-taking! Look, in the mirror.' She pulled the woman towards her.

'I won't, thank you.'

'Come!'

'No. There's no need.'

Jocelyn frowned. 'What is it?'

'I'm not comfortable, dressed up like this.' Her mouth trembled.

Jocelyn gently reached for Doreen's hand. 'What is it? You look beautiful.'

'Sorry.' Doreen rushed behind the screen again and tugged off the dress. Without saying anything else, she put her clothes back on and hurried out of the bedroom, down the stairs.

The front door closed, and the house was quiet. Jocelyn stood in the bedroom, frowning. What was that all about? Had she said something that had upset Doreen?

She felt silly now, standing in the gown, her clothes strewn over the bed. She changed back into her shirt and trousers, then returned Kate's dresses to the closet and close the doors.

***

Later on Friday, after work, Jocelyn had walked with Rosa to the reservoir that Max and she had passed in the car that first day. They had met outside Heather Cottage and walked along the road to the bridge, and then, just past it, climbed a stile and made their way up a steep track up the hillside. The warm afternoon air was mellowing. On the opposite hillside, the Welsh ponies were specks amongst the gorse, but the whinnies of the mares to their foals carried clearly across the basin of the valley.

'So, you are a lawyer?' Rosa was leading the way through the bracken. 'That must be a challenging job.'

'Well, it demands a lot of my time and attention. I love it though. I was very fortunate to get into a family firm with an ethos that goes with the grain of my personality. I'll stay put there until they carry me out!' Jocelyn swiped at some strands of hair that were falling over her face and annoying her, and Rosa handed her a hairband from the pocket of her chunky-knit cardigan. She took it gratefully and they stopped walking while she scraped her hair back in a high ponytail.

'Wow, that style makes you look young!'

'I'll probably burn my face, now.'

'Not at this time of day. But it does suit you; you should wear it like that more often.' She carried on walking. 'So, is your husband - Jonathan - a lawyer, too?'

Jocelyn followed. 'He is. We are specialised in different legal areas, but his job is equally as demanding; we understand each other in that way. We met at university and we both knew that our careers were our priority; we've been in lockstep throughout the journey, and it's certainly strengthened our relationship. I don't think either of us would have survived in different relationships; other people wouldn't have put up with us!'

At the top of the track, they stopped to catch their breath and to watch a small blue butterfly feeding on a thistle head, then they looked back on the town, this time from a different vantage point to that of their first walk five days earlier - before continuing across the open grassland, dotted with the woolly forms of grazing sheep. In the light, the waving heathland grasses glowed rust-orange, as if alight.

They reached the lake. It stretched, dark and calm, to the bank on the other side; the sky, clouds, and pine trees on the opposite side mirrored perfectly in its surface. Apart from a 'plop' and then a few dispersing ripples - from a jumping fish or something near the middle - the whole scene was still, and the women stood for a moment in awe.

'Gosh, it does looks inviting,' Jocelyn said, her voice echoing across the silent waters so that she lowered it to finish, 'I wish I could just dip my toes in.'

Rosa shook her head. 'It's dangerous to swim here. It looks safe but it's cold and very deep!'

She gestured to the track running along the lake's edge, and they turned onto it and strolled along, breathing in the wonderful scent of peat and damp pine needles; the only sound their shoes crunching on the red shale. They walked for an hour, passing only a man with a dog and a few weary-looking sheep with large hungry lambs butting persistently at their sides. Then the track ended at the huge, sweeping arc of the dam; a man-made barrier between the lake and the steep gorge of valley beyond it.

They looked over the wall at the river churning out of the dam base far below, all white and frothy, and flowing away down the valley. The noise was loud.

'It's amazing!' Jocelyn mouthed. She picked up a pebble from the ground and tossed it over the wall, and Rosa copied her, and they watched the stones disappear against the vast backdrop of the dam. They stood quietly for a while, resting their chins on their arms and looking over the wall.

Then, as the sun began to drop behind the hills beyond the reservoir and the air grew cooler, they turned to retrace their steps back home. Stonechats escorted them through the gorse, to the top of the hill above town.

'What is it about water that makes you feel alive?' Jocelyn said as they walked along it.

'Tell me about it! Do you swim?'

'No! Well, I *can*.... It's been a long time, though.'

'Do you want to go up to the waterfall?' Rosa's eyes twinkled.

'Waterfall? Really? Where?'

'Just north of town. We can follow the river up, from the bridge.'

'Sounds tempting, I must say.'

'And... bring your bathers!'

'I don't have any bathers! Jocelyn laughed, 'But I'm still keen to see them. How about you take your bathers and I'll take the picnic.'

'Great!'

They made their way back down the hillside; Rosa, ever the perfect tour guide, pointed out plant- and animal-life as they walked. It was dusk when they reached the main road and meandered along it, over the bridge and back to Heather Cottage. They agreed to meet again on Monday evening for a hike to the waterfall, and then parted company.

That evening on the phone, Jocelyn told Jonathan about the bizarre incident with Doreen. 'There's something going on, something odd I can't put my finger on.'

'Do you need to get involved?' he queried. 'You 're only there for another week.'

'I don't want to - you know I've never been one to intrude in other people's business - but I feel like I'm already in the middle of it. Perhaps it's something to do with Kate.'

'What could Kate have to do with anything?'

'I don't know,' Jocelyn frowned. 'Doreen used to spend a lot of time with Kate, I think.'

'She probably misses having her to talk to.'

'I expect so. Doreen is very reserved.'

'And Kate was private too, or so you said. Perhaps in Kate's passing, Doreen has lost someone she felt able to trust.'

'I think you are right Jonathan. I think I must invite Doreen round. I'll do it tomorrow.'

Day 16 - Saturday

'Alan wouldn't notice me; it wouldn't matter what I was wearing.' Doreen tried to laugh off her comment, but her eyes were filling up and she stared into her teacup.

Earlier that morning, Jocelyn had gone over to the farm shop, as she had done the previous Saturday, and had been pleased to find Doreen opening the store again. She had taken the time to make conversation with the woman, strolling slowly around the produce aisles under the pretence of being unable to choose ingredients to make a soup. Did Doreen have any suggestions? Persuading her to pay a social visit to the Coach House after lunch to share her recipes had been surprisingly easy, considering the unusual departure Doreen had made the previous day.

Jocelyn put her own cup down on the table, then reached out a hand and laid it softly on Doreen's forearm. 'What makes you say that?'

'Oh, I shouldn't trouble you with it.'

'Not at all. You have been nothing but kind to me, Doreen. Is there something you want to share?'

At first, they had politely discussed recipes for carrot soup and lamb cawl and then the conversation had come back around to Kate's wardrobe. Now Doreen twisted and untwisted the fabric of her pinafore in her hands. She opened her mouth, but no words came out. Her cheeks flushed more. Jocelyn looked at her, and waited patiently until she was ready to continue.

'He doesn't notice me anymore. He doesn't look at me. I know I'm old now and not how I was.'

'Who, Alan?'

'Yes!'

'Nonsense! You're an attractive woman…'

'But I'm not a woman! Not a whole one. I don't feel like a woman and Alan doesn't see me as one.'

'I don't understand.'

Doreen moved her mouth silently, and tears sprung forth and rolled down her cheeks. She slumped down on the bed; her head hung low. 'I had cancer,' she said. 'It was five years ago. They took away parts of me and now I'm left feeling like... *this*.'

She looked down at the dress and tugged at a handful of fabric. 'No fancy clothes nor jewels can bring back my womb!'

***

The grandfather clock ticked loud and slow.

'Here, fresh tea.' Jocelyn handed a cup to Doreen and sat back down beside her.

Doreen took a sip and gazed out of the window. 'I'm sorry, I shouldn't have shouted at you.'

'You are very welcome to shout at anyone you like.'

Doreen sighed and placed the cup down. 'I haven't shouted at all, until just then.' She rubbed her temple with one hand. 'There's been times I've wanted to scream and scream. I didn't. Nobody notices me.'

Doreen glanced up. Jocelyn didn't speak but kept her hand on the woman's arm. She had just become Doreen's confidant, and she felt privileged.

She nodded, encouraging Doreen to continue.

'Somehow, it feels easier to let it all out to you,' Doreen breathed. 'Perhaps it's because you're a stranger - well, you know what I mean.'

Doreen started talking. She told Jocelyn about the first symptoms - knowing in her heart that something was wrong but pushing it aside, hoping she was mistaken. The day of the diagnosis; watching the doctor's lips moving and knowing that dreadful words were coming out but nodding and wondering where the beach was in the picture hanging on the wall behind him. The fear and confusion that accompanied the formal letters that followed. The stay in the city hospital, the bustle of white coats and blue uniforms and the smell of illness and disinfectant. Lying in line with the other frail patients, wanting to be anywhere on earth but here. Then, the slow convalescence - and a fresh battle; that with anxiety, just when she thought things would start getting better.

And finally, the hopelessness; being unable to see a way forwards in putting back the pieces of her life, when life had been irreversibly changed.

All afternoon, they talked - and Doreen cried, and laughed, and cried again. Jocelyn listened to it all patiently and without interruption. She only paused the conversation to get up and make more tea and cut more cake for the two of them.

Giving her time to Doreen was the most unselfish thing she had done in years.

Eventually Doreen fell quiet, purged of all her angst, and exhausted. She lifted her red-rimmed eyes to Jocelyn.

'And there you have it; my story. I know they say beauty isn't skin deep, but what about when you are rotten *inside*, too?'

'Doreen, I can't pretend to understand what you have been through.' She took hold of her hands and squeezed them. 'But I do know this. In front of me, I see a woman whose warm eyes reflect a genuine soul. A woman who doesn't gossip - and for me, there is no more desirable quality than one who does not judge nor tongue-wag. A woman whose gestures to others are not out of duty, but of kindness; who puts herself in the shoes of another and thinks, now, what can I do to make this person's life a little easier? A woman who is gentle and patient. Integrity, compassion, a soul free of prejudice... there *is* no greater beauty. And your courage, Doreen. What you have had to battle, alone - you are made of steel! Radiant is the person who possesses those qualities - and *you* do, in abundance! I think beauty does not come from physical appearance but from the willingness to love and be loved.'

Doreen listened to Jocelyn, and a tear trickled down her cheek. She blew her nose. 'Oh my.'

Jocelyn stood up and moved around the table. 'A hug does wonders,' she lifted her arms to embrace her. They hugged and then both started to laugh; a laugh between two friends when souls have been bared and a new bond of trust forged.

'So, now… *will* you join me, madam, in a little dressing up?' Jocelyn said.

'Well, I think you might have persuaded me.'

'Good. Follow me.' They tidied up the table and then made their way back upstairs to Kate's bedroom. 'Now, you fix your dress and face in the mirror, and I shall dress here.' Jocelyn selected another dress from the rail. 'Meanwhile, I shall try this.'

Doreen tidied herself while Jocelyn exchanged her gown for a colourful ankle-length kaftan in Moroccan colours. For a while, the only noise was of rustling fabric, and then the two women convened at the floor-length mirror.

'That dress does look good on you Doreen - but I think the look would be more complete with your hair down.'

'Down? Loose?' Doreen said, 'Not at my age! I never wear it down.'

'Nonsense! May I style it for you?' Jocelyn steered Doreen to the dressing table and sat her down in front of the mirror. She gently eased out the rubber band holding up Doreen's bun and shook out her hair with her fingers. It was thick and glossy, unspoilt by styling products, and her natural silver streaks gave her a stunning maturity.

'Beautiful. No, don't look away. I said *beautiful*.'

Doreen looked in the mirror. A shy smile spread across her face and she flushed.

'Doreen, you must take this dress home with you. Kate would want you to have it.'

'It is beautiful,' Doreen agreed, 'But I'd never wear it!'

'That doesn't matter! Just put it on when you need uplifting. I have dressing up evenings by myself sometimes - I even dance around the bedroom alone! Now, let's find you some matching shoes.'

The two women spent a decadent afternoon trying on gowns and shoes and experimenting with jewellery and hairstyles. With each outfit change, Doreen would steal behind the changing screen, and only come out when she was fully clothed. Eventually, they were exhausted with the effort of changing outfits, and Jocelyn's stomach was rumbling. Laughing, they began to put everything back onto hangers and into cover bags, to return them to the wardrobes.

Jocelyn turned to Doreen and took her hands. 'Now, there is one more thing we must do today.'

'Oh?'

'Yes, and it is imperative. Aunt Kate and I used to do this every day when I stayed here.'

'Oh?' Doreen repeated, puzzled.

Jocelyn grinned and her eyes flashed. 'For this, we must remove these restrictive gowns.'

'What?'

'Come on. Off with it!' She undid the zip of her own gown and began wriggling out of it, indicating for Doreen to do the same. 'Off with it!'

'What? No, no, Jocelyn; I can't…'

'Doreen, my friend. You can. Off!'

'Oh dear.' Doreen stood frozen.

Dressed in her underwear, Jocelyn climbed onto Kate's big bed. 'Now. We must bounce.' She started to jump on the bed.

Doreen watched her with wide eyes. Jocelyn was windmilling her arms, laughing. 'Come on!'

'What, in just my underwear?'

'Well, you can't bounce in a ballgown.'

Doreen looked down at her dress.

'It is abs…ol…utely and un…doubt…edly the one… thing that will… lift our spirits. Totally exhilarating!' Jocelyn said between jumps. 'You cannot but smile after ten minutes of bouncing. Wee hee!'

'But…' Doreen hadn't moved.

Jocelyn stopped jumping and caught her breath. 'Doreen,' she panted, 'Look at this bed! It's huge, it's soft, it's calling out to be jumped upon. And if Kate could do it, Doreen Hughes, then so can you!'

Doreen knew she wouldn't win. 'Oh well…' She unzipped her dress, took it off with a sigh and lay it over the stool.

'Right, my beautiful friend. Up!'

The old bedsprings creaked as Doreen joined Jocelyn on the bed. She started to laugh. 'I don't think I've ever met anyone like you, Jocelyn Anderson. Getting me into trouble like this!'

Jocelyn grabbed her hands. 'And I've never met anyone like you, Doreen Hughes! Yahoo, let's bounce!'

They jumped and jumped on Kate's old four poster bed, dislodging the pillows, and ruffling the covers; laughing until they could barely breathe and oblivious to the racket they were making.

***

In the garden around the side of the Coach House, Alan began tidying away his gardening equipment. He'd spent the afternoon weeding the borders and planting seedlings. Carrying seed trays, a trowel and a hand fork, he wandered slowly around the front of the house, hoping that Jocelyn would be there at the table to offer him a cup of tea before he had to go home.

He stopped and frowned. Raucous laughter floated down from the bedroom window above him. Puzzled, he took a few steps backwards onto the lawn, for a better view, and looked up.

The sight that met him made him drop his tools all over the floor. 'What the…?'

The laughter continued.

'Jocelyn? And… *Doreen*?!

Unaware of their spectator, the underwear-clad women whooped and bounced on the bed. Alan stood frozen, his mouth hanging open; knowing that he shouldn't be gawping, but unable to peel his eyes away. 'Well, I'll be…' He scratched his head and looked around him. The street was empty. He looked back up at the window, his cheeks reddening.

'I can see I'm going to have to up my game around here.' He bent down and hastily gathered up the tools. Then he stood up and scurried towards the shed, stealing one last glance at the laughing women.

***

'Hello Jonathan, darling.'

'Jocelyn, sweetheart, how are you?'

'I'm fine. Well, there is a lot happening up here, but I won't go into it now. How is work, and the flat? Is everything well?'

'Yes, everything here is the same as usual. But I'm more concerned about you! How are you coping with the house and the packing?'

'Oh, I don't really want to think about that right now. Sorry darling, but as I said, there a lot going on and I'd prefer to deal with things as they arise.'

'What sort of things? Are you sure you don't want me to come over there? At a push, I could rearrange my schedule here and come mid-week.'

'Goodness, no. I only have one week left. I'll be home on Saturday evening.' She yawned.

'You sound tired, sweetheart. Would you like me to call you tomorrow morning instead? We could have one of our lazy Sunday mornings over the telephone…'

'No, sorry darling, I'm going hiking on the common with a friend in the morning.'

'You're doing what?'

'Yes, I know - not my usual thing. But as I said, there's a lot going on that I can't wait to tell you about in person. But I'm mindful of the cost of these long-distance calls…'

'Don't worry about the cost Jocelyn, we can afford it.'

'Yes, but I prefer chatting in person.'

'But I miss you sweetheart. It's nice to hear your voice.

'And you. I'm dreadfully tired though. I'm just about to go upstairs'

'Oh, all right. Well, as long as you are managing by yourself.'

'I am.'

'I'll let you go to bed, then.'

'Thank you, Jonathan. I miss you darling.'

'I miss you very much!'

'Goodnight.'

Day 17 - Sunday

On Sunday lunchtime, Jocelyn had prepared another pot of soup. This time, she made lamb cawl, with leek and parsnips. Doreen had written the recipe on a piece of paper before she left the day before.

She washed and chopped the vegetables swiftly and got the pot simmering on the stove in no time. When it was ready, she filled a bowl with the broth and then cut a slab of Caerphilly cheese and a pot of tea. Smiling and hungry, she took the tray out to the garden table.

Alan was in a corner of the garden, tying up young green vines to a row of bamboo canes. She placed the tray down, pulled out a chair and sat down. 'Hello Alan. I didn't hear you arrive. Would you like some tea?'

Alan stood up. 'Ah yes, all right. Thank you.' He tucked the roll of garden string in his trouser pocket, dusted off his hands and walked over to the table.

Jocelyn poured tea and nodded at him to take a seat. A hoverfly danced above the lavender and Jocelyn watched it. She smiled and looked over to see if Alan was also watching, but he was staring across the valley, sipping his drink in silence. He lowered his head and frowned.

'How are you today, Alan? You seem a little… subdued.'

He looked up and laughed, then his cheeks flushed and he focused on the teacup again.

'Has something happened?' she asked.

'No, no.'

Jocelyn watched him for a minute, waiting for an answer. He didn't want to talk, and she didn't want to press him to. She stretched back in her chair, enjoying the sun's warmth. 'I admire your passion for gardening,' she said, 'You don't seem to tire of it.'

'Well, you know I would never speak for anyone else, but the way I see it is - what use is this life, if there is no time to follow your passion?'

'Mm, I suppose,' she said. 'My job, I'm passionate about that. That takes all of my time.'

'I'm sure it does. You help people; it sounds very important.'

'It is satisfying.' She leaned her head back and looked up at the blue sky. 'It's more than a passion though. It's my identity.'

'I think of the garden more as a friend,' said Alan. 'It's *there* for me. I mean, what if the job isn't there anymore? If it's your identity, who are you then?'

Jocelyn raised her eyebrows. 'I'll always have my job. Why wouldn't I?' She placed her cup down.

He shrugged.

'Although I certainly wouldn't refer to it as my companion,' she finished.

Alan looked down at his hands. 'There's many an hour I've spent in the garden. I have laughed with her, and I have cried with her.'

'Oh?'

He nodded. 'I assume Doreen told you of her illness?' he asked, staring at his hands. 'You two seem to have grown close.'

Jocelyn paused. She looked at Alan, but he continued to stare down.

'Yes,' she said gently, 'She told me that she had had cancer and needed a hysterectomy.'

Alan's shoulders heaved with a sigh, and he looked across the valley. 'When Doreen was first diagnosed, I didn't know what I would do. I can't imagine life without her. I went to the garden every day and I sat on the ground and I focused. Focused on pulling the weeds, hoeing the soil, tending the seedlings...'

Jocelyn gently nodded and waited for him to continue.

'I could lose myself for hours in the garden. It gave my mind a rest from going over and over the *What Ifs*. I've never dug so hard as those months when she was having her treatment. I dug so hard I couldn't move my shoulders in the mornings; but it helped, just pounding at the soil, ripping up the clods and smelling the earth as I turned it.' He looked at Jocelyn and his eyes were full. 'It was something I could do, something I was good at, where I was failing everywhere else.' He lowered his forehead into his hands.

'Failing?'

'Yes, failing. Well and truly, utterly, miserably failing.'

'How were you failing, Alan?'

'I didn't know how to talk to Doreen. I was feeling so sorry for myself, I didn't know how to talk to her.'

'I see.' Jocelyn paused. 'And… what would you have liked to say to her?'

'I wanted to say, *Doreen, you cannot leave me! It's been forty years and you are the only woman I have ever loved! There is nothing in this world if you are not in it with me!* But I said nothing. I just went to the garden and dug.' His shoulders heaved.

Jocelyn let the man sob, big silent heaves. She put her hand on his shoulder and left it there, thinking carefully how to help him. When he eventually stopped, and sighed, she spoke quietly. 'You could say it to her now.'

'I can't. It's too late! I didn't want it to be happening, so I pretended it wasn't. I left her alone at the one time in forty years that she needed me the most. And now, things have changed between us.' He looked up. 'Oh don't get me wrong, we wake up, we go to bed, we follow our routine. But that closeness, that special bond where two people think and speak as one; it's gone and it'll never return. It's all my fault.'

'Oh, Alan.' Jocelyn let her hand stay on Alan's shoulder as the man hung his head and battled his grief. They sat for a few minutes.

Eventually, Alan spoke. 'I'm sorry to be pouring all of this out onto you. It seems easier somehow, because you are a, well, a stranger - if you know what I mean.'

'I know exactly what you mean, and I am glad you poured this out onto me.'

He wiped his eyes, then picked up his cap and put it on. 'I'll carry on now.'

'Wait, Alan. There is something you must do.'

'What's that?'

'You must go home immediately to Doreen.'

Alan waited for her to explain.

'You must sit down with her and you must talk to her. Tell her everything you have just told me.'

'But...'

'No, you must. And then, you must say *Now, Doreen, it is your turn,* and you must insist that she talks to you.'

Alan's voice was cracking. 'I can't...'

'Alan, you must. Go now. There is not a minute in this short and wonderful life for Doreen and you to lose.' She stood up and escorted him towards the path. 'Go!'

Alan looked at her and she thought for a minute that he might flatly refuse her instruction, but then he nodded, straightened his hair and scuttled off down the garden path.

Jocelyn watched him until she was sure he had headed to his cottage. Then she returned to the table. She collected up the teacups, thinking about this gentle couple and the pain they were enduring because they were too reserved to talk openly to each other.

She went into the house and deposited the tray in the kitchen. Then, in the privacy of the sitting room with the lace curtains closed, she plonked down in the armchair and sat in silence. She wished Jonathan was there. Jonathan always knew how to take care of things.

She tried calling him, but there was no answer from the London apartment. She left a message on the answerphone, putting on a breezy voice so as not to alarm him, and telling him that all was fine because she decided at the last minute that she'd feel worse if she worried him with dramas from a town two hundred miles away. By the time Jonathan called back, she was in the shower and missed the call.

Day 18 - Monday

'Another cup?'

'Go on then, since it's your final week here.' Max pushed his mug across the table and Jocelyn poured him a fresh brew. It was dawn, and the sun was just starting to throw its rays across the valley. They sat back and watched the cows, who had ventured up to the fence across the road and were looking back at them, slowly chewing their cud as they observed the tea-drinkers, and occasionally tousling each other with big soft muzzles. They were slick and muscular, and their coats shone brilliant rust-brown in the sunlight.

'Old Dai Jones' prize Limousin herd,' Max nodded.

Max had a smile on his face because of an earlier incident involving a slow worm, which had been under a piece of slate that he had moved to prop open Kate's garden gate. Jocelyn had seen it and thought it was a snake, and she had had to apologise profusely for swearing in front of the man.

He hadn't been offended. It had amused him to see her lose her cool and run to a perceived safe spot -

stood on top of the garden bench. He could see that she was still embarrassed, so he made polite conversation to change the subject. 'The lavender is putting on a good show this year.'

'It is. And these flowers that the bees love so much. What is this?' She pointed to a silver bush.

'Rosemary. And those in the border over there are chives.'

'Alan suggested I grow herbs in a window box.'

'Oh yes.' Max lifted his mug to his lips and sipped his tea.

Jocelyn's gaze moved across the street, where a familiar figure was emerging from his cottage. 'Bob does a lot of gardening too.'

'Yes.'

'Do you?'

'Oh, no.' Max said. He looked away.

'I suspect Bob spends time in his front garden because he likes talking to passers-by,' she whispered with a smile.

'He used to come over for morning tea,' Max said.

'What, over here? To sit with Kate?'

Max nodded.

'No one mentioned that,' Jocelyn frowned. She looked down at the tea set spread over the table. 'Do you think he'd like to come over now?'

'I'm sure he would if you asked him.'

'Well, he probably doesn't want to. He doesn't know me.'

'You could still ask him and let *him* decide whether or not to come.'

Jocelyn looked at Max and he winked back at her.

'It really is a lesson a day from you, isn't it?' she said.

Max laughed.

***

'Hello Bob.'

Bob touched his cap at the smart young woman from London, now addressing him over his garden wall.

'I was wondering if you'd like to join Max and me for a cup of tea?'

She spoke in an accent that surely meant she had a very important job in the city, but she held his gaze with blue eyes that were genuine, and she reminded him of Kate. 'I'll just wash my hands,' he said. He disappeared under the low door of his cottage.

Jocelyn waited. She looked back across the street at the elevated garden of the Coach House. Bob had watched her host people at the table and she had never thought to invite him over. She kicked herself. Six years of law training and seventeen years in practice, and yet she was still on the steep part of the learning curve on the social skills front.

Bob emerged from his house and they crossed the street together. Max was still seated at the table and soon the three of them were sitting in the morning sunshine, drinking, and sharing observations on the garden. Jocelyn smiled and listened to the two men. The idle conversation they were sharing was a pleasant complement to the buzzing of insects and chirruping of birds. Jocelyn breathed slowly and let her mind wander.

Then Alan arrived and he too joined the table. His face was tranquil, and Jocelyn didn't try to read him any more than that. At seven thirty, Rosa wandered past with Will and a girl of around fourteen - Jocelyn assumed it to be her daughter, Emily - and at first they politely declined the offer of tea, but after a second invitation Rosa and Will agreed to join the party. Emily continued on her way. Now there were six around the table and Jocelyn had to return to the house for a fresh pot and more cups. She remembered the shelf of mugs in the kitchen; perfectly suited to a table full of friends.

So, this is how you spent your mornings, Kate!

When Doreen arrived, Max fetched an extra chair from the side of the house. Jocelyn looked around the table of faces. This was a very different way to spend a Monday morning - and it was nice.

At nine, the party dispersed, and Jocelyn went indoors to start working. Alan remained in the garden and later that morning, when Jocelyn looked out of the window, she saw that Doreen was helping him plant something in the vegetable patch.

***

At lunchtime she wandered outside and found the couple enjoying sandwiches that they had brought with them, and in the afternoon, she quizzed them over different plants and shrubs. They had all the time in the world to show her the spring onions just starting to poke through the soil, the row of sweet peas that would give a blaze of colour against the brick wall in a few weeks' time. They showed her how to take cuttings of rosemary so she could propagate more plants of her own - cutting off the newest part of the stem just below the leaf node, dipping the ends in a little of the white rooting powder from Kate's shed and potting them in compost, in little terracotta pots.

Later that afternoon, she sat at the window table with Kate's books open alongside her client files. In between reading she watched, through the binoculars, a tiny bird - not a wren, but a goldcrest, she learned - hopping among the shrubbery and the unexpected sight of a green woodpecker, a flash of bright plumage, bolting through the trees.

Rosa arrived at five thirty, carrying a small rucksack with a bottle of juice tucked into a mesh side pocket, and a rolled-up towel strapped on the top. The door of the Coach House was already open, to let in the afternoon breeze.

'I'm a little late, sorry,' she called as she kicked off her shoes, 'I was leaving a paella for Will and Emily. Are you ready?'

Jocelyn was tidying her paperwork. She came out into the hallway, greeted Rosa, and then grabbed her trainers. 'I'm ready. I've got sandwiches for us both and an apple each; is that enough?' She picked up her own bag and slipped it onto her shoulders.

'I'm sure it is. We don't want to carry too much.'

Jocelyn closed the door behind her, and the two women set off in the direction of the river. The sun was still high and they walked in the shade of the trees that lined the road, until they reached the bridge. They leaned over the thick stone walls to peer below and, for a few moments, delighted in the noise of the white water rushing over the rocks and the cool misty spray rising from it. Then Rosa pointed over the wall to a flat, earthy path that was running alongside the river down below them. 'We're going to follow that, up to the waterfalls.'

Jocelyn nodded. She followed Rosa over a stone stile and down some rough steps that twisted down the steep grassy bank at side of the bridge, onto the track. The valley was mossy and cool, shaded by steep sides and tall trees. A flash of blue heading downstream made Jocelyn start, and she gasped, and then slowly smiled; she had seen her first ever kingfisher.

The path was wide enough to walk side-by-side and they strolled together. 'So you cook Spanish cuisine?' Jocelyn asked.

'I do. Emily is a great cook and she's keen to learn about her heritage. Do you like to eat Spanish food?'

'I don't know. We tend to eat Italian in London. I'm sure I would like it.' She frowned, 'Although I can't think of any Spanish restaurants near us.'

'You could cook some simple tapas yourself easily enough.'

'Oh no, don't you start, please! I've already got Doreen teaching me everything she knows about stews,' Jocelyn laughed.

'Then you must come over to my place,' Rosa said, 'And I will cook for you, or rather, we will cook together.'

They headed upstream of the tumbling river. The riverbed was lined with huge slabs of grey rock, jagged in parts where it jutted up out of the water and covered in green algae, and in other parts worn pale grey and smooth by the frothy flow. Farther along, the track passed right beside the town, which sat above them on the northern bank. As usual, Rosa pointed out various bird and plant life, and Jocelyn listened and absorbed it all with genuine interest. They left the town behind them and continued walking. After about an hour, they reached a flat area with a wooden picnic bench, and a wide wooden gate, beyond which a single-track lane stretched back in the direction of town.

They passed through the picnic area, and on the other side of it the path narrowed to a single track. Rosa checked on her companion. 'It gets a little harder now. Are you still okay to go on?'

Jocelyn was gazing above them, at the lichen-covered tree boughs that arched to form a magical canopy over the narrowing valley. There was no sound apart from rushing water and a lone bird call somewhere upstream. She nodded silently and they walked onwards.

The track hugged the very edge of the river now, and the going was indeed tough; they scrambled over huge boulders and hopped cautiously over muddy pools. Ferns sprouted all around, and the air smelled of leaves and damp soil. Still, Jocelyn kept up the pace, exhilarated by the fresh air and the closeness of cool, cascading water. They hiked steeply upwards, in parts having to use hands and knees to tackle rocky shelves, until they reached a plateau where the trees thinned and the sun's rays shone on their shoulders once again.

Jocelyn scrambled up onto the ledge, moved forwards to safety and stood up. Before them lay a huge, round pool of water, deep and clear. Above the pool at the far end, a waterfall streamed down a sheer, fern-dotted rockface. The shower landing on the surface made it dance and sparkle in the evening sunlight.

The women stood in silent awe of the scene; Jocelyn, who had never in her life stood at the foot of a waterfall and experienced her senses being awakened by the sound and the spray, and Rosa, who made the hike to the waterfall regularly and yet never tired of its magnificence. Then Rosa turned and gestured behind Jocelyn, and Jocelyn followed her gaze around behind her, down the valley where they had come from. She could see the picnic spot far below them; the rest of the valley as far as the eye could see was filled with trees, with the occasional glimpse through the canopy of the river flashing in the sunlight.

They turned back to the pool and Rosa spoke first. 'A dip?' She peeled off her t-shirt and shorts, revealing a figure tanned and toned from hours spent hiking the moors. Jocelyn didn't know how to reply; she watched as the woman stepped carefully over the slippery rocks and eased herself slowly into the chilly spring water with a gleeful gasp.

'I told you, I don't have a swimsuit!' Jocelyn laughed, partly in disbelief that Rosa really was going to swim in the pool.

Rosa took a breath and launched herself fully into the pool with a little squeal, and swimming breaststroke to the middle. Then she trod water and turned back to face Jocelyn laughing on the bank, 'Then come in your birthday suit!'

'I don't think so!'

'Come on! There's no one around. It's eight o'clock; no one ever comes up here at this time.'

Jocelyn looked around her.

'Come on! I can see you want to.'

'I really can't.'

'It's not deep. Look, I can touch the bottom - as long as we stay away from the base of the fall.'

It was true. Although the pool looked deep, Rosa was able to stand up in almost all of it - except where the water showered down the rock face, where its force had hollowed out a deeper basin on the pool floor. She swam back to the side and climbed carefully out over the stones.

'Are you tempted?'

'Not naked, I'm not. I'm sorry.'

'I will too if it makes you feel better.' Rosa slipped out of her bathing suit and quickly scrambled back into the water, laughing, "I don't usually do this either!'

'Oh my gosh, are you actually skinny-dipping?'

'Is that an English expression?'

'Yes! I can't believe you're doing it!'

'Come in! It's amazing, I promise. You can leave your underwear on.'

'I don't have a towel.'

'You can borrow mine. Any other excuses?'

Jocelyn looked around again. It was true, she was out of excuses and… Was she really going to do this?

She slipped off her shoes and socks, unbuttoned her trousers and laid everything on a dry rock, groaning to herself and yet feeling a giggle rise in her throat. She took off her shirt with a grimace.

'Oh my gosh, oh my gosh…'

'Come on! Woo hoo!'

Folding her arms over her chest in a feeble attempt at modesty, Jocelyn picked her way over the stones to the pool's edge and dipped her toes into the water. It was delightfully refreshing on feet freed from the heat and confinement of trainers after an hour-and-a-half's hike.

'But it's rather cold! How will I get in?'

'You just have to go for it.' Rosa was swimming around in circles.

Jocelyn hesitated.

'Jocelyn, I expected a girl like you would do this easily.'

Jocelyn looked at Rosa indignantly and pushed her foot a little deeper along the gravelly bottom. Rosa winked back. 'Kate always went in.'

Jocelyn stopped in surprise. 'Kate swam here?'

'Naked!' Rosa laughed.

Jocelyn nodded - yes, Kate *would* have gone in. Kate was never afraid to take the plunge; it was what set her apart from everyone else. 'Right.' She waded determinedly into the pool, sucking her breath at the sudden chill on her skin, but determined not to back out now. Deeper, to her waist and then a little further. 'I think this is far enough!' She could barely speak through the gasps, and it made both women giggle.

'You've got to get your shoulders under, now.'

'Ok. Right. One, two, three…' Jocelyn jumped up and then lifted her knees up on the way down, reasoning that so long as she willed herself to keep her feet up, gravity would do the rest in getting her body submerged.

She went under the water to the neck, then planted her feet on the floor and shot up again with a shriek. Rosa laughed.

'Again! Do it three times, and then you will be accustomed to the cold.'

She ducked under twice more, and then felt her breathing relax a little. The smile on her face seemed to stretch to both ears.

'Oh! It's wooonderful.' She sank under, closed her eyes against the low sun and felt the water lapping around her neck. She could hear Rosa still swimming in circles around the pool.

The women managed to stay in the pool for ten minutes, splashing and chatting, and then the chill became too much. Rosa clambered out first, breathless and happy. Jocelyn politely avoiding looking at her dripping form - although Rosa didn't seem embarrassed. She stood up, facing down the valley and stretching and smiling as the sun warmed her bare skin - and then she dropped her arms and gasped.

'There's a vehicle in the lane!'

'What?' Jocelyn froze.

Rosa giggled and scurried back to the pool.

'A car! At the picnic spot.'

'Oh my. Oh gosh.' Jocelyn didn't move; she didn't know what to do. Rosa had plunged back under the water.

'Is anyone coming?'

'I don't know.'

'Well, let's get dressed!' Jocelyn scrambled out of the water as fast as she could safely do so and grabbed Rosa's towel from her rucksack. Rosa followed her and was standing naked and dripping behind her, trying to stifle laughter.

'Oh no, you need the towel more than I do!' Jocelyn thrust the towel at her so that she could cover herself, and then she started to laugh too, so that they were both almost choking as they hurriedly dried themselves in turn and dressed.

Jocelyn stood up so that she could see over the ledge down the track. 'I think someone's coming! I can hear rustling!'

'Really?' Rosa was trying to wrestle herself into underpants, and in her haste, she put her legs into the wrong holes so that when she pulled them up above her knees, they became twisted and stuck. She said something in Spanish as she fumbled, giggling, and then took them off to start over. Jocelyn had been trying not to look, but then she had seen the kerfuffle and was doubled over with laughter.

'Oh no, I am so close to wetting myself!' She whispered, crossing her legs and jiggling.

Finally, Rosa got her clothes on, and Jocelyn was able to wrap the towel around her own damp body. No one had appeared over the ledge, and she dressed while Rosa kept watch. 'I think you were mistaken; no one is coming up here. There are people sitting at the bench; its looks like a couple and a dog.'

Jocelyn turned to her and they locked eyes, and then began giggling again like two children. Jocelyn shook her head in disbelief and wiped tears from her eyes.

Afterwards, they sat on a boulder near the edge of the plateau gazed down the valley below them, eating the sandwiches that Jocelyn had brought and drinking elderflower cordial, home-made by Rosa. Jocelyn's skin was tingling, and she felt a warmth spreading through her body that was invigorating. She mentioned it to Rosa

'There's nothing like a dip in river water.' Rosa agreed. 'I don't know why more people don't do it.'

'I didn't know you were allowed to swim in rivers. I never imagined it would feel so good.'

'Well then, here's to pushing boundaries,' Rosa smiled, and she offered her glass for Jocelyn to meet with her own.

'Cheers to that.'

They finished the picnic as the sun was beginning to dip behind the hills. 'We'd better head home,' Rosa said, 'There's only an hour of daylight left. We can get onto the road by the picnic spot - that'll take us through town rather than walking back by the river. We will be faster walking home because it's downhill.'

They gathered up their things, wrestled rucksacks back onto shoulders and then set off the way they had come, treading carefully in the dusk light around the rocks and logs and other obstacles along the track. They reached the lane in half an hour and the couple and their dog had gone. They followed the lane until it intercepted the north end of the town's main street and followed it right through the heart of town. Llanfairyn's inhabitants had clearly settled for the night; the only sound as they trudged, weary but happy down the centre of the empty road, was of gentle laughter floating through an open window of the town's one pub, The Black Sheep.

At the corner of the street by the Coach House, they had parted company after agreeing to a paella supper at Heather Cottage on Wednesday evening. It was eleven o'clock by the time Jocelyn had showered, hung her wet underwear to dry and snuggled into her soft warm bed.

Day 19 - Tuesday

Jocelyn spent Tuesday morning working happily by the sitting room window, which she had opened to release a trapped butterfly - a Gatekeeper, according to Kate's guide - and then left open to enjoy the singing of a male blackbird. In the afternoon, she sat in the armchair with a notepad and pen, her lips pressed together. Only four days of her stay in Llanfairyn remained. Llan-via-rin; she thought the word over in her mind. On Saturday she would need to instruct the solicitor on dispersing Kate's estate.

She thought about Kate's possessions and her own minimalist apartment in London. No-one wanted other people's junk. She would instruct them to arrange a house clearance firm to auction off the belongings and then the money could go to a charity.

She leaned over and picked up a small pile of books beside the armchair, running her fingers over them. Then she looked along the shelf at the row of little ornaments in carved wood and china. Trinkets from Kate's travels. She pictured Kate sitting here, talking to

Will. Did she light the open fire in the winter, and sit deep in conversation with the boy? She pictured them eating cake from the rose-painted plates as snowflakes fell outside the window and over the common. She pictured Kate sitting in the window, perhaps eating cawl, watching her garden creatures with the binoculars.

Jocelyn wandered upstairs to the bedroom, ran her hands along the row of necklaces on the dresser. Then across to the wardrobes, to scan the rows of gowns and racks of shoes. She plonked herself down on the bed and stroked the crocheted blanket that covered it.

What would Kate want her to do with all this? Why had Kate left it in her hands in the first place? She had hoped that her stay would provide answers. But with only four days remaining, she felt no closer to any.

Not liking the sadness stirring in her, she left the room, closed the door and went downstairs.

Later that evening, Will came round and they ate cawl together in front of the crackling open fire, and then spent the rest of the evening sharing stories. Will told of his escapades up on the common and in the pine forests by the reservoir. When he'd been at school, he'd had a group of friends who shared his adventures but as they grew older, the boys had either gone away to study or had started families of their own. Will wasn't bothered though; he loved working with Max because he met lots of people. Everyone in the town knew him and made time to have cake with him, and in the evenings, he loved playing board games with his mam and Emily.

Jocelyn talked of her home and Jonathan and the places they used to visit before work became too busy. She told Will of their picnics in Hyde Park and her visits to the city's museums. Then they had taken out books from the bookshelf and read together, in silence, for one hour, only pausing to place a few more pieces of coal onto the glowing embers in the grate.

As Will was leaving, he had asked Jocelyn if they could cycle again soon, and they fixed a date for Thursday evening. She had gone outside afterwards, to try her hand at a spot of gardening - taking cuttings of marjoram and sage and pulling out a few dandelion shoots from among Alan's sweet peas, as the darkness fell and the honeysuckle came to life with moths.

Day 20 - Wednesday

On Wednesday evening, Alan, Max and Bob were finishing the last of their tea when Jocelyn emerged from the house. She spoke to the three men as she skipped past the table. 'Don't rush your tea. I can tidy up the tray when I get back.'

The men nodded and stayed sitting at the table. Alan had been mowing the lawn and Max and Will had painted all the downstairs window frames of the old house, so that the place looked cheerfully inhabited and loved. The maintenance on Kate's property was continuing as usual until its fate was decided.

Jocelyn crossed the road and made her way to Heather Cottage, the end one in the row of cottages opposite. She smiled as she walked in the evening air; Rosa was going to teach her how to cook paella, it was going to be fun.

Heather Cottage was miniscule compared to the Coach House. She bent to open the garden gate and walked up the gravel path. On each side of the path, large flowerpots were spilling with brilliant red and orange begonias. It took only three strides to reach the front door, which was also miniaturised. Anyone over five feet five would have to bend their head to step inside.

Rosa answered the door and they kissed on each cheek. 'Come in! Welcome to tiny Heather Cottage!'

Rosa's home was beautiful, but in stark contrast to the scale and grandeur of Coach House. The ceilings were low enough to touch if you reached up. The front door led directly into the lounge, which Rosa had decorated in bold modern colours - rusty reds, warm orange, bright greens. There was a little two-seater couch with colourful plump cushions on, and a brown leather bean bag in the corner by the wood burner. A set of narrow wooden stairs led upstairs from the lounge, and rock music floated gently down from behind a closed bedroom door.

Jocelyn looked around the room in delight. The walls were hung with contemporary paintings, in the same brilliant colours. A side table by the sofa held a lamp whose base was a marble carving of two entwined figures.

Rosa closed the door behind them. 'Now, tea, coffee? Or something a little more Spanish?' she grinned.

She led the way through a little doorway off the lounge with a bead curtain hung over it, and through it Jocelyn could see a tiny kitchen and then a view of the fields at the rear of the house. From the kitchen, the sound of music floated - a male voice singing in Spanish she assumed. She followed Rosa into the kitchen.

'I love to listen to music while I cook,' Rosa said. She hummed along to the gentle sound of guitar. The kitchen counter was laden with ingredients - big red tomatoes, onions, peppers, peas still in their pods, a chunk of cured meat of some sort - and two chopping boards and knives. 'Now, you put this pinny on, and take this chopping board.'

The women set to work, chatting as they shelled peas and chopped vegetables and chorizo. Rosa showed Jocelyn how to set hot vegetable stock and saffron strands to infuse, how to fry the vegetables in olive oil and garlic and stir in paprika, how to combine the ingredients together in a large round pan, stirring with a big flat wooden spoon. Soon, the kitchen was filled with the aroma of vegetables, olive oil and spices, and the sound of rice simmering gently. The pan steamed with pleasant scents and its colours were appropriately vibrant for a meal cooked by Rosa.

They ate at a round table on a paved patio at the back of the cottage, from bright, hand-painted crockery, overlooking the valley as the sun dropped lower. First though, they had begun the meal with a toast to Kate. Rosa had fetched a bottle of Pernod - Kate's favourite aperitif, she explained - on a tray along with a jug of iced water and two small heavy-bottomed glasses, and they raised their drinks in honour of the lady who had brought them together. Then they feasted on paella and drank glasses of light Navarra rosé, laughing and conversing in the comfortable armchairs as the evening sun turned everything around them pink.

Jocelyn turned to speak. 'I have to say, it has been lovely to be able to walk with you. I have really appreciated the company. All this business with Kate's house, it's knocked me off balance. I'm usually on top of things.'

'Well, thank you. Here's to friendship.' Rosa raised her glass to Jocelyn's. 'And for me, it's been nice to have some female company.' She paused and gazed across the valley. 'It's been two years since Joe died.'

Jocelyn followed Rosa's gaze. A heron rose from the river in the distance, beating its huge wings gracefully. The two women watched it disappear over the trees.

'I was sorry to learn about Joe,' said Jocelyn.

'Oh, well, thank you. Most of the time I'm all right, and I've got Will to keep me busy!' Jocelyn looked at her and she smiled back. 'It's usually just Will and me. Emily, love her, nowadays she wants to be locked away in her bedroom or out with friends.'

'Are you managing without Joe?

'Yes,' Rosa put down her wine glass, 'We miss him terribly, but it wasn't totally unexpected. He'd had a few health problems in recent years.'

Jocelyn wasn't sure how much Rosa wanted to share, so she asked her questions carefully. 'Did you meet in London?'

'Yes, we did.'

'Were you both studying?'

'Not exactly. I was a nursing student and Joe… he was a professor in my department.'

'Ah.'

'We just connected,' Rosa explained. 'We felt the same way about the things that were important to us. We knew what the other was thinking. I was twenty and he was forty-five but to us, there was no age difference.' Jocelyn nodded and sipped her wine, allowing her to continue, 'Of course, we couldn't make our relationship public in the faculty. I knew I would have to drop out of my course if I wanted to be with him.'

'And?'

'And so, I did. What we didn't expect - perhaps we were naive - was the University, and our families, would disapprove so strongly.' She looked at Jocelyn and smiled, 'That's how we came to move up here. Away from the gossip. We started the cafe together.'

'So, you both gave up your careers to be together?'

Rosa brushed a strand of curly hair behind her ear, 'It depends on how you view it. The cafe has been profitable, and we loved running it; our project together.'

'I see.'

'Don't you view that as a career?' Rosa smiled.

'Oh, it's not that. I've just been conditioned to think differently about work.'

'Ah yes, University can do that to you.'

Jocelyn shrugged. 'The thing is, I did very well at school, and so the only path for me was an academic one.'

'You mean the only career path you *understand* is an academic one?'

Jocelyn sighed, 'Pretty much, yes.' She returned her gaze to the valley. 'I thought I was wise, but Llanfairyn certainly is opening my eyes.'

'To other ways of living?'

'Yes, and other ways of thinking.' She frowned. 'People seem… open-minded, here.'

'They are,' Rosa agreed. 'We moved into Heather Cottage one freezing cold January. Do you know, not a single person in Llanfairyn ever made a comment about the age difference between Joe and me or suggested that our relationship was inappropriate. We were just two ordinary people in love. Will came along a couple of years later. We had thirty wonderful years.

Of course, we were mindful that because of Joe's age and health, I might one day find myself alone with the children, but that only motivated us to cherish every moment we had as a family.'

'True love. Some people have relationships that follow the social norms - they are a similar age or they move in identical circles - but a few years down the road they find themselves in unhappy marriages. What is it in a relationship that matters? Joe was my best friend; he had the same interests and the same values as I. That was enough for us.'

'It must have been hard for you though, to face a choice between your relationship, or your family and career.'

'No, it wasn't hard. It was what I wanted. But anyway, it's a long time ago and I don't hold any grudges. My family thought they had my best interests at heart. I think they hoped that if they put the pressure on - you know, made their disapproval known, that our relationship would fizzle out. That doesn't work; it brings you closer. I was cross at first, hurt and disappointed. But we all made peace in the end. It's important to be the bigger person and reach out the olive branch, if necessary. Life is too short to hold grudges - and feeling sorry for yourself is a waste of precious energy.'

'I imagine Will and Emily are wonderful companions.'

'Emily has been so resilient - she's being a rebellious teenager at the moment, but she is just finding her way in life. And Will is precious. He adored your aunt, you know. When he was born, she fell in love with him - used to come and keep me company while I was finding my feet with motherhood! She was like an aunt to me too, and was wonderful with my babies. She used to say it was because she could have the best bits of them, and then hand them back to me! Will's face would light up when she came knocking and do you know, he would fall asleep on Kate for hours - the two of them on my sofa. I can still see them now. Her presence brought such calm to my home. I like to think her serenity rubbed off onto me. Of course, Will would have me awake all night; she didn't see that side of things.'

'He was a darling, fixing her bicycle.' Jocelyn finished the last of her wine.

'Oh, he was always fixing it for her. She used to spend hours chatting with him. She used to tell him all about her work and travels, and he just lapped it up.'

'She didn't make him feel restless?'

'No, no. Will is a homebird. Anyway, he wouldn't manage without me.'

Then they heard the stairs creaking from footsteps, and Will appeared in doorway to the patio.

'And here he is now,' Rosa smiled, putting down her glass. Would you like to eat, my darling? We have saved paella for you.'

The night was dark; it was time to leave. Rosa refused the offer of help to tidy away the dishes and so, after thanking her for a wonderful evening, Jocelyn picked up her handbag and made for the door.

'I'm leaving on Saturday,' she said, turning in the doorway to kiss her friend on each cheek. 'Shall we walk again on Friday?'

Rosa smiled. 'We must.'

Day 21 - Thursday

On Thursday, after morning tea with the usual crowd of Max, Bob, Alan and Doreen, Jocelyn had worked quietly at her window seat for three hours and finished a significant piece of writing that she'd been tackling since arriving at Kate's. She sat back and clapped her hands together, smiling. She was on top of things.

She stood up and stretched, then wandered over to the shelves. She pulled out a book called *Natural Remedies* and thumbed through it. It contained the herbs that she had discussed with Alan, as well as many more. Each page contained a beautifully painted picture of foliage, and a description of ailments and conditions that each could be applied to. There was a bookmark inserted into the pages describing the benefits and properties of lavender and she grinned. There was certainly plenty of the stuff in the garden borders! Kate must have loved it.

There were also four leather photograph albums on the same shelf. Jocelyn hesitated at opening those; she wondered what can of worms lay inside. She wasn't ready for pictures of Kate or her mother. She looked along the shelf at the ornaments. It would be a pity for all these things Kate had collected and loved to go to the charity shops, but what else could she do with them?

On Thursday evening, Jocelyn and Will had cycled to the top of the common with a picnic supper and found a flat dry spot to sit and watch the town below. They ate ham and cheese sandwiches and pickled onions, and swigged elderflower cordial - all from the farm shop.

'That was a great picnic, Josey. You're a great cook!' Will was lying on his back, looking up at the sky.

Jocelyn laughed 'I think that's the first picnic I've made in… well, I don't know how long. I can't remember last having one.' She watched as swallows flitted and swooped in the evening sky.

'They're feeding on flies,' said Will, watching her.

She smiled and was silent for a while. The town below was quiet and still, with the occasional vehicle moving through the streets - toy-sized from up here and too far away to be heard.

'Being in Llanfairyn,' she said eventually, 'It's making me think about my life. I'm going to miss this place, the people, so much.'

Will turned to her. 'You could always stay here.'

'Stay?'

'Yes, at Kate's. You don't have to go back to the city.'

She laughed. 'Of course I do.'

'Why? We've only just made friends.'

'Well, I have work for a start, and I have a house and my life.'

'You can find a job here.'

'And my house?'

Will shrugged. 'Dunno. Sell it?'

'And there are Jonathan's wishes to consider, and…'

'He can come if he wants to, or he can stay in the city. You can ask him which he prefers.'

She thought for a moment how to answer. A tiny Small Heath butterfly had settled in the grass beside the picnic blanket, folding its wings gently together to reveal brilliant, rust-coloured tips on the undersides and a bold black dot in the centre. She watched it.

'It's not that simple really, Will.'

'Well, it seems simple to me,' he frowned. 'You like it here. You never get to ride your bicycle in the city; here you can.'

Jocelyn laughed. 'Oh Will. I have a lot of commitments.'

'But if you'd rather be here, then stay.'

'Kate's house is too big for me. I like my small apartment. Look, don't get me wrong, I'm very happy in the city; there are just aspects of my life that perhaps I need to address.' She gazed across the town.

For a while they sat in silence, and then Will picked up a twig from the ground beside him and rolled it slowly between his fingers. 'I feel sad,' he said quietly.

Jocelyn looked up from the butterfly, and turned to him, 'Oh dear, Will. Why?'

'Because my dad left, and then Kate left, and now you are going to leave.' Will carried on staring at the twig, wrapping it around his middle finger. Jocelyn watched him, waiting for him to continue.

'Would you like to talk about Kate?' She asked.

'Well,' he looked up and shrugged, 'Kate was my friend. I used to go to her house every day. She always talked to me, she was never too busy, like other people sometimes are. She used to tell me about London and places I'll never visit.' His shoulders dropped, 'And then suddenly, she left. And now, I feel an aching in here, in my heart, every time I think about her. I miss her so much. Sometimes, when I'm lying in bed and I close my eyes, I can see her face, smell her hair.'

Jocelyn studied the boy's face, the long eyelashes that framed his eyes, now lowered to the ground. 'I see.'

'Mum told me she's riding on the clouds, watching me. But I know she can't be, not really. Where do you think she is?'

'When people die… their bodies are gone. But I like to think that they are everywhere. They are not in one single place, but rather, they are here, in our hearts and in the space around us. Everywhere we go.'

Will frowned. 'But we can't talk to them.'

'We can talk to them.'

'But they can't answer us.'

'No, they can't answer,' Agreed Jocelyn, 'And that is the part that is sad, that is the hardest to accept. But we can always, always talk to them. And we can think of them and hold them in our hearts.'

'It's not the same.'

'I know.' Jocelyn had not been close to her mother, but still the grief she had felt at the loss of the one who had known her for longer than any other person was deep and raw. She looked at Will in his oversize t-shirt with his dusty hands and his eyes lowered to the ground, and she saw for the first time the grief locked within him. She was not familiar with a situation such as this, and she thought for a moment before speaking.

'Will, do you have any photographs of Kate?'

'No.'

'Any of her treasures?'

'No.'

She stood up. 'Come with me.'

'Where are we going?'

'Back to the Coach House. I'd really like you to help me sort Kate's photographs out, and some of her precious things. There are so many to look through, I've been putting it off. It would be great to have someone to help me.'

Will blushed. 'All right then.'

'Fabulous. Pick up your bicycle. Let's go.'

Jocelyn had telephoned Rosa a while later, to explain that Will was at the Coach House and would be home by ten unless she wanted him back sooner. Rosa wasn't worried; Will came and went as he wished and could be home later if that suited their evening's plans better. She thanked her for the call, all the same. Jocelyn and Will then spent three hours looking through the photograph albums and trinkets on the bookshelves; Jocelyn telling Will as much as she could recall of the places and faces in the black-and-white images, Will telling her the origins of the treasures on the mantel: The elegant figurines in flamenco costume, from Kate's year in Barcelona. The wooden carvings from her tour of Southern Africa. The tiny soft bear that a child had given her after a show in Rome. The Christmas bauble with 'Best Friend' painted on it, a treasured gift from a fellow actress following a long run at the West End.

By the end of the evening, Jocelyn and Will were laughing and crying at the same time, and they both felt that their emotions had been soothed. Jocelyn found a box and Will selected the objects that he wanted to keep. They wrapped each in newspaper and placed it carefully in the box for him to take home. Jocelyn had decided she would keep three of Kate's hardback nature books, as well as two photographs of Kate - one of her on stage, and one of her standing in the garden in front of the Coach House. It was an old image; Kate looked younger and the honeysuckle that now covered the porch was just knee-high. She was wearing gardening gloves and holding a trowel and she smiled serenely at Jocelyn out of the photograph.

Jocelyn packed the pictures carefully in her briefcase. The books, she decided, could go into her suitcase at the expense of some clothing she would leave behind.

When Will was leaving, Jocelyn followed him outside to say goodnight and watched him leave on his bike, the box held securely under one arm. The night was navy and cool. The lamp in the sitting room shone a pool of light on the lavender in front of the porch. Jocelyn bent and inhaled the scent of the flowers, and then had one last wander around the garden, to check her herb cuttings and give them a spot of water from the watering can, which she filled from the rain tub next to the shed. When she was satisfied all was well in the garden, she sat for a while in the quiet, and watched a fox trot down the road and away around the corner. Then she retired for the night.

Day 22 - Friday

Jocelyn now knew which mug belonged to which visitor and she poured tea into them as Max, Bob, Alan and Doreen settled themselves in their chairs around the garden table. Max had the one that read *Genius at Work*, which made him roar with laughter every time she set it in front of him. Alan's read *If You Like My House, Wait Until You See My Garden* and Bob's simply said *Older, Wiser.* Doreen always preferred the china teacups. This morning, as it was almost the end of Jocelyn's stay Rosa joined the crowd, so all seats around the table were full again and all Kate's novelty mugs were out of the cupboard. Jocelyn looked around at the smiling faces sharing idle conversation.

This was how it had been before Kate had left them; Kate had been the pillar of this circle of friends.

At eight, the friends got up one-by-one and left to go about their day and Rosa and Jocelyn departed for their last walk together. They took the route towards the reservoir, intending to cross the dam and walk in the pine forest.

Jocelyn climbed over the stile onto the common first - and disturbed a pair of rabbits grazing on a patch of purple selfheal. She watched, with a smile, their white tails bob as they hurried into the bracken, and waited for Rosa to join her. Then they strode off towards the summit, feeling the pleasure of their leg muscles working and their lungs filling with clear air. A robin hopped along the track in front of them, guiding the way up the hillside for the two laughing women. Once the path levelled out, their breathing eased and they fell into comfortable conversation.

'Will you use your walking shoes back in London?' said Rosa.

'I'm going to try! I might walk some of the way to work.'

They reached the banks of the lake and Rosa bent to pick up a flat pebble. She turned it over in her hands, brushing soil from the smooth surface. 'Or you could walk around London's parks. There are some beautiful open spaces in the city.'

Jocelyn looked out across the still water. 'I'm certainly going to spend more time outdoors. Hyde Park is nearby, so I'll drag Jonathan out for a weekend walk around the Serpentine.'

'Or for a swim in it? Now you've had a taste of wild swimming!' She bent over to skim the pebble across the surface of the lake. It bounced four times across the glassy surface, leaving perfect little ever-increasing circles behind it, before disappearing into the darkness.

Jocelyn also picked up a pebble and copied Rosa's technique. Her pebble disappeared at first contact with a plop. They laughed at the poor show, and then searched around for more smooth stones to skim.

'My Spanish relatives can't believe how much walking I do,' said Rosa, in between throws. 'It is a source of amusement for them.' They left the water's edge and made their way to the dam, then crossed the cobbled path over the dam to the forest on the other side. Inside was cool and quiet. They conversed quietly now, because turning down the volume in this tranquil space felt the right thing to do.

'So, you haven't always been a keen hiker?' asked Jocelyn.

'No! I was a very glamorous twenty-year-old. I mean, we are talking *heels*! We used to visit our relatives back home in Spain every summer and I'm telling you, Madrid by night is *very* different to Llanfairyn!' They laughed and disturbed a plump wood pigeon, which clattered loudly away through the branches, and carried on walking one behind the other over the rusty pine needle carpet.

'You're still glamorous! Rosa… I've been meaning to talk to you about Will.'

'Oh?' Rosa continued walking, watching her step over the occasional tree root.

'I noticed that he has some…' Jocelyn searched for words.

Rosa spoke for her, 'Yes, I know.'

'I'm sure there would be support available to help him. I'm talking about bursaries, so that he could study.'

Rosa smiled gently. 'Thank you; we've tried that already.'

Jocelyn continued, 'He could train for a profession. There are bound to be more opportunities for support in London than here, and…'

Rosa stopped walking. 'You'd have him leave his home and friends and the life he enjoys?

'He'd make new friends. And the job possibilities would be so much greater…'

'But Will loves working with Max.'

'Max is getting old.'

'He's not old!' Rosa quipped, and she seemed offended. Then she calmed again, and explained gently, 'Will is learning Max's trade and getting to know his customers. He will be able to take over the business from him.'

'Will that… profession suit him?' Jocelyn was probing carefully now.

'Oh, people like you and I will always need our lawns mowing, our gardens weeded, or our windows painted. And I know for sure that I am not capable of unblocking my drains or clearing my gutters by myself!' In her unique, serene way, Rosa had communicated her point very clearly. Jocelyn nodded in understanding.

They carried on walking for a while, and then Rosa broke the silence. 'I was a little abrupt with you and I didn't mean to be.

'Don't apologise, I deserved it.'

They emerged from the forest at the far end of the lake and re-joined the track around the edge. The sun was climbing higher in the sky now.

'We'd better head back,' Jocelyn said with a note of sadness, because this was her last walk. 'And I am sorry for suggesting Will leave Llanfairyn. I just thought there might be something I could do to help you all out in some way.'

'I am privileged to have Will as mine, Jocelyn. He is the most loving soul. He has brought me more joy, and less heartache, than many other mothers' children.'

They headed back along the lake to the dam, and crossed it, and then strode back down the hillside, as the town was coming to life. The sound of the school choir rehearsing in the hall floated up, and behind that singing was the distant rumble of vehicles in the town centre. They climbed down the last of the sheep track, over the stile and hopped onto the road. As they came side-by-side on the pavement, Rosa turned to speak. 'The biggest help you can be to Will is to be his friend.'

Jocelyn nodded thoughtfully, and then after a few paces she replied, 'I could write to him from London.'

'He's not big on writing letters, but he likes postcards, if you could send those.'

'It would be a pleasure.'

'You will indeed find it a pleasure; when you make a friend of Will, you make a friend for life.

Jocelyn stifled a sigh, 'Well, if you think that is the best I can do for you all…'

'Will is happy, Jocelyn. He is surrounded by people who cherish him. He will always be all right in this community, so please don't think that something about his life needs to be changed.'

'But what about you? Are *you* all right?' Jocelyn searched Rosa's eyes but found only serenity.

Rosa replied firmly, 'I'm absolutely fine, and I appreciate your concern.'

They arrived outside the Coach House just Emily was slamming the door of Heather Cottage and dashing up the path. 'Hi mam! I'm late! I've had the last crisps for my lunchbox, sorry.'

'All right my darling. Jocelyn, I don't think you've been introduced to Emily yet!'

Jocelyn smiled at the attractive girl. 'Good morning.'

Emily looked at her and flicked her long dark hair back over her shoulder. 'Hiya. Mam's talked a lot about you.'

'Oh, I see,' Jocelyn felt flattered.

The girl went on, 'Will you be joining in the carnival parade tomorrow?'

'Carnival?' Jocelyn looked towards Rosa for an explanation, 'I don't know anything about that.'

'It's the Llanfairyn Annual Carnival,' Emily said, 'And there is a procession through the town at one. Everyone joins in, and we all dress up in costume.'

'Oh, I see...'

'So, will you be joining in?'

Jocelyn laughed, 'No, I'm returning to London early tomorrow morning.'

'Can't you stay one more day. You shouldn't miss the carnival.' Then Emily turned to her mother, 'Sorry mam, I'm late, I have to go!'

Rosa kissed her and said something gentle in Spanish and Emily replied, then she hurried off across the road, pulling her school rucksack onto one shoulder as she went.

Jocelyn looked again at Rosa, who just shrugged and said, 'What's one more day?'

'I would have to stay until Sunday, though, and I don't think there are trains to London on a Sunday.'

'There are from Cardiff. I'm sure Max would drive you to Cardiff if you wanted to stay another day.'

Jocelyn briefly considered the prospect of a trip in Max's car all the way to Cardiff, and Rosa appeared to read her thoughts. 'It's not as far as you are thinking; you don't need to go the same way you came. You can head straight over the common in that direction,' she gestured Eastwards, 'And drive down the valleys straight to the city. Stay one more day Jocelyn, that's all. Then London can have you back!'

'Well, all right then. But I won't dress up. I'll just watch, with the others.'

'Oh, but everyone joins in - everyone dresses up. You'll feel left out if you don't!'

'I see. What sort of costumes do people wear?'

'Anything you like! Just make sure that you make an effort,' Rosa teased, 'Otherwise you will stand out for being the one who didn't.'

'I'll think about it.'

'Well, I thought I would have to say goodbye to you in the morning, but a carnival send-off is a far better option!'

Jocelyn rolled her eyes. 'And what will you be wearing in the parade?'

'I have no idea!' Rosa pulled a face. 'I shall have to pull out some costume from the back of my wardrobe.' They laughed and then said their farewells.

Jocelyn headed back to the Coach House. On the way she passed Bob, in his usual spot in his vegetable patch. 'Bore da Bob!'

Bob stood up and smiled. 'Bore da. Beautiful day.'

'It is! Oh, don't forget to collect the rosemary cuttings before I leave tomorrow. I've put them aside for you. Did you want some of the mint too? I can dig up a root for you.'

Bob nodded and put up a grubby thumb in acknowledgement. Jocelyn waved at him and made her way up her own garden path.

At nine thirty, she made her final long-distance call to Trudy. At noon, she took off her reading glasses and rubbed her eyes. Outside was sunny but the sitting room was shaded and cool. That would have to be enough for today. It was time to begin packing to return home. On Monday, she would be back in her office. She went upstairs, tidied the bedroom and folded her clothes. She dragged the suitcase from under the bed and began packing it neatly. She had chosen some items to leave out to make room for Kate's books, and these clothes she left in one of the drawers. She placed the books in the case carefully, making sure that each was cloaked in fabric to protect the edges. She went to Kate's bedroom, opened the wardrobe doors and looked at the garments, hanging in all their splendour on the rails. The house clearance company would see to all the belongings. Soon, the dresses and shoes, the scarves and jewellery would be packed up and disposed of.

Kate lifted Jocelyn onto the stool and slipped the silver gown over her head. It spilled in long shimmering folds to the floor. The diamante detail around the neckline sparkled against her pale collar bones.

'Oh, it's beautiful!' said the child.

'This dress was handmade in Paris, to be enjoyed by the grandest of all audiences!' Kate whispered in her ear.

Of course! Jocelyn hurried back down the stairs and picked up the telephone.

***

In the afternoon, Max tapped on the door and Jocelyn ran down to greet him.

'Hello love.' He was standing in overalls and had a tin of paint and a pot with two brushes on the ground beside him.

'Max, hi!'

'I'll finish the door frame this afternoon if it won't disturb you.'

'No that's fine. I'm just packing.' It was warm outside, and Jocelyn lifted her hand to brush away a fly that was flitting between them.

'There we are then.' He picked up the painting gear and went to walk away.

'Wait! Would you join me for tea, first?'

He laughed. 'I thought you'd never ask!' He wandered over to the garden table and Jocelyn followed him a few minutes later with the tea tray. She set it down, and then sat beside the man.

'Max, I'm grateful of how much love Alan and you put into the Coach House.'

The man just laughed and dismissed it with a hand.

'No, I mean it,' she said, 'I am very grateful.'

'Oh, there we are,' he said, and his cheeks reddened a touch. 'So, it's your last day tomorrow.'

'Yes, and I wanted to talk to you about that. I was wondering - and I feel very cheeky asking this - I was wondering whether you could possibly take me to Cardiff, on Sunday, instead?'

'Ah yes, Rosa mentioned it to me. Yes, that's grand.'

'Wonderful! It's just that Rosa and Emily really wanted me to stay an extra day, and I didn't know how to say no…' She poured the tea.

Max was grinning. 'Oh, I understand. You mustn't say no to the carnival without a good reason.'

'Well, it is hard to say no to Rosa! First, she got me out hiking, then I ended up swimming beneath a waterfall! Well, she told me that Kate would have gone in the water - so I took the plunge.' She passed Max his mug. 'Kate *did* say that, you know. Dither on the banks or take the plunge! So much of what she taught me is coming back to me now. Anyway, then Rosa persuades me to stay for a fete. Yes, Rosa is very hard to say no to!'

Max smiled, but he didn't reply, just drank his tea and stared across the valley.

'Also, Max, I'm taking some items of Kate's back to London with me. It's just that, well, your car… is a little small to fit it in.'

'Ah yes, no problem. I'll get Edwin Thomas to run any extra baggage down to the station in his van. I can call him later.' He paused to take a sip of tea, and then continued, 'I take it you have enjoyed your stay, then?'

'Very mixed feelings, really. The joy of discovering - or should I say re-discovering Llanfairyn - mixed with the sadness of having to sort and sell Kate's house.'

'Is there much left to pack?'

'No, not really. I'm glad that Will has taken what he wanted. I've kept Kate's favourite books for myself. The house clearance people will sort the rest.'

As they drank, they watched the Limousins in the valley ambling over to a stone water trough in the afternoon sun. They flicked away flies with their tails, and as they walked their hooves made little dust clouds rise from the dry ground.

After a while, Jocelyn put down her cup and leaned back in her chair. She spoke thoughtfully, 'What makes people stay here, Max?'

He took a sip of tea and rocked his foot slowly up and down on the table foot. 'They are happy here.'

Jocelyn slowly brushed away a fly. 'Three weeks ago, I would have assumed people would want to move somewhere better...'

'Define *better*. They have their friends and family here.'

'I mean, a place where they could seek better jobs?'

'Why?'

'Well, one can earn a lot of money in the city.'

Max laughed. 'Like you do?'

Jocelyn shrugged.

He breathed in and stretched out his arms grandly. 'Move to the city - and live without this space and freedom?'

'Our house in London is worth a lot of money.'

'It doesn't have a garden.'

'It's still worth a lot of money...' her voice trailed off.

'It still doesn't have a garden.'

'So, you think one should sacrifice a lucrative career for space and freedom?'

Max brought his arms back down to his sides and looked at her. 'That's not what I'm suggesting. Isn't life all about knowing what is important to you - because everything has a cost? Take Alan, for example. For him, it's all about his garden. He doesn't need to feel wealthy; he needs to feel alive - and he feels alive when he's gardening. He's willing to trade wealth. Trade, not sacrifice.'

Jocelyn thought about that for a minute. Everything she had been conditioned to believe - that an outstanding profession would follow an outstanding education, and that a happy and successful life would follow both, with no other ingredients necessary - was shifting. She looked down, puzzled at her own change in perspective of how success was defined. Eventually, she moved on. 'Do you think they will be all right; Doreen and Alan?'

'I know they will.'

The animals finished drinking and wandered away down the valley, to find fresh grass.

'And what about Rosa, Max? Will she be all right - and Emily and Will?'

Max smiled fondly. 'Ah Will, wonderful, wonderful Will. He views the world through a child's eyes. We could all take a lesson from him; to allow our minds to be free of clutter.'

'He calls me Josey.'

Max laughed. 'It suits you; now you've let down your hair and got a bit of colour in your cheeks! He showed me the box of Kate's treasures you gave to him.'

'I hope it helps him to have things he can look through, when he wants to feel her near him.'

'I expect it will. It wasn't something we had thought of, you know; to let him go in and choose things of Kate's. And of course, we didn't want to touch anything before you arrived - it wasn't our place to.'

Jocelyn looked over at the man, 'Oh, I don't know about that, Max. this feels like your place more than mine. How often did you all drink tea?'

'Oh, most mornings,' he winked.

Jocelyn smiled to herself and thought about them all sitting together, looking over the valley and chatting about everything and nothing - around about the same time that she was pressed into a sweaty tube train in London.

'You didn't tell me at first.'

'Well, what could I say? Anyway, you figured it out for yourself.'

'Including Doreen?'

'No, Doreen never joined us. Not until now.' He smiled at her.

Jocelyn looked back across the fields. 'I hope that Rosa and Emily will be all right, too.'

'Did they give you a reason to think otherwise?'

Jocelyn didn't know how to answer that, but she understood his point. They finished their tea.

'Max, in such a short time, you have taught me so much.'

'And you me, cariad,' he replied, and Jocelyn frowned, wondering what she could possibly have taught a wise old fellow like Max. Then he placed his cap on his head. 'People here have certainly warmed to you. They've opened up to you.'

'Well, I'm a stranger.'

'No, you're a listener.'

Jocelyn blushed at his compliment, and that surprised her, because she wasn't accustomed to feeling embarrassed. 'Oh, I don't know about that. I didn't make much time for people when I first arrived.'

'You just needed to remember how.' He finished his drink. 'Now, I think it's time for you to carry on packing.'

'Max, is there anything of Kate's that you would like to take?'

'Me? Oh no, no! Thank you. I like to keep my life simple.' He pushed under the chair and Jocelyn stood up and placed the cups on the tray.

'I hope whoever buys the Coach House will keep Alan on as the gardener,' she said.

Max nodded quietly. They parted company - Max to finish painting the door frame and Jocelyn to pack the last of the folders into her leather briefcase, ready for the journey home.

***

'Hello Jonathan, it's me.'

'Hello stranger! I haven't heard from you in a while. How are things up there?'

'Oh, fine. Missing you terribly, of course.' Jocelyn looked out of the window onto the darkening street.

'Are you sure? You sound a little deep in thought.'

'Mm. Oh, you know, just the usual.'

'And the house? It's your last day tomorrow - how are you coping with the packing?'

'I'm all done. I shall call Daniel Rhys on Monday, to give instructions to empty the house and put it on the market. It's all rather sad… but it must be done.' She traced the pattern in the carpet with her bare toes.

Jonathan paused. 'Sweetheart, there's no need to rush things, if you need more time to decide what to do.'

'No, it's what I wanted; tie everything up and get back to normal life. I'll press on.'

'All right, darling.'

'Oh, Jonathan, I'm going to be travelling back on Sunday now, not tomorrow.'

'Oh? Is there a problem with anything?'

'No. There's just some little fete or something that I've been talked into attending. It's the least I can do to show my face at it before I leave this place and take all trace of Kate with me.'

Her comment hung for a while.

'Oh, well, a little fete sounds nice,' Jonathan said gently. 'Call me when you have an arrival time then, and I will meet you at Paddington.'

'I will. Goodnight.'

'I love you, sweetheart; you've handled all of this remarkably. Did you hear me, Jocelyn?'

He waited for a reply, but Jocelyn had already hung up.

Day 23 - Saturday

When the shy tap on the door came at ten o'clock on the morning of the carnival, Jocelyn had rushed to answer it with excitement and apprehension. Now, twenty minutes and several enthusiastic introductions later, five women from Doreen's drama circle, along with Doreen herself, paraded half-dressed around Kate's bedroom.

Jocelyn had called Doreen the morning before, to say that she wanted to invite the ladies from Llanfairyn Amateur Dramatics Society to use costumes from Kate's wardrobe for the carnival parade, and would Doreen be so kind as to contact them with the proposal. Doreen was hesitant at first and she offered to give Jocelyn their phone number instead. Doreen hadn't joined in the group for several years. Despite her friends' best efforts to support her when illness had struck, the shy woman had isolated herself and afterwards, the thought of putting herself in a social setting and having to re-form those lost connections was overwhelming.

Jocelyn suspected all of this. She gently nudged Doreen, and Doreen eventually agreed to call the Chairwoman, Maggie and put the offer to them. The response from Maggie was immediate and full of appreciation. She telephoned Jocelyn within the hour. Kate had been well respected in the town as a professional actress, and they would be honoured to gain access to the costumes for the parade. Maggie sounded so flattered that without much extra thought, Jocelyn went on to suggest that the society take whatever of Kate's collection they wished, for the drama society's own wardrobe. The two women chatted for over an hour and by the end of their conversation, there was a plan in place for purchasing glass cabinets for the foyer of the church hall for the display of Kate's highest-profile outfits. Maggie would bring four other ladies from the group over on Saturday morning to try on outfits for the carnival - and she was determined they would re-connect with Doreen and bring her with them.

And so it was. The women had explored Kate's collection of gowns, shoes and accessories with awe, and they had treated the collection with such respect that Jocelyn was convinced, she had made the right decision for its fate. Saturday morning passed in a flurry of giggles and changing and catwalking around the bedroom in ball dresses and jewels and high-heeled shoes. Jocelyn had put together a plate of cheese and pineapple sticks - and seven crystal glasses containing a modest splash of Dom Perignon, given the time of day - which she had found in Kate's wine cabinet in the dining room. The women munched and gossiped as they tried outfits. As for Doreen, she joined in the dressing up too - shyly at first, for she hadn't been in the company of the ladies for a long time, but Jocelyn watched with relief as they took Doreen back into the fold of their friendship, and soon she was laughing as much as the others.

Max and Alan had met on the lawn of the garden and looked up to see seven half-naked women dancing and giggling in Kate's bedroom. Max had lifted his cap and scratched his head, but Alan just said, 'Oh yes, that's how Jocelyn likes to socialise.' The two men had raised their eyebrows to each other, and then ambled off to their respective tasks around the Coach House.

At eleven thirty, the women departed, with two binbags each of lovingly folded clothes and boxes of shoes. Kate's collection was destined for a home where it would be enjoyed for years to come. Then, Jocelyn and Doreen dressed in the costumes they had chosen for themselves to wear in the parade; tasselled 1920's flapper dresses complete with long, knotted strings of pearls, and sequinned headbands which they had fixed with hair grips to their loose waved hairstyles.

Just before one, they locked up the house and made their way to the corner of the main road, where Doreen had said the procession would pass on its way from town to the recreation field on the other side of the bridge. Other townsfolk were also coming out of their houses and either milling around in gardens, chatting over walls or waiting on the pavement. All were dressed in some costume or another, even toddlers and baby prams had been decorated for the occasion.

Jocelyn looked down at herself. 'Oh, my Doreen; this dress, can I get away with it? Is it suitable, or too much?'

'No, it will be fine.' Doreen reassured her. 'It's a very colourful parade.'

'I can see Kate now, on stage in the West End…' The distant sound of drumming broke the conversation, and at the same time, the attention of the people around them turned towards the main street. 'Oh! Is that the procession?' Jocelyn pointed up the street. 'Yes, I see it!' She felt a wave of excitement fill her chest, and giggled. This was absurd; she was forty-two, too old to dress up and join in carnival parades!

The drumming grew closer and from the direction of the High Street, they could see a vast crowd of people approaching, filling the road. In front, there were two rows of drummers - men and women dressed in smart black jackets with gold trimming and black peaked hats. They marched in line, banging out a drumbeat so deliciously rhythmic that it set Jocelyn's body moving in time. As they marched nearer, a troupe of dancers came into view behind them - girls in white leotards with blue sequined skirts over the top, and white knee-high socks and plimsolls - clapping and moving to the beat, and then behind them, a row of decorated vehicles filled with waving children.

The noise of the drumming and laughter grew louder as the procession drew closer. Jocelyn looked across the street, as Bob stood up from his vegetable patch and Rosa, Will and Emily emerged from Heather Cottage - Rosa and Emily in long, colourful flamenco dresses and Will with his hair gelled into spikes and a t-shirt that read something like *Never Mind The Bollocks…* Jocelyn couldn't make out the rest.

Rosa looked across and gave Jocelyn a thumbs-up. Then, as the procession arrived, residents of the cottages and the houses lining the main road spilled out onto the pavement, and as it passed, joined back of the swaying crowd to move along with it. Rosa pushed her way over to Doreen and Jocelyn, meeting them in the middle of the sea of people and greeting them with a kiss and a laugh because it was too noisy to speak. Everyone was swaying to the rhythm of the drums, walking along in the sunshine and waving back at the costumed children on the backs of the floats.

'I thought it was just a small fete!' Jocelyn said to Doreen, but Doreen was laughing and Rosa dancing and neither heard her, so she danced along with them and clapped her hands above her head in time with the beat. The sun shone warm on the parade as it continued, towards the party field by the river.

***

Afternoon turned into evening as the folk of Llanfairyn revelled. At eight o'clock, the festivities moved undercover, into a big white marquee, and a local band took up their instruments and played the rest of the night away. People drank and danced until they were filled to the brim with joy and community spirit.

It was midnight when Jocelyn, Rosa and Doreen wandered home, linking arms, with Jocelyn carrying her sandals in one hand. 'Oh, that was the best night I've had in a very long time! My poor feet! But the band were fabulous! I didn't want to stop dancing.'

Alan, Max and Will followed close behind, deep in conversation. Max looked up, and agreed, 'Here here!'

'It's safe to say it's the best night for all of us in a long time,' said Doreen, looking back at Alan. He winked at her, and she giggled. Her sequinned headband was crooked now, and she had two red cheeks thanks to the beer tent's plentiful supply of cider.

'It was certainly an entertaining way for you to spend your last night in Llanfairyn.' said Rosa, hitching up her long dress to avoid tripping over it, and revealing that she was still wearing men's socks and trainers. 'We only party like this once a year, so we like to do it well!'

'It's the only night of the year mum stays up late.' Will put his arms around Rosa's shoulders and squeezed her, and she laughed and tousled his hair.

They stopped at the corner, and Jocelyn turned to face the friends. 'Well, here we are then. Tea at seven thirty in the morning - if you can all get up in time!' and dropping her voice, she added, 'I shall wish you all farewell then.'

In turn, they each gave her a hug, and then the atmosphere fell silent, because there was nothing more anyone could say.

'Right then,' Max made the first move, 'Come on you rowdy lot. Jocelyn needs her sleep tonight.'

The tired party dispersed for their own homes and Jocelyn made her way up the path onto the lawn of the Coach House, then turned back to the street and watched them disappear into the night.

She took a deep breath and turned for the house and was still fumbling in her bag for the house keys when two female figures appeared walking up the road, from the recreation field. She recognised Rosa's daughter.

'Oh, Emily!'

Emily looked across the road, 'Hiya.'

'Emily, I'm glad I spotted you.' Jocelyn walked back down the path and into the street, 'Do you have time for a quick word? I won't keep you long; I'm sure you want to get home.'

Emily looked at her companion, who, sensing that Jocelyn wanted to speak to Emily in private, said goodnight and left the two of them by the gate.

'Well, first, I want to thank you for encouraging me to join in today.'

The teenager shrugged. 'You shouldn't miss out. Any relative of Kate's is part of our community.'

'Well, thank you. I haven't had the opportunity to get to know you at all, and now I am leaving tomorrow.'

The girl looked back at her, waiting.

'Emily, I just wanted to make sure that you knew that if there is anything I can do to help your mother, Will or you...'

'That's very kind; we are fine,' Emily said.

'Are you sure?'

Emily looked straight at her, smiling, and then spoke with a wisdom far beyond her years. 'You mean well, I can see that - and my mam is really fond of you - but sometimes we can look for a problem where there isn't one.'

'Oh.' Jocelyn was taken aback.

'Did you know that my mum has been seeing Max?'

'No, I didn't know that!' Jocelyn blinked wide-eyed at Emily a few times. Then, realising that her mouth was hanging rather loosely open, she shut it, and worked to transform her shocked expression into a casual smile. 'Although they'd have no obligation to tell me; it's none of my business.'

Emily just smiled, and Jocelyn noticed she had the same chestnut eyes and long black eyelashes as her mother.

'And… are Will and you all right with that, Emily?'

'Of course!' Emily said. 'More than all right. Mum had a tough time caring for dad, and it must have been lonely for her, you know, relationship-wise. We've known Max for years and we love him.'

'Well, that's wonderful!'

Emily nodded and her dark eyes shone.

'I hope it works out for them -' Jocelyn said, '- for all of you.'

'Will and I do, too,' a slight furrow appeared on Emily's brow, 'We're just sorry they can't find a way for us all to live together, as a family.'

'Oh!' Jocelyn waited for an explanation, but it didn't come. She asked, 'Couldn't Max move in with you?

'Oh no, not until I move out of Heather Cottage. Will isn't going anywhere any time soon and the cottage is too small for four adults.'

Jocelyn nodded slowly in agreement; Heather Cottage was certainly quaint. 'What about Max's place?'

Emily's frown deepened. 'Max's? Don't you know where Max lives?'

'No. He never mentioned it.'

'Max lives in a caravan, down the lane there.'

Jocelyn's gaze followed Emily's; she was gesturing to an overgrown lane beyond the farm shop and school. It was true that Max always emerged from up the main road, but Jocelyn had never ventured much further than the farm shop - apart from the one time she had walked home at dusk with Rosa, and then she had been tired and filled with thoughts of the waterfall and hadn't taken much notice of anything else.

Seeing Jocelyn's surprise, Emily continued. 'For years he lived with his partner in town, a lady from a wealthy family. But she wouldn't marry him and the house was always in her name. Anyway, turned out she preferred her business partner. She kicked Max out. Broke his heart and left him with nothing.'

'Oh!'

'It's a while ago now, though.' Emily shrugged and smiled. 'You'll never see him feeling sorry for himself. He just gets on with life, always cheerful. It's just that, well, he's afraid now, to move out of his caravan. I guess he feels safe there.'

'I didn't realise.'

'I know you didn't. But you see, we're all fine.'

Jocelyn did see. 'Well Emily, I wish the four of you the very best.'

Jocelyn watched Emily hurry away for home, thinking to herself how fortunate Rosa was to have such a strong young daughter, and then went up the path to the porch. She took the key from her handbag, unlocked the door, reached in to flick on the hall light and then stepped inside. There was a sliding noise as she pushed the door open; she put her head around it to find a package and a letter were lying on the floor. She bent down and picked them up. They were both addressed to her; the package was from London and had Jonathan's handwriting on it, and multiple scribblings out on the front indicated that it had been redirected several times before finally finding its way to the Coach House. Jocelyn opened it. It was the migraine tablets that he had posted two weeks ago. She'd forgotten all about those.

She put them on the table and then turned to the letter, an expensive looking cream envelope with her name, *Jocelyn Anderson,* hand-written on the front. No address, and no stamp; it had been delivered by hand. Frowning, she opened it and pulled out the matching cream letter; an A4 sheet that had been folded twice.

Clipped to the front was a compliments slip: From Rhys & Dean Solicitors, and Daniel Rhys had penned on the front 'Regards, Daniel Rhys.'

Jocelyn slowly unfolded the letter, and her breath caught. The page was filled with rows of elegant handwriting, written with a fountain pen - and it was Kate's writing. She started to read.

Dearest Jocelyn - my great-niece,

You are reading this letter, which means that I have finally popped my clogs! As instructed, my solicitor Daniel Rhys has arranged delivery of this letter to you, three weeks after you arrived at the Coach House.

Don't be sad my dear girl; I am now at one with Nature, as is the way of life.

I am sorry we didn't see much of each other in recent years - but those long summer holidays we spent together when you were a child were so precious! I hope you remember them as vividly as I do. You are so dear to me, and I watched - albeit from afar - as you grew into a young woman with courage, determination, compassion and self-discipline; values akin to my own.

Now, why did I summon you for three weeks, you ask? Well, anyone can take a vacation for two weeks, can they not? We sometimes need that little bit longer, to really notice what's been in front of us all along. To remind ourselves of who we really are.

I hope you have experienced the journey that I did when I retired to Llanfairyn thirty five years ago. Oh, I refer not to the physical one - although the rocking train that grows quieter as the miles fall away, the drive from the tiny station by the sparkling ocean, over the open hills to our colourful town nestled by its reservoir - are all sights to behold, are they not?!

No, I mean the spiritual journey. Your journey closer to your true self.

You have spent three weeks living in my home, amongst my friends; the folk who live and breathe for these hills. Now, it's time for you to distribute my estate. It's entirely up to you what you do with it. Keep it all for yourself if you wish. Or give it away. It doesn't matter to me anymore!

But for you, Jocelyn, this is your time - to be.

Carpe diem, my girl!
Kate.

Jocelyn stared at the letter, written for her with this moment in mind.

She walked back outside to the garden table and sat down, laying the letter carefully on the table in front of her. The night was clear and the moon a brilliant white disc over the shadowed valley. Jocelyn sat quietly for almost an hour.

***

'Darling, I've made a decision about the house!'

The telephone ringing on the bedside table tore Jonathan from a deep sleep. He tried to prise his eyelids open. 'Oh, that's good sweetheart. But it's one in the morning.'

'I know and I'm sorry for waking you. It's just that I've made my decision and I needed to talk it through with you straight away. Oh gosh, my mind has been all over the place this last week and I didn't know what I was going to do, and now Jonathan, now it is all so obvious! But I need to talk with you. I only have tomorrow morning to sort everything out - and there is so much to sort out.'

Jonathan sat up in bed, rubbing his hair. 'Just give me a minute.' He moved the receiver away from his face, and then used his free hand to slap his cheek twice. On the other end of the telephone, Jocelyn giggled at the sound.

'Right,' he said, 'Sort what out?'

'Get yourself comfortable, Jonathan. I *know* you can do this for me…'

He smiled. 'Go ahead, I'm listening.'

Day 24 - Sunday

Max collected Jocelyn at eleven thirty on Sunday morning. The day was promising to be hot and so she had chosen to travel in a flowery, halter-neck dress of Kate's with a bright cardigan over the top and flat sandals. Her hair hung loose over her shoulders, and her bronzed complexion was bare of makeup. She had sat alone in the garden since the first streaks of dawn, when the singing of the skylarks on the common had roused her through the open bedroom window. At nine, Kate's friends, *her* friends, had dropped by to say their goodbyes. Now, she stood on the pavement as Max heaved her suitcase into the car.

'All ready to go?' Max pulled the front seat back into position. 'I arranged for the extra baggage to go on ahead, so it'll be waiting for you to collect in Paddington. Is someone coming to meet you to help you get it home?'

'Yes, Jonathan will meet me.'

'So, we've got plenty of time; your train is at three, and…'

Jocelyn placed a hand on her chest. 'Oh.'

Max stopped what he was doing and turned with a frown. 'Is everything all right?'

'Yes, I…'

'Are you sure? It doesn't look like it is.' He put a hand under her forearm, as if afraid she might faint.

'Oh dear, Max. I've got a strange sensation, just here in my chest. It's the opposite of that feeling I described on my first day here.'

'Oh yes, I remember, that feeling of…' he gestured with his arms, '…the pleasure of interacting with people?' He chuckled and let his arms down.

'Yes. This, this is different.' Her shoulders dropped. 'I think it's… I think it's heartache.'

'Oh yes. I expect so,' he said kindly. He watched her.

Jocelyn bit her lip. 'I hadn't realised until now that I learned most of my values from Kate. I wish I had spent more time with her; I still have so much to learn.'

'We all learned from Kate, and we're all still learning,' he said softly. 'Would you like to sit back down for a few minutes?'

'No, no. I'd better not. If I sit down now, well,' she looked at him apologetically, 'I might never get up again.' She took a deep breath, pulled her cardigan together and tucked her hair behind her ears. 'No, it's time for me to go home.'

She looked behind her at the big house, and then across at the valley. Bob raised a hand in farewell from his garden. She waved back at him, and as their eyes met, she held his gaze for a moment. 'Just give me a minute Max,' she said.

She hurried across the street to Bob's wall and faced the man. 'Hwyl fawr, Bob; goodbye.'

'Hwyl fawr, Jocelyn.' The old man placed a withered hand over hers. 'It's been a pleasure to know you.' He smiled and his weathered face crinkled up in the morning light - the lines of a thousand tales, she thought to herself, and she regretted she hadn't more time to listen to some of them.

She walked back to Max's car. 'Oh goodness,' she sniffed, blinking hard. 'Right, thank you for everything, Max. I'm going to miss the life here.'

'I think it's us that needs to thank you,' he said. 'You say you'll miss the life here, but a little of that life is departing this morning.'

She looked at him, and then up and the Coach House. 'All right, Let's go,' her voice wavered.

But Max didn't get in the car. Instead, he walked around to her and put his great arms around her shoulders, and she lowered her face until her forehead rested lightly on his jumper. Her shoulders moved and Max wasn't sure if she was crying, but he knew better than to speak. Eventually, when she was ready to compose herself, she straightened up, forced a smile and tidied her hair and clothes, and repeated, 'Now let's go.'

There followed some mild excitement when the old car refused to start, and Max had had to jump out again and insert a starting handle into a hole in the front bumper to fire it up. Jocelyn had muttered 'Never a dull moment…' to herself, and grinning, she tucked her hair behind her ears and waited. The journey from Llanfairyn to Cardiff took just under two hours. There was little conversation between them. Jocelyn stared out of the window, watching the miles fall behind them. The dun mare and foal were grazing apart from the rest of the herd of ponies and the foal looked up, tiny ears pricked forwards, as they passed. In the sky, the red kite circled silently.

The little car gave them no more trouble as it rumbled across the open moor, although Jocelyn did clutch at the seat firmly as they headed over the last brow of the common and took a sharp turn onto the main road. The brakes held up just fine though, and they both smiled at Jocelyn's reaction, although they didn't look at each other.

By three, Jocelyn was on the train for London. It was quiet at first, with few passengers, but as the miles passed and each station it stopped at marked a step closer to the southeast of England, the train grew busier. It picked up speed as it raced across the flat green fields, hurrying her homewards.

***

London is alive, whatever the time of day, or night, or the season. In the summer, the evening air is warm and smells of hot bricks and tarmac, and steaks sizzling through bistro extractor fans. Restaurants throw their windows and doors open to let the heat out and the breeze in. People mingle on the streets and in the bars; designer suits, dresses with heels, boho fashions and underground styles. Everyone laughing, drinking, relishing everything the city has to offer.

Tonight, the sound of a piano floated from a wine bar somewhere down the street, accompanied by soft laughter and the chinking of wine glasses. Jocelyn leaned against the back of a bench and listened.

'Jocelyn!' Jonathan arrived, breathless, 'I'm so sorry I'm late. I was held up.'

'It's absolutely fine,' she smiled quietly, 'I'm just standing here, enjoying the sights and sounds.'

'Really?' he was relieved. 'That's not like you.'

She stood up, wrapped her slender arms around her husband and held him tightly, enjoying the smell of his aftershave, and he returned the embrace. Then he pulled away to savour the sight of her, putting his hands on her shoulders and stroking her cheek as she smiled up at him. His dark hair had grown a little and curled around his ears, and he looked even more handsome than she remembered.

'I've really missed you! I'm so glad you are home!' He cupped her cheeks with his hands and kissed her lips slowly.

'Mm, I've missed you!' she murmured. She felt safe again. 'I'm glad to be home.'

'You seem to have acquired a bicycle on your travels,' he said, looking over her shoulder and gesturing to Kate's bike, leaned against the wall.

'Yes! It's mine - well, it was Kate's and so now it's mine.'

'Splendid.' He pulled her back around to face him. 'What are you going to do with it?'

'I'm going to ride to work on it.'

'Excellent. Do we need to get you some stabilisers?'

'No, we don't! I've learned to ride again.'

'Go you! But how will we get it home?'

'We'll walk! It's a beautiful evening.'

Jonathan looked at his wife in amazement. 'Well, it's good to have you back. You look radiant! I haven't seen that dress before.'

'Oh, I'm just experimenting with some new styles,' she grinned.

I thought you might decide to stay.'

'Ha! Well, I, I must confess I did fall in love.'

'Oh?'

'Yes,' her eyes grew distant for the briefest moment. Then she looked straight at him and said, 'But this is home. Here, with you.'

Jonathan smiled.

'There are a few changes I'd like to make though, Jonathan.'

'Oh no,' he teased, 'You're not thinking of replacing me, are you?'

She chuckled, 'No, you are a keeper!' they hugged again and as she pulled away, her face grew serious, 'Jonathan, you are my hero, my best friend. I just want us to start thinking about… living in the moment a little more.'

'Oh, music to my ears!' Jonathan pretended to punch the air, 'How many years have I waited for you to say that?'

'Have you? You never said.'

'Well…'

'Jonathan, do you know - while I was in Llanfairyn I only worked from nine until five thirty - and I took weekends off entirely. And yet… I achieved more than usual. I am on top of my work.' She frowned as she tried to make sense of her statement.

Jonathan just smiled.

'Go on, say 'I told you so'.'

'I never say that!' he objected.

'I know. But you could.'

'So what changes are you planning?'

'Well, the first thing I'm going to do is take Trudy out for lunch tomorrow.'

'Gosh! And then?'

'And then you and I need to plan a break.'

'Hurrah! I shall send you up to Llanfairyn for three weeks again, if this is the effect it has on you. Here, let me take the bags.' He lifted the suitcase. 'Golly, what on earth is in here? It's twice as heavy as when you left.'

'Nature books.'

Jonathan tried to hide his surprise. 'So, how were Alan and Doreen when you left?' he asked.

'Well, I saw them walking together as we left for Cardiff - and they were holding hands. Max said they would be fine.'

'And Max and Rosa?'

She stopped and turned to face him. 'They were thrilled at the suggestion that they all move into The Coach House. Rosa cried - and Max said that he was ready to take the plunge. In all my years of Very Important Work, I don't think I've ever seen anyone so appreciative of a gesture that cost me so little - and in the end, it was such an obvious decision.'

'And tiny Heather Cottage?'

Jocelyn reached into the pocket of her dress, pulled out a set of housekeys and held them in the air. 'Tiny Heather Cottage will suit the two of us in retirement just perfectly.'

'I can't wait to visit it,' he said.

'You will love it, I'm sure of it.'

He grinned and put his hands over hers. They kissed, oblivious to the people passing by, and the buses and cars on the street - only moving apart to make way for two men in business suits who were walking towards them.

'Good evening,' Jocelyn nodded as they passed. The men glanced at her briefly, then resumed their conversation.

Then Jonathan picked up the bags, and Jocelyn grasped the bike, and they started to wander home.

ABOUT THE AUTHOR

Cal Heath was born in North Staffordshire and trained as a Microbiologist, receiving a doctorate from the University of Bath. She worked in scientific research in the U.K. and South Africa, travelling and studying extreme global habitats, before settling on the South Wales coast in 2012 to start a family. She lives with partner Lance, their two children and the family cat, and divides her time between caring for her brood, getting wet in the sea, and writing audio and stage plays.

Printed in Great Britain
by Amazon